THE
PLANTAGENETS

THE PLANTAGENETS

Adapted by
the Royal Shakespeare
Company
from
William Shakespeare's
Henry VI Parts I, II, III
and *Richard III* as

HENRY VI

The Rise of
EDWARD IV

RICHARD III,
His Death

INTRODUCTION BY
ADRIAN NOBLE

faber and faber
LONDON · BOSTON

First published in 1989
by Faber and Faber Limited
3 Queen Square London WCIN 3AU

Photoset by Wilmaset, Birkenhead, Wirral
Printed in Great Britain by
Richard Clay Ltd
Bungay, Suffolk

This adaptation © Royal Shakespeare Company, 1989
Introduction © Adrian Noble, 1989
Photographs taken by Richard Mildenhall

A CIP record for this book is available from the British Library

ISBN 0-571-14176-5

CONTENTS

INTRODUCTION

I: THE PLAYS

I became interested in Shakespeare's first tetralogy (*Henry VI Parts I, II, III* and *Richard III*) when I was a student at the Drama Centre in London in the early seventies. I was on the directors' course and for one term our group worked with young designers from the Sadlers' Wells Design Course, on a project supervised by the late Michael Ware, an actor-cum-writer-cum-director-cum-designer of great personality and generosity. We read aloud all four plays, with Michael – like Bottom – reluctantly taking on, in succession, the roles of Humphrey of Gloucester, the Duke of York and then Richard of Gloucester. Each director was assigned a design partner, and we were given the Easter holiday to conceive and present the outline for a production of the tetralogy in a theatre of our choice. My designer and I chose the Round House, a space that had housed some of the most memorable theatrical events of our time: the Mnouchkine '1789'; The Living Theatre; a Royal Shakespeare Company experimental season. We sought an arena, rather than a theatre, and designed three leather-bound, overlapping angular stages; an angry epic space – thrilling to look at, impossible to act upon. Michael Ware wisely pointed out that, although the great public scenes might relish such a space, the narrative proceeds through very precise and delicate political manoeuvres, not at all suited to such Wagnerian proportions. We had, of course, designed our emotional responses to the plays rather than a space in which the plays might happen in performance; in other words, a response in sculpture. But those original responses have remained with me – the violence of the world, the teeming panorama of people and their politics, and most of all the extraordinary energy of the plays.

The reasons for this energy are of course obvious, but need to be recognized. We have a young playwright/actor, still in his twenties, who for one of his first ventures chooses (or was encouraged to choose) the great dynastic power struggle that led to the establishment of the Tudor dynasty; a young writer dealing with contemporary history, for indeed, the collapse of the English empire in France and the appalling civil war that followed was modern history to the Elizabethans. (As one reads the plays in the twentieth century, one is forcibly struck by the potential for violence latent in most of the political confrontations, and the energy with which this is communicated through the language; and increasingly in the plays, by an almost overwhelming desire for peace.)

The plays are written for an audience listening to and, perhaps for the first time, achieving some sense of its own history. Shakespeare is telling the story of his race. Perhaps it would be more accurate to say that Shakespeare was *creating* the story of his race. It is, of course, well known that he was following a Tudor tradition in misrepresenting Richard III as a misshapen psychopath, but throughout the tetralogy there are numerous incidents of historical inaccuracy: for example, men being killed in battle who were, in fact, hundreds of miles away at the time; several historical figures being merged to create one dramatic figure. There are many reasons why Shakespeare did this; the clear narrative convenience of reducing the number of protagonists the audience is asked to follow (a process which we have continued in the version printed here); the dramatic advantages of shape and focus achieved by running several events into one (again, a process of elision which we have taken further in *The Plantagenets*); the need to simplify the actuality of politics both to enhance and illuminate the dramatic stature of an individual and also to marshal the events in order to achieve a particular dramatic effect. (Again, in *The Plantagenets*, we have taken this further; an example of the first is our inclusion of Clarence in many early scenes in *Edward IV*, to bind him more fully into the family structure; an example of the second is our juxtaposition of York's great soliloquy plotting the Cade rebellion, with the scene of public condemnation of the Eleanor of Gloucester faction.)

The apparently cavalier way in which Shakespeare re-ordered and edited actual historical events begs two questions. First, was he aware of the discrepancy between his version and what subsequent generations of historians would testify to be the actuality? And, second, did he care? An examination of his source material (Edward Hall) leads one to believe that more often than not he was at least aware of previous chroniclers' versions of history and decided for artistic reasons to depart from these. He was a writer of fiction and, like subsequent generations of artists, refused to worship at the shrine of actuality. It is interesting to note that in the 1980s, the controversy of history-versus-fiction arose again with the production of 'drama documentaries' on television, which were accused of political bias, i.e. a marshalling of events to lead the viewer to a particular conclusion. I would argue that it is an absolutely proper ambition for the artist to attempt to lead his audience to a conclusion. The objection comes, of course, when one does not agree with the conclusion.

It is in this context that I must address the accusation that the plays upon which we based our *Plantagenets* are spectacular exercises in Tudor propaganda. It was a question we continually posed during the preparation and rehearsals for our production in Stratford. I believe that Shakespeare quite knowingly and deliberately set out to lead his audience to certain conclusions. To deduce from this that Shakespeare was a propagandist for a right-wing monarchy strikes me as being as imprecise and paranoid as some of the accusers of recent drama documentaries.

I myself have concluded that Shakespeare's primary purpose in the plays is moral. Sometimes this is didactic. The arrangement of the material in the extraordinary sequence which begins with Henry's molehill speech and is developed in the Father-who-kills his son/Son-who-kills-his-father episodes is one of the best examples of didactic drama in the language. It is morally explicit in its condemnation of civil war; it is touchingly human in the small details of characterization; and it is in no way sentimental, principally because of the master stroke of the juxtaposition of the king's fantasy of a life of no responsibility, with the appalling results of this actual lack of responsibility.

Sometimes Shakespeare is brutally contemptuous, as in the Cade scenes (look what happens when noblemen cynically mislead a hungry, ignorant mob!); but even here the morality is complex. While satirizing Cade's populism (and indeed many subsequent demagogic populists) it is also clear that what the rebels most want is strong government and a revival of national pride – a Peronist rebellion ultimately suppressed by another conservative orator (Clifford).

More often than not the plays revolve around a private and individual moral choice coming into harsh conflict with a complicated and violent political scenario. Examine the events leading up to the Battle of Wakefield in our *Edward IV*: the Duke of York takes an oath not to go to war if the king swears to disinherit his own son in favour of the York heirs. In the next scene we hear young Richard persuade his father, York, that the oath had no legal basis and that they should straightaway take arms against the king; immediately a messenger enters to say the queen is approaching their castle with a mighty army. The battle commences. Who is responsible for the slaughter that ensues? Is the king guiltless because he has kept to his oath, even though it disinherited his son? Is the queen justified in performing some of the most barbaric actions of the cycle (in the molehill scene) because of her natural, maternal instincts to protect her son's rights? Is York justified by the fact that the war stems right back to the original usurpation of the throne by Bolingbroke in *Richard II*, even though his obsession with what is his by right leads to the civil war, and even though England inherits his children, the last of whom will make 'this earth our hell' in *Richard III*?

The treatment of Joan of Arc in *Henry VI Part I* deserves special consideration because of what it teaches us about Shakespeare's attitude to his material. At first glance, the portrayal of Joan is at best opportunistic (she offers exciting narrative opportunities) and at worst downright xenophobic. Joan, to the English, is a witch who uses demonic powers to defeat the otherwise invincible Talbot; however, to the French she is a great heroine, a peasant girl who humbles and chastens the callow and often hubristic French aristocracy and inspires the nation to victory. Shakespeare quite deliberately keeps the two views of her separate, with the exception of the odd line such as, after Burgundy's miraculous conversion, 'Done like a Frenchman, turn and turn again!' In other words, we have two distinct and opposing views of the same phenomenon – both totally credible and accurately portrayed. A modern audience is faced with a simple question: who are right, the French or the English? Is she a witch, or isn't she? Then, very late in the day we, the audience, are given privileged information, when Joan conjures the devil and demons appear on the stage. Joan goes to her death with no trial and no proof of witchcraft given. In this case, it becomes not an issue of right and wrong, but one of faith. In our editing of this section of the play, we tried to portray Joan as positively as possible to the French, underplaying the suggestions of her promiscuity, while in other scenes stressing the English view of her as a witch. In this way we attempted to focus what we saw as Shakespeare's essential purpose and to retain the truth behind the myth-making of war: the profound understanding Shakespeare had of soldiers and their need to re-shape the enemy into something worthy of slaughter, of their need of rhetoric to give others – but mostly to give themselves – courage; of their heroism and of their degradation.

II: THE PRODUCTION

Thoughts about the *Henry VI* plays recurred over the years; I was asked to direct them twice abroad, in East Germany and by Nuria Espert in Spain, but it was not until 1987 that I seriously considered tackling them in England. Terry Hands, the Artistic Director of the RSC, had invited me to take responsibility for the Stratford end of the company, with artistic responsibility for all three auditoria: the main house, the Swan and The Other Place. I decided to accept, and while seeking to create separate identities for the repertoire of each auditorium, I sought a large-scale project for the main house which I would direct myself, something around which to form a company, something with sufficient challenge to really stretch the actors and something unusual enough to fire the imagination of the whole organization.

History cycles have consistently fitted this bill since the RSC was formed in 1960. John Barton and Peter Hall's *Wars of the Roses* in 1963 created the RSC identity and made it an international theatrical force. In the mid-1970s, at a time of low artistic ebb, Terry Hands embarked on a history series in partnership with Alan Howard, which gave a whole new energy to the company. I had directed Kenneth Branagh as Henry V in 1985 and Bob Crowley, the designer, and I felt we had discovered principles of playing and staging that we were keen to follow up. The *Henry VI* plays seemed most appropriate for the 1988 Stratford season, with their vast gallery of characters, their high-octane theatricality, their simple but exhilarating metrical pulse – all ideal for training a new company.

The excitement of re-reading the texts was balanced by two major worries. First, I found sections of the *Henry VI* plays not only clumsy, but fairly tedious. I felt that *Henry VI Part I* had great theatrical possibilities, but contained many *longueurs* and seemed repetitive. *Part II* seemed the best of the three, a major play. *Part III* seemed to wither alarmingly in the last two acts. My second concern was whether or not to risk playing *Richard III* alongside. Terry Hands advised against this; Trevor Nunn felt *Richard III* should be included. The more I read the plays the more convinced I became that our cycle should indeed take us through the pageant, through the heroics, through the whole convulsive world of Henry VI into the more closeted, dangerous, claustrophobic world of Richard III; that this narrowing of the focus was part of Shakespeare's purpose. I also perceived an added advantage: the *Henry VI* cycle would shed light on *Richard III* by demonstrating that what are traditionally 'star-turn' cameos (Clarence, Edward, Margaret etc.) are, in fact, final expressions of guilt and grief that have built up over several hours in the theatre and over decades of history. Starting from this conviction it was an easy and pragmatic choice to adapt the *Henry VI* plays into two and complete the cycle with an edited *Richard III*.

The first stages of the adaptation were done in collaboration with Charles Wood. I believe him to be the greatest living writer on war and soldiers. The early discussions were heady and far-reaching. We were fascinated by France and determined that it should be a colony worth fighting for and keeping, not just for its wealth but for its culture, its 'otherness'. We were intrigued by what I called Shakespeare's 360 degree universe, a cosmos with an active and real demonology where this earth was an active battleground in the fight between good and evil. We were fascinated by the role of the women in the play and Shakespeare's ambivalent attitude towards them: Joan of Arc, the devil child, who manages to create a nation out of an arrogant aristocracy and a demoralized army; Margery Jourdain, the witch; Eleanor of Gloucester, tainted by pride and ambition; and, of course, Margaret of Anjou, Shakespeare's first great female characterization, who in many ways embodies the journey of our Plantagenets

– from innocent formality in her early scenes with Suffolk, through the terrible transformation brought about in her by civil war, to the refugee in *Richard III* who hands on, quite crucially, the gift of cursing to the grieving Queen Elizabeth, whose encounter with Richard changes the course of that play.

We also had a strong sense of a changing, developing style in the plays and felt that this was to be embraced rather than eschewed. This was to be a vital part of our rich feast – we would allow the style to change as Shakespeare's relationship with the material changed; we would not try to homogenize it or bend it to one view of history. This relish of the contradictions and paradoxes in the world of the Plantagenets became central to the adaptation. For example, in one of the few instances of textual addition, a common soldier confronts the burning Joan of Arc with Jesuitical zeal; this is immediately followed by the scene of political dealing between Henry VI and Gloucester, known as 'marriage letters', a scene which we played on the same set. This is followed in turn by the arrival of the newly created Cardinal to enforce a peace – to the disgust of the soldiery. Finally we learn that he has bribed his way to office – two and a half minutes of theatre rich in paradox and noisy in contradiction.

Rehearsals began in May 1988 in Stratford with a company of forty-two actors playing literally hundreds of characters. No design decisions had been made and only a first-draft adaptation of the first play was in existence. The early weeks of rehearsals centred around passionate debate about the script and extensive improvisations of battles and acts of violence which led directly to much of the final physical manifestation of the productions. The emphasis was continually on how to use the acting company as a tool of narrative, how to create vivid, poetic images with human bodies, rather than scenery. Only at a later stage, after the whole production had been 'blocked', did Bob Crowley design the sets as eventually seen.

But continually the debate returned to the script – was the scene order right? Had the correct material been deleted? And most important of all, was the play an entity within itself? For our play *Henry VI*, the central decision of adaptation had been to have three long narrative sections – first, a section containing five scenes all in England, taking the story from the funeral of Henry V to his son's embarkation for France; second, a French section showing the English victories and defeats, taking us through the whole Joan of Arc story as far as the wooing of Margaret by Suffolk; then a section back in England largely concerning itself with the fall of Gloucester and its terrible aftermath. Each section had its own working title ('the Cathedral of England'; the 'Cathedral Garden of France' and 'the Hunt'). This structure seemed to hold up under the glare of the rehearsal lights, although several of the early, more filmic images in the script were dropped. More of Shakespeare's line order was restored and the play was extended to include the banishment and death of Suffolk in order to provide a more 'resolved' sensation at the end of the play. We found many of the devices of condensation, such as 'the March' (SCENE 2, p. 9) and the cross-cut 'despatches' section in France between York and Somerset, worked particularly well, as did the elision of several Talbot battles and sieges into two major confrontations, at Orleans and at Bordeaux.

The rehearsals turned out to be a genuine workshop, a foundry if you like, in which the script was hammered out! Decisions were fought over and perhaps the greatest tribute I can pay to the acting company is that they rapidly learned to balance the need to project and develop their own character with the needs of the work as a whole. We all had to learn to value narrative over 'character moments' and to value story-telling over psychology. One of the most ego-less and purposeful companies imaginable emerged surely and deftly in Stratford.

Henry VI had to be left after only five weeks, a tottering infant still blinking in the light. But time was passing. *Edward IV* proved an easier play to develop. Again we felt the need to reduce the number of battles and council scenes, and we had the added problem of informing an audience who had not seen *Henry VI*. But a clear pattern was emerging; there genuinely did seem to be a world, a style if you like, that was created by each king, but this did not emerge until half-way through each play – the first half of *Henry VI* takes place, in part, in the shadow of *Henry V*; the reign of Henry VI which then ensues, though pious and monastic at the centre, is dangerous and treacherous in its extremity; Edward IV's soft world, with its false illusions of peace and prosperity, begins in optimism half-way through *Edward IV*, but ends with the brutal oppression of court and nation as Richard ascends the throne half-way through *Richard III* to begin his bored, pointless reign.

Richard III, His Death is a fairly straightforward reading of the play from a textual point of view. But it is in production that I believe the real rewards of the adaptation lie: we discovered a landscape of death, of mourning, of grieving, that is the true counterpoint to Richard's inventive genius and so becomes the seed-bed for his downfall. There is a sterility in Richard's success, a taste of ash in the mouth after his coronation. But this bleak, divided, brutalized world is healed by the Tudor Richmond, who 'unites the white rose and the red'. This sense of healing, of renewal, is perhaps my lasting memory of *The Plantagenets*, and perhaps the strongest 'message' of the tetralogy – an anguished cry for peace.

HENRY VI

Henry VI was first performed at the Royal Shakespeare Theatre, Stratford-upon-Avon, on 29 September 1988, and subsequently transferred to the Barbican Theatre, London, on 16 March 1989.

The cast was as follows:

THE ENGLISH
For Lancaster

HENRY VI	Ralph Fiennes
JOHN, DUKE OF BEDFORD, REGENT OF FRANCE	Raymond Bowers
HUMPHREY, DUKE OF GLOUCESTER, PROTECTOR	David Waller
ELEANOR, DUCHESS OF GLOUCESTER	Cherry Morris
THOMAS BEAUFORT, DUKE OF EXETER	Nicholas Smith
HENRY BEAUFORT, BISHOP OF WINCHESTER	Antony Brown
JOHN BEAUFORT, DUKE OF SOMERSET	Tom Fahy
WILLIAM DE LA POLE, EARL OF SUFFOLK	Oliver Cotton
LORD TALBOT	Robert Demeger
JOHN TALBOT	Mark Hadfield
BASSET	Trevor Gordon
SALISBURY	Jeffrey Segal

For York

RICHARD PLANTAGENET, *later* DUKE OF YORK	David Calder
EDMUND MORTIMER, EARL OF MARCH	Jeffrey Segal
RICHARD NEVILLE, EARL OF WARWICK	David Lyon
VERNON	David Morrissey

THE FRENCH
CHARLES THE DAUPHIN, *later*
   CHARLES VII   Simon Dormandy

REIGNIER, DUKE OF ANJOU   Richard Bremmer
MARGARET, *later* WIFE OF
   HENRY VI   Penny Downie
DUKE OF BURGUNDY   Darryl Forbes-Dawson
DUKE OF ALENÇON   Edward Harbour
BASTARD OF ORLEANS   Patrick Robinson
JOAN LA PUCELLE   Julia Ford

Directed by Adrian Noble
Designed by Bob Crowley
Lighting by Chris Parry
Music by Edward Gregson
Fight Director Malcolm Ranson
Sound by Paul Slocombe
Company voice work by Cicely Berry and Andrew Wade
Music Director Michael Tubbs
Assistant Director Stephen Rayne
Stage Manager Michael Dembowicz
Photographs by Richard Mildenhall

CHARACTERS

KING HENRY VI

DUKE OF GLOUCESTER, uncle to the King, and Lord
  Protector

ELEANOR, his wife

DUKE OF BEDFORD, uncle to the King, and Regent of France

DUKE OF EXETER, great-uncle to the King

EARL OF SALISBURY

EARL OF SUFFOLK

EARL OF WARWICK

DUKE OF SOMERSET

RICHARD PLANTAGENET, later DUKE OF YORK

BISHOP OF WINCHESTER, great-uncle to the King, later
  CARDINAL BEAUFORT

EDMUND MORTIMER, Earl of March

LORD TALBOT

JOHN TALBOT, his son

WATKINS, a soldier

BASSET, of the Lancaster faction

VERNON, of the York faction

MAYOR OF LONDON

JOHN HUME, a priest

JOHN SOUTHWELL, a priest

MARGERY JOURDAIN, a witch

ROGER BOLINGBROKE, a conjuror

SIMPCOX, an impostor

SIMPCOX'S WIFE

CHARLES, Dauphin

DUKE OF ALENÇON

DUKE OF BURGUNDY

REIGNIER, Duke of Anjou, titular King of Naples

MARGARET, his daughter, later Queen to Henry VI

BASTARD OF ORLEANS

Lawyer, Sergeant, Legate, Messengers and Posts, Murderers,
  Keepers, Servingmen, Servants

5

BASTARD OF ORLEANS
Lawyer, Sergeant, Legate, Messengers and Posts,
Murderers, Keepers, Servingmen, Servants

ACT ONE

SCENE I

Chapter House. Enter BEDFORD *with the dead king's shield;*
WARWICK, *with the dead king's helmet and crest;* EXETER, *old, his*
gauntlets; GLOUCESTER, *his mourning sword;* SOMERSET, *the*
dead king's gipon on a cross. WINCHESTER. *They unhelm, food*
brought, a brazier, the requiem sung at their back. Their squires ease
their black-draped armour.

BEDFORD: Hung be the heavens with black, yield day to night!
    Comets, importing change of times and states,
    Brandish your crystal tresses in the sky,
    And with them scourge the bad revolting stars,
    That have consented unto Henry's death –
    Henry the Fifth, too famous to live long!
    England ne'er lost a king of so much worth.
GLOUCESTER: England ne'er had a king until his time.
    Virtue he had, deserving to command:
    His brandish'd sword did blind men with his beams:
    His arms spread wider than a dragon's wings:
    He ne'er lift up his hand but conquered.
EXETER: We mourn in black: why mourn we not in blood?
    Upon a wooden coffin we attend;
    Henry is dead and never shall revive.
WINCHESTER: He was a king bless'd of the King of kings.
    The battles of the Lord of Hosts he fought;
    The Church's prayers made him so prosperous.
GLOUCESTER: The Church! Where is it? Had not churchmen pray'd,
    His thread of life had not so soon decay'd.
    None do you like but an effeminate prince,
    Whom like a school-boy you may overawe.
WINCHESTER: Gloucester, whate'er we like, thou art Protector,
    And lookest to command the Prince and realm.
BEDFORD: Cease, cease these jars, and rest your minds in peace;
    Henry the Fifth, thy ghost I invocate:
    Prosper this realm, keep it from civil broils,

7

Combat with adverse planets in the heavens.
A far more glorious star thy soul will make
Than Julius Caesar or bright –
(*A shout*:)
MESSENGER: Awake, awake English nobility!
(*The black and gold mass sways and parts*.)
Guienne, Champaigne, Rheims . . .
(*Enter* MESSENGER.)

       . . . Rouen, Orleans,
Paris, Guysors, Poictiers, all are quite lost!
Dauphin Charles is crowned king in Rheims:
The Bastard of Orleans is with him join'd:
Reignier, Duke of Anjou, doth take his part.
EXETER: How were they lost? What treachery was us'd?
MESSENGER: No treachery, but want of men and money.
Amongst the soldiers this is muttered –
That here you maintain several factions:
And whilst a field should be dispatch'd and fought,
You are disputing of your generals.
GLOUCESTER: If Henry were recall'd to life again,
These news would cause him once more yield the ghost.
MESSENGER: My gracious lords, to add to your laments,
I must inform you of a dismal fight
Betwixt the stout Lord Talbot and the French.
WINCHESTER: What! Wherein Talbot overcame, is't so?
MESSENGER: O no: wherein Lord Talbot was o'erthrown:
Retiring at the siege of Orleans
He was encompassed and set upon.
BEDFORD: Is Talbot slain? Then will I slay myself,
For living idly here, in pomp and ease.
Give me my steeled coat: Regent I am of France.
Away with these disgraceful wailing robes!
An army have I muster'd in my thoughts,
Wherewith already France is overrun.
EXETER: Remember, lords, your oaths to Henry sworn,
Either to quell the Dauphin utterly,
Or bring him in obedience to your yoke.
(WARWICK *lays the helm and crest on the high altar*,
SOMERSET *sets up the gipon*. BEDFORD *presents the huge*

8

shield with its arms of England and blue of France.
GLOUCESTER *goes up to lay the sword.*)

BEDFORD: I do remember it, and here take my leave
To go about my preparation.
(EXETER *lays the gauntlets.*)

GLOUCESTER: I'll to the Tower with all the haste I can
To view th'artillery and munition;
And then I will proclaim young Henry king.

ALL: Amen.

EXETER: To Eltham will I, where the young King is,
Being ordain'd his special governor;
And for his safety there I'll best devise.
(*Exit* EXETER, WARWICK, SOMERSET, GLOUCESTER, *all
their separate ways.*)

WINCHESTER: Each hath his place and function to attend:
I am left out; for me nothing remains;
But long I will not be Jack out of office.
The King from Eltham I intend to steal,
And sit at the chiefest stern of public weal.
(*Exit* WINCHESTER.)

MESSENGER: Cropp'd are the flower-de-luces in your arms;
Of England's coat one half is cut away.

SCENE 2

*Marching men. Among them an archer with his huge arrow bag, his
bows wrapped, a red cross tacked to his brigandine.
The* MESSENGER *with* SERGEANT.

SERGEANT: Is Sir John Talbot then slain?

MESSENGER: No leisure had he to enrank his men;
He wanted pikes to set before his archers;
Instead whereof sharp stakes pluck'd out of hedges
They pitched in the ground confusedly
To keep the horsemen off from breaking in.
More than three hours the fight continued;
Where valiant Talbot, above human thought,
Enacted wonders with his sword and lance:
Hundreds he sent to hell, and none durst stand him.

His soldiers, spying his undaunted spirit,
'A Talbot! a Talbot!' cried out amain,
And rush'd into the bowels of the battle.
A base Walloon, to win the Dauphin's grace,
Thrust Talbot with a spear into the back.
SERGEANT: I ask you, is the man slain? Talbot dead?
MESSENGER: He lives but is took prisoner.
(*Enter* BEDFORD.)
BEDFORD: His ransom, there is none but I shall pay:
I'll hail the Dauphin headlong from his throne;
His crown shall be the ransom of my friend.
On, on, on!
(*Exit* BEDFORD, SERGEANT, MESSENGER.)

SCENE 3

Garden. Inner Temple. Silence. Birds. A far off bell tolling.
Enter SOMERSET, SUFFOLK, WARWICK, RICHARD
PLANTAGENET, BASSET, LAWYER *and* VERNON.

PLANTAGENET: Great lords and gentlemen, what means this
silence?
Dare no man answer in a case of truth?
SUFFOLK: Within the Temple Hall we were too loud;
The garden here is more convenient.
(*Silence. All the young men glaring at each other.*)
PLANTAGENET: Since you are tongue-tied and so loath to
speak,
In dumb significants proclaim your thoughts:
Let him that is a true-born gentleman
And stands upon the honour of his birth,
If he suppose that I have pleaded truth,
From off this brier pluck a white rose with me.
SOMERSET: Let him that is no coward nor no flatterer,
But dare maintain the party of the truth,
Pluck a red rose from off this thorn with me.
(*From the hedge of pikes they pick their colours.*)
VERNON: I love no colours; and without all colour
Of base insinuating flattery

I pluck this white rose with Plantagenet.
SUFFOLK: I pluck this red rose with young Somerset.
BASSET: And I too.
WARWICK: Stay, lords and gentlemen, and pluck no more
    Till you conclude that he upon whose side
    The fewest roses from the tree are cropp'd
    Shall yield the other in the right opinion.
SOMERSET: My Lord of Warwick, it is well objected:
    If I have fewest, I subscribe in silence.
PLANTAGENET: And I.
WARWICK: Then for the truth and plainness of the case,
    I pluck this pale and maiden blossom . . .
SOMERSET: Prick not your finger as you pluck it off,
    Lest, bleeding, you do paint the white rose red.
LAWYER: Unless my study and my books be false,
    The argument you held was wrong in law;
    In sign whereof I pluck a white rose too.
    (SOMERSET *angry*. PLANTAGENET *dangerously elated. He*
    stops, asks quietly himself:)
PLANTAGENET: Now, Somerset, where is your argument?
SOMERSET: Here in my scabbard, meditating that
    Shall dye your white rose in a bloody red.
    (*The parties shuffle, the pikemen range in their parties.*)
PLANTAGENET: Hath not thy rose a canker, Somerset?
SOMERSET: Hath not they rose a thorn, Plantagenet?
PLANTAGENET: Ay, sharp and piercing, to maintain his
    truth.
SOMERSET: Well, I'll find friends to wear my bleeding roses.
PLANTAGENET: I scorn thee and thy fashion, peevish boy.
SUFFOLK: Turn not thy scorns this way, Plantagenet.
PLANTAGENET: Proud Pole, I will, and scorn both him and
    thee.
SUFFOLK: I'll turn my part thereof into thy throat.
    (PLANTAGENET *and* SUFFOLK *close, both mingling angry*
    breath, hands to swords. SOMERSET *close to them both.*)
SOMERSET: Away, away, good William de la Pole!
    We grace the yeoman . . .
WARWICK: Now, by God's will, thou wrong'st him,
                            Somerset;

(WARWICK *ranges with* PLANTAGENET.)
His grandfather was Lionel Duke of Clarence,
Third son to the third Edward, King of England!
SOMERSET: Was not thy father, Richard Earl of Cambridge,
For treason headed in our late king's days?
And by his treason stand'st not thou attainted.
Corrupted, and exempt from ancient gentry?
And, till thou be restor'd, thou art a yeoman.
PLANTAGENET: My father was attached, not attainted . . .
LAWYER: Sic.
PLANTAGENET: Condemn'd to die for treason, but no
traitor . . .
LAWYER: Non constat.
PLANTAGENET: And that I'll prove on better men than
                                    Somerset,
Were growing time once ripen'd to my will.
Look to it well, and say you are well warn'd.
SOMERSET: Ah, thou shalt find us ready for thee still;
And know us by these colours for thy foes,
For these my friends in spite of thee shall wear.
PLANTAGENET: And, by my soul, this pale and angry rose,
As cognizance of my blood-drinking hate,
Will I for ever, and my faction, wear,
Until it wither with me to my grave,
Or flourish to the height of my degree.
SUFFOLK: Go forward, and be chok'd with thy ambition!
(*Exit* SUFFOLK.)
SOMERSET: Have with thee, Pole. Farewell, ambitious Richard.
(*Exit* SOMERSET *and* BASSET. PLANTAGENET *puts his hand
on* VERNON's *shoulder and speaks to him but looks hard at*
WARWICK *the while.* PLANTAGENET, *looking still at*
WARWICK, *takes his time and then says:*)
PLANTAGENET: How I am brav'd and must perforce endure it!
WARWICK: This blot that they object against your house,
Shall be wip'd out in the next Parliament,
Call'd for the truce of Winchester and Gloucester;
And if thou be not then created York,
I will not live to be accounted Warwick.
Meantime, in signal of my love to thee,

Against proud Somerset and William Pole,
Will I upon thy party wear this rose.
PLANTAGENET: Good Master Vernon, I am bound to you,
That you on my behalf would pluck a flower.
(VERNON, *an instant adherent, proud:*)
VERNON: In your behalf still will I wear the same.
LAWYER: And so will I.
PLANTAGENET: Thanks, gentlemen.
Come, let us four to dinner.
(*Shouts off.*)
VOICES: Stones! Stones!
(*Enter Servingmen of Gloucester with blood pouring from a
split head, pursued by large crowd.*)
PLANTAGENET: This quarrel betwixt Gloucester and
Winchester
I dare say will drink blood another day.
(*Exeunt all except* WARWICK. WARWICK, *at the smear of
blood left by the wounded Servingman:*)
WARWICK: And here I prophesy; this brawl today,
Grown to this faction in the Temple Garden,
Shall send between the Red Rose and White
A thousand souls to death and deadly night.
(*Exit* WARWICK.)

SCENE 4

The death of Mortimer.
Enter MORTIMER, *brought in a chair, and keepers.*

MORTIMER: Kind keepers of my weak decaying age,
Let dying Mortimer here rest himself.
But tell me keeper, will my nephew come?
KEEPER: Richard Plantagenet, my lord, will come:
We sent unto the Temple, unto his chamber . . .
MORTIMER: Enough: my soul shall then be satisfied.
Poor gentleman! his wrong doth equal mine.
(*Enter* RICHARD PLANTAGENET.)
KEEPER: My lord, your loving nephew now is come.
PLANTAGENET: Your nephew, late despised Richard, comes.

MORTIMER: Direct mine arms I may embrace his neck
And in his bosom spend my latter gasp.
PLANTAGENET: This day, in argument upon a case,
Some words there grew 'twixt Somerset and me;
He did upbraid me with my father's death;
Therefore, good uncle, declare the cause
My father, Earl of Cambridge, lost his head.
MORTIMER: That cause, fair nephew, that imprison'd me,
And hath detained me all my flowering youth;
Henry the Fourth, grandfather to this king,
Depos'd his nephew Richard, lawful heir
Of Edward king, the third of that descent;
During whose reign the Percies of the north,
Finding his usurpation most unjust,
Endeavour'd my advancement to the throne.
For since King Richard did beget no heir
I was the next by birth and parentage;
But mark: as in this haughty great attempt
They laboured to plant the rightful heir,
I lost my liberty, and they their lives.
Long after this, when Henry the Fifth,
Succeeding his father Bolingbroke, did reign,
Thy father, levied arms for to redeem
And reinstall me in the diadem;
But, as the rest, so fell that noble earl,
And was beheaded. Thus the Mortimers,
In whom the title rested, were suppress'd.
PLANTAGENET: Of which, my lord, your honour is the last.
MORTIMER: True; and thou seest that I no issue have,
And that my fainting words do warrant death.
Thou art my heir; the rest I wish thee gather:
But yet be wary in thy studious care.
PLANTAGENET: But yet methinks my father's execution
Was nothing less than bloody tyranny.
MORTIMER: With silence, nephew, be thou politic;
Strong-fixed is the house of Lancaster,
And like a mountain, not to be remov'd.
But now thy uncle is removing hence,
As princes do their courts when they are cloy'd

14

With long continuance in a settled place.
And so farewell; and fair befall thy hopes,
And prosperous be thy life in peace and war!
PLANTAGENET: And peace, no war, befall they parting soul!
In prison hast thou spent a pilgrimage,
And like a hermit overpass'd thy days.
Well, I will lock his counsel in my breast;
And what I do imagine, let that rest.
Here dies the dusky torch of Mortimer,
Chok'd with ambition of the meaner sort;
And for those wrongs, those bitter injuries,
Which Somerset hath offer'd to my house,
I doubt not but with honour to redress;
And therefore haste I to the Parliament,
Either to be restored to my blood,
Or make mine ill th' advantage of my good.

SCENE 5

Parliament.
WARWICK, GLOUCESTER, HENRY, RICHARD PLANTAGENET,
WINCHESTER, EXETER, SOMERSET, SUFFOLK *and lords.*

GLOUCESTER: Accept this scroll, most gracious sovereign.
(GLOUCESTER *offers to put up a bill;* WINCHESTER *snatches
it, tears it.*)
WINCHESTER: Com'st thou with deep-premeditated lines,
With written pamphlets studiously devis'd,
Humphrey of Gloucester? If thou canst accuse
Or aught intend'st to lay unto my charge,
Do it without invention suddenly.
GLOUCESTER: Presumptuous priest, this place commands my
patience,
Or thou shouldst find thou hast dishonour'd me.
Hear, prelate; such is thy audacious wickedness,
Thy lewd, pestiferous, and dissentious pranks,
As very infants prattle of thy pride.
Thou art a most pernicious usurer,
Froward by nature, enemy to peace;

And for thy treachery, what's more manifest,
In that thou laidst a trap to take my life,
The King, thy sovereign, is not quite exempt
From envious malice of thy swelling heart.
WINCHESTER: Gloucester, I do defy thee.
If covetous, ambitious, or perverse,
As he will have me, how am I so poor?
And for dissension, who preferreth peace
More than I do? – except I be provok'd.
No, my good lords, it is not that offends;
It is not that that hath incens'd the Duke;
It is because no one should sway but he,
No one but he should be about the King;
But he shall know I am as good –
GLOUCESTER: As good!
Am I not Protector, saucy priest?
WINCHESTER: And am not I a prelate of the church?
GLOUCESTER: Yes, as an outlaw in a castle keeps,
And useth it – to patronage his theft.
WINCHESTER: Unreverent Gloucester!
GLOUCESTER: Thou art reverent
Touching thy spiritual function, not thy life.
WINCHESTER: Rome shall remedy this.
GLOUCESTER: Roam thither then.
WARWICK: Methinks his lordship should be humbler;
It fitteth not a prelate so to plead.
SOMERSET: Yes, when his holy state is touch'd so near.
KING HENRY: Uncles of Gloucester and of Winchester,
The special watchmen of our English weal,
I would prevail, if prayers might prevail,
To join your hearts in love and amity.
Believe me, lords, my tender years can tell
Civil dissension is a viperous worm
That gnaws the bowels of the commonwealth.
(*Enter* MAYOR. *Stones fall into the parliamentary area. The*
MAYOR *looks aghast at the stones. Whistles, shouts, running
feet.*)
MAYOR: Pity the city of London, pity us!
The Bishop and the Duke of Gloucester's men

Do pelt so fast at one another's pate
That many have their giddy brains knock'd out:
Our windows are broke down in every street,
And we for fear compell'd to shut our shops.
(*Enter three servants.*)
KING HENRY: We charge you, on allegiance to ourself,
To hold your slaughtering hands and keep the peace.
Pray, uncle Gloucester, mitigate this strife.
FIRST SERVANT: Nay, if we be forbidden stones, we'll fall to it
with our teeth.
SECOND SERVANT: Do what ye dare, we are as resolute.
KING HENRY: O, how this discord doth afflict my soul!
Can you, my Lord of Winchester, behold
My sighs and tears, and will not once relent?
WARWICK: My Lord Protector, yield; yield, Winchester.
WINCHESTER: He shall submit, or I will never yield.
GLOUCESTER: Here, Winchester, I offer thee my hand.
You of my household, leave this peevish broil,
And set this unaccustom'd fight aside.
WARWICK: Behold, my Lord of Winchester, the Duke
Hath banish'd moody discontented fury . . .
KING HENRY: Fie, uncle Beaufort! I have heard you preach
That malice was a great and grievous sin . . .
WARWICK: For shame, my Lord of Winchester, relent!
WINCHESTER: Well . . .
(WINCHESTER *considering his move, then reluctantly:*)
. . . Duke of Gloucester, I will yield to
thee;
Love for thy love and hand for hand I give.
(WINCHESTER *puts out his hand.* GLOUCESTER *with the*
MAYOR. *Enter* RICHARD PLANTAGENET. GLOUCESTER *to
them aside:*)
GLOUCESTER: Ay, but, I fear me, with a hollow heart. –
See here, my friends and loving countrymen,
This token serveth for a flag of truce
Betwixt ourselves and all our followers:
So help me God, as I dissemble not!
WINCHESTER: (*Aside*) So help me God, as I intend it not!
KING HENRY: O loving uncle, kind Duke of Gloucester,

How joyful am I made by this contract!
Away, my masters! trouble us no more,
But join in friendship, as your lords have done.

THIRD SERVANT: Content; I'll to the surgeon's.

FIRST SERVANT: And so will I.

SECOND SERVANT: And I will see what physic the tavern
affords.

WARWICK: Accept this scroll, most gracious sovereign,
Which in the right of Richard Plantagenet
We do exhibit to your Majesty.

GLOUCESTER: Well urg'd, my Lord of Warwick; for, sweet
prince,
You have great reason to do Richard right,
For those occasions I told your Majesty.

KING HENRY: And those occasions, uncle, were of force;
Therefore, my loving lords, our pleasure is
That Richard be restored to his blood.

WARWICK: Let Richard be restored to his blood;
So shall his father's wrongs be recompens'd.

ALL: Ay.

WINCHESTER: As will the rest, so willeth Winchester.

KING HENRY: If Richard will be true, not that alone
But all the whole inheritance I give
That doth belong unto the house of York,
From whence you spring by lineal descent.

PLANTAGENET: Thy humble servant vows obedience
And humble service till the point of death.

KING HENRY: Stoop then and set your knee against my foot;
Rise, Richard, like a true Plantagenet,
And rise created princely Duke of York.

PLANTAGENET: And so thrive Richard as thy foes may fall!
And as my duty springs, so perish they
That grudge one thought against your Majesty!

ALL: Welcome, high Prince, the mighty Duke of York!

SOMERSET: (Aside) Perish, base Prince, ignoble Duke of York!

GLOUCESTER: Now will it best avail your Majesty
To cross the seas and to be crown'd in France.
The presence of a king engenders love
Amongst his subjects and his loyal friends,

As it disanimates his enemies.
KING HENRY: When Gloucester says the word, King Henry
                                                    goes;
    For friendly counsel cuts off many foes.
GLOUCESTER: Your ships already are in readiness.
    (*Sennet. Flourish. Exeunt all but* EXETER.)
EXETER: Ay, we may march in England, or in France,
    Not seeing what is likely to ensue.
    This late dissension grown betwixt the peers
    Burns under feigned ashes of forg'd love,
    And will at last break out into a flame;
    As fester'd members rot but by degree
    Till bones and flesh and sinews fall away,
    So will this base and envious discord breed.
    And now I fear that fatal prophecy
    That Henry born at Monmouth should win all,
    And Henry born at Windsor should lose all:
    Which is so plain that Exeter doth wish
    His days may finish ere that hapless time.

SCENE 6

The cathedral garden of France.
Enter CHARLES, ALENÇON, REIGNIER.

CHARLES: Mars his true moving, even as in the heavens
    So in the earth, to this day is not known.
    Late did he shine upon the English side;
    Now we are victors, upon us he smiles.
    At pleasure here we lie near Orleans,
    The whiles the famish'd English, like pale ghosts,
    Faintly annoy us one hour in a month.
ALENÇON: They want their porridge and their fat bull-beeves.
    Either they must be dieted like mules
    And have their provender tied to their mouths,
    Or piteous they will look, like drowned mice.
REIGNIER: Let us end the seige; why live we idly here?
    Talbot is taken, whom we wont to fear;
    Remaineth none but mad-brain'd Salisbury,

And he may well in fretting spend his gall –
Nor men nor money hath he to make war.
CHARLES: Sound, sound alarum; we will rush on them.
Now for the honour of the forlorn French.
Him I forgive my death that killeth me
When he sees me go back one foot, or fly.
(*Exeunt. Alarum; they are beaten back by the English, with
great loss. Re-enter, breathless,* CHARLES *defeated. Re-enter,
breathless,* ALENÇON, REIGNIER.)
Who ever saw the like? What men have I!
Dogs! cowards! dastards! I would ne'er have fled
But that they left me 'midst my enemies.
REIGNIER: Salisbury is a desperate homicide.
ALENÇON: Lean raw-boned rascals! Who would e'er suppose
They had such courage and audacity?
CHARLES: Let's leave this town; for they are hare-brain'd
                                                    slaves,
And hunger will enforce them be more eager:
Of old I know them; rather with their teeth
The walls they'll tear down than forsake a town.

REIGNIER: By my consent, we'll even let them alone.
ALENÇON: O, be it so.
   (*A shout. The* BASTARD OF ORLEANS *shouts:*)
BASTARD: Where's the Prince Dauphin? I have news for him.
   (*Enter* BASTARD.)
CHARLES: Bastard of Orleans, thrice welcome to us.
BASTARD: Be not dismay'd, for succour is at hand:
   A holy maid hither with me I bring,
   Which, by a vision sent to her from heaven,
   Ordained is to end this tedious siege
   And drive the English forth the bounds of France.
   The spirit of deep prophecy she hath,
   What's past, and what's to come, she can descry.
   Speak, shall I call her in? Believe my words,
   For they are certain and unfallible.
   (CHARLES *gasps, still short of breath.*)
CHARLES: Go call her in. But first, to try her skill,
   Reignier, stand thou as Dauphin in my place;
   Question her proudly; let thy looks be stern;
   By this means shall we sound what skill she hath.

Enter SALISBURY *and then* TALBOT.
SALISBURY: Talbot, my life, my joy, again return'd!
   Say by what means gots thou to be releas'd?
TALBOT: The Earl of Bedford had a prisoner;
   For him was I exchang'd and ransom'd.
SALISBURY: How wert thou handled, being prisoner?
TALBOT: With scoffs and scorns and contumelious taunts.
   In open market-place produc'd they me
   To be a public spectacle to all;
   Here, said they, is the Terror of the French,
   The scarecrow that affrights our children so.
   Then broke I from the officers that led me,
   And with my nails digg'd stones out of the ground
   To hurl at the beholders of my shame.
   My grisly countenance made others fly;
   None durst come near for fear of sudden death.
   So great fear of my name 'mongst them were spread
   That they suppos'd I could rend bars of steel!

Enter PUCELLE.

PUCELLE: Dauphin.

TALBOT: What stir is this? What tumult's in the heavens?
 Whence cometh this alarum, and the noise?

SALISBURY: A holy prophetess new risen up.

REIGNIER: Fair maid, is't thou wilt do these wondrous feats?

PUCELLE: Reignier, is't thou that thinkest to beguile me?
 Where is the Dauphin? Come, come from behind;
 I know thee well, though never seen before.
 Be not amaz'd, there's nothing hid from me.
 In private will I talk with thee apart:
 Stand back, you lords, and give us leave awhile!
 Dauphin, I am by birth a shepherd's daughter,
 My wit untrain'd in any kind of art.
 Heaven and our Lady gracious hath it pleas'd
 To shine on my contemptible estate.
 Lo, whilst I waited on my tender lambs,
 And to sun's parching heat display'd my cheeks,
 God's Mother deigned to appear to me,
 And in a vision full of majesty
 Will'd me to leave my base vocation
 And free my country from calamity:
 Her aid she promis'd, and assur'd success.
 My courage try by combat, if thou dar'st,
 And thou shalt find that I exceed my sex.

CHARLES: In single combat thou shalt buckle with me;
 And if thou vanquishest, thy words are true.

PUCELLE: I am prepar'd: here is my keen-edg'd sword,
 Deck'd with five flower-de-luces on each side.

CHARLES: Then come, o' God's name; I fear no woman.

PUCELLE: And while I live I'll ne'er fly from a man.
 (*They fight.*)

CHARLES: Stay, stay thy hands; thou art an Amazon.

PUCELLE: Christ's Mother helps me, else I were too weak.

CHARLES: Excellent Pucelle, if thy name be so,
 Let me thy servant and not sovereign be.

PUCELLE: I must not yield to any rites of love,
 For my profession's sacred from above:

When I have chasèd all thy foes from hence,
Then will I think upon a recompense.
REIGNIER: My lord, methinks, is very long in talk.
ALENÇON: My lord, where are you? What devise you on?
Shall we give over Orleans, or no?
PUCELLE: Why, no, I say: distrustful recreants!
Fight to the last gasp; I will be your guard!
CHARLES: What she says I'll confirm, we'll fight it out.

SCENE 7

TALBOT: What chance is this that suddenly hath cross'd us?
Where is my strength, my valour, and my force?
Our English troops retire, I cannot stay them;
A woman clad in armour chaseth them.
WATKINS: A witch! A witch.
TALBOT: A witch by fear, not force, drives back our troops.
My thoughts are whirled like a potter's wheel;
I know not where I am, nor what I do.

SALISBURY: O Lord, have mercy on us, wretched sinners!
TALBOT: How far'st thou, mirror of all martial men?
    One of thy eyes and thy cheek's side struck off!
    In thirteen battles Salisbury o'ercame;
    Henry the Fifth he first train'd to the wars;
    Heaven, be thou gracious to none alive,
    If Salisbury want mercy at thy hands!
    Frenchmen, I'll be a Salisbury to you.
    Puzzel or Pussel, dolphin or dogfish,
    Your hearts I'll stamp out with my horse's heels
    And make a quagmire of your mingled brains.
    They call'd us, for our fierceness, English dogs;
    Now like to whelps we crying run away.
    Hark, countrymen! either renew the fight,
    Or tear the lions out of England's coat.
    (*Enter* PUCELLE *and French.*)
    Here, here she comes. I'll have a bout with thee;
    Devil or devil's dam, I'll conjure thee:
    Blood will I draw on thee, thou art a witch,
    And straightway give thy soul to him thou serv'st.
PUCELLE: Come, come, 'tis only I that must disgrace thee.
    (*They fight.*)
TALBOT: Heavens, can you suffer hell so to prevail?
    My breast I'll burst with straining of my courage.
PUCELLE: Talbot, farewell; thy hour is not yet come:
    I must go victual Orleans forthwith.
    This day is ours, as many more shall be.
    (*Exit* PUCELLE *and army.*)
TALBOT: (*Lunging after* PUCELLE) Puzzel is enter'd into Orleans
    In spite of us or aught that we could do.
    O, would I were to die with Salisbury!
    The shame hereof will make me hide my head.
    But I will chastise this high-minded strumpet!
    (*A shout of French triumph heard. The battlefield full of
    dispirited English, archers, sergeants, men at arms.*)
    Stand!
    (*Englishmen stand. Archers form. Enter French on the walls.*)
PUCELLE: Advance our waving colours on the walls;
    Rescu'd is Orleans from the English.

REIGNIER: Why ring not bells aloud throughout the town
　　To celebrate the joy that God hath given us?
ALENÇON: All France will be replete with mirth and joy
　　When they shall hear how we have play'd the men.
CHARLES: 'Tis Joan, not we, by whom the day is won;
　　For which I will divide my crown with her,
　　And all the priests and friars in my realm
　　Shall in procession sing her endless praise.
　　(*The group of soldiers moves, murmurs, is quietened by*
　　TALBOT.)
　　No longer on Saint Denis will we cry,
　　But Joan de Pucelle shall be France's saint.
　　Come in, and let us banquet royally
　　After this golden day of victory!
　　(*Exit the French. Silence from the English group, then one of*
　　the soldiers breaks, and with a cry.)
WATKINS: Stand!
TALBOT: Wait.
　　(TALBOT *and his small tight group of defeated men remain.*)

25

Dawn.
Silence, first light. The tight group of men about TALBOT *just seen.*

(*A hoarse whisper challenges:*)
WATKINS: Who comes?
(*Enter* BEDFORD.)
BEDFORD: Bedford!
(*Enter* BURGUNDY, VERNON *and* BASSET.)
BURGUNDY: Burgundy!
WATKINS: Advance, my lords, and be recognized your claim.
BEDFORD: Who challenges?
TALBOT: Talbot.
(BURGUNDY *and* BEDFORD *are absorbed into the* TALBOT
group, their banners furled, lance points bright above. Quiet
greetings; three commanders assess the field.)
Lord Regent, and redoubted Burgundy.
This happy night the Frenchmen are secure,
Having all day carous'd and banqueted,
Embrace we then this opportunity,
As fitting best to quittance their deceit,
Contriv'd by art and baleful sorcery.
BURGUNDY: But what's that Pucelle whom they term so pure?
TALBOT: A maid, they say.
BURGUNDY: A maid! and be so martial!
(*Ladders come up out of the group.*)
BEDFORD: Coward of France, how much he wrongs his fame,
Despairing of his own arm's fortitude,
To join with witches and the help of hell!
BURGUNDY: Traitors have never other company.
TALBOT: Well, let them practise and converse with spirits;
God is our fortress, in whose conquering name
Let us resolve to scale their flinty bulwarks.
BEDFORD: Ascend, brave Talbot; we will follow thee.
TALBOT: Saint George, his cross!
SOLDIERS: Saint George, his cross!

SCENE 9

Enter VERNON, *sporting his white rose. Enter* BASSET, *badged with his.*

VERNON: Lackey of Somerset!
BASSET: Minnow of York!
VERNON: Dar'st thou maintain the former words thou spak'st?
BASSET: Yes, sir, as well as you dare patronage
    The envious barking of your saucy tongue
    Against my lord the Duke of Somerset.
VERNON: Sirrah, thy lord I honour as he is.
BASSET: Why, what is he? As good a man as York!
VERNON: Hark ye, not so: in witness take ye that!
    (VERNON *strikes* BASSET. BASSET, *getting to his feet, wiping the blood from his mouth:*)
BASSET: Villain, thou knowest the law of arms is such
    That whoso draws a sword, 'tis present death,
    Or else this blow should broach thy dearest blood.
    But I'll unto his Majesty, and crave
    I may have liberty to venge this wrong.
VERNON: Well, miscreant, I'll be there as soon as you;
    And, after, meet you sooner than you would.
    (*They exit.*)

SCENE 10

BASTARD: I think this Talbot be a fiend of hell.
REIGNIER: If not of hell, the heavens, sure, favour him.
ALENÇON: Of all exploits since first . . . [I followed arms]
    (*Enter* PUCELLE, *in armour, with sword.*)
CHARLES: Is this thy cunning, thou deceitful dame?
PUCELLE: Improvident soldiers! had your watch been good . . .
CHARLES: Duke of Alençon, this was your . . . [default]
ALENÇON: Had all your quarters been as safely kept,
    We had not been thus shamefully surpris'd.
BASTARD: Mine was secure!
REIGNIER: And, so was mine . . .
CHARLES: And for myself, most part of all this night,

Within her quarter and mine own precinct,
I was employ'd, in passing to and fro
About relieving of the sentinels.
Then how or which way should they first break in?

PUCELLE: Question, my lords, no further of the case,
How or which way; 'tis sure they found some place.
Let frantic Talbot triumph for a while
And like a peacock sweep along his tail;
We'll pull his plumes and take away his train!
(*Exit* PUCELLE *and* CHARLES. *Exit* ALENÇON, BASTARD,
REIGNIER. *A shout off:*)

WATKINS: A Talbot! A Talbot!
(*They flee.*)

SCENE II

Enter WATKINS.

WATKINS: I'll be so bold to take what they have left.
The cry of 'Talbot' serves me for a sword;
For I have laden me with many spoils,
Using no other weapon but his name.
(*Exit* WATKINS. *Enter* TALBOT *and* BURGUNDY.)

TALBOT: Lost, and recover'd in a day again!
This is a double honour, Burgundy:
Let heavens have glory for this victory!

BURGUNDY: Warlike and martial Talbot, Burgundy
Enshrines thee in his heart, and there erects
Thy noble deeds as valour's monuments.

TALBOT: Thanks, gentle Duke. But where is Pucelle now?
I think her old familiar is asleep.
Now where's the Bastard's braves, and Charles his gleeks?
What, all amort?
Now will we take some order in the town.
Placing therein some expert officers,
And then depart to Paris to the King,
For there young Henry with his nobles lie.

BURGUNDY: What wills Lord Talbot pleaseth Burgundy.

TALBOT: But yet, before we go, let's not forget

The noble Duke of Bedford, late deceas'd . . .
(PUCELLE *shouts:*)
PUCELLE: Bedford! Bedford!
 What will you do, good grey-beard? Break a lance
 And run a tilt at death within a chair?
TALBOT: A braver soldier never couched lance.
 Foul fiend of France and hag of all despite!
 A gentler heart did never sway in court;
 But kings and mightiest potentates must die,
 For that's the end of human misery.
(*Exit* TALBOT.)

SCENE 12

CHARLES: A parley with the Duke of Burgundy!
BURGUNDY: Who craves a parley with the Burgundy?
PUCELLE: The princely Charles of France, thy countryman.
CHARLES: Speak, Pucelle, and enchant him with thy words.
PUCELLE: Brave Burgundy, undoubted hope of France,
 Stay, let thy humble handmaid speak to thee.
BURGUNDY: Speak on, but be not over-tedious.
PUCELLE: Look on thy country, look on fertile France,
 And see the cities and the towns defac'd
 By wasting ruin of the cruel foe;
 As looks the mother on her lowly babe
 When death doth close his tender dying eyes,
 See, see the pining malady of France;
 Behold the wounds, the most unnatural wounds
 Which thou thyself has given her woeful breast.
 O, turn thy edged sword another way;
 Strike those that hurt, and hurt not those that help!
 One drop of blood drawn from thy country's bosom
 Should grieve thee more than streams of foreign gore.
BURGUNDY: Either she hath bewitch'd me with her words,
 Or nature makes me suddenly relent.
PUCELLE: Who join'st thou with but a lordly nation
 That will not trust thee but for profit's sake?
 See then, thou fight'st against thy countrymen,
 And join'st with them will be thy slaughter-men.

Come, come, return; return, thou wandering lord;
Charles and the rest will take thee in their arms.
BURGUNDY: I am vanquished; these haughty words of hers
Have batter'd me like roaring canon-shot.
Forgive me, country, and sweet countrymen!
My forces and my power of men are yours.
PUCELLE: Done like a Frenchman! – turn and turn again.
CHARLES: Welcome, brave Duke! thy friendship makes us fresh.
BASTARD: And doth beget new courage in our breasts.
BURGUNDY: So farewell, Talbot; I'll no longer trust thee.
CHARLES: Now let us on, my lords, and join our powers,
And seek how we may prejudice the foe.
(*Exeunt.*)

SCENE 13

Paris.

GLOUCESTER: Lord Bishop, set the crown upon his head.
WINCHESTER: God save King Henry, of that name the sixth!
ALL: God save King Henry, King of France and England.
TALBOT: God save King Harry, King of France and England.
My gracious Prince, and honourable peers,
Hearing of your arrival in this realm,
I have awhile given truce unto my wars
To do my duty to my sovereign:
In sign whereof, this arm, that hath reclaim'd
To your obedience fifty fortresses,
Twelve cities, and seven walled towns of strength,
Beside five hundred prisoners of esteem,
Lets fall his sword before your Highness' feet.
KING HENRY: Welcome, brave captain and victorious lord!
When I was young, as yet I am not old,
I do remember how my father said
A stouter champion never handled sword.
Yet never have you tasted our reward,
Because 'till now we never saw your face.
Therefore stand up; and for these good deserts
We here create you Earl of Shrewsbury;

And in our coronation take your place.
(*Enter* EXETER.)

EXETER: My gracious Sovereign, as I rode from Calais,
To haste unto your coronation
A letter was deliver'd to my hands,
Writ to your Grace, from th' Duke of Burgundy.

GLOUCESTER: What means his Grace, that he hath chang'd his
style?

No more but plain and bluntly 'To the King'!
What's here? 'I have, upon especial cause,
Mov'd with compassion of my country's wrack,
Forsaken your pernicious faction
And join'd with Charles, the rightful King of France.'
O monstrous treachery! Can this be so —

KING HENRY: What! doth my uncle Burgundy revolt?

GLOUCESTER: He doth, my lord, and is become your foe.

KING HENRY: Why then Lord Talbot there shall talk with him
And give him chastisement for this abuse.
My lord, how say you, are you not content?

TALBOT: Content, my liege!

KING HENRY: Then gather strength and march unto him
straight.

TALBOT: I go, my lord, in heart desiring still
You may behold confusion of your foes.
(*Exit* TALBOT. *Enter* VERNON *and* BASSET.)

VERNON: Grant me the combat, gracious sovereign.

BASSET: And me, my lord, grant me the combat too.

YORK: This is my servant: hear him, noble Prince.

SOMERSET: And this is mine: sweet Henry, favour him.

KING HENRY: What is the wrong whereof you both complain?

BASSET: This fellow here, with envious carping tongue,
Upbraided me about the rose I wear.

VERNON: Yet know, my lord, I was provok'd by him,
And he first took exceptions at this badge,
Pronouncing that the paleness of this flower
Bewray'd the faintness of my master's heart.

BASSET: Saying the sanguine colour of the leaves
Did represent my master's blushing cheeks!
I crave the benefit of law of arms.

VERNON: And that is my petition, noble lord.
KING HENRY: Good Lord, what madness rules in brainsick
    men.
SOMERSET: The quarrel toucheth none but us alone;
    Betwixt ourselves let us decide it then.
YORK: There is my pledge; accept it, Somerset.
KING HENRY: Good cousins both, of York and Somerset,
    Quiet yourselves, I pray, and be at peace.
BASSET: Confirm it so, mine honourable lord.
GLOUCESTER: Confirm it so! Confounded be your strife!
    And perish ye, with your audacious prate!
    Presumptuous rascals, are you not asham'd
    With this immodest clamorous outrage
    To trouble and disturb the King and us?
    And you, my lords, methinks you do not well
    To bear with their perverse objections.
    Let us persuade you take a better course.
KING HENRY: Come hither, you that would be combatants:
    Henceforth I charge you, as you love our favour,
    Quite to forget this quarrel, and the cause.
    And you, my lords, remember where we are:
    In France, amongst a fickle wavering nation;
    If they perceive dissension in our looks,
    And that within ourselves we disagree,
    How will their grudging stomachs be provok'd
    To wilful disobedience, and rebel!
    Beside, what infamy will there arise
    When foreign princes shall be certified
    That for a toy, a thing of no regard,
    King Henry's peers and chief nobility
    Destroy'd themselves and lost the realm of France!
    O, think upon the conquest of my father,
    My tender years, and let us not forgo
    That for a trifle that was bought with blood!
    Let me be umpire in this doubtful strife.
    I see no reason if I wear this rose,
    (*plucking a red rose from* BASSET)
    That any one should therefore be suspicious
    I more incline to Somerset than York:

Both are my kinsmen, and I love them both;
And therefore, as we thither came in peace,
So let us still continue peace and love.
Cousin of York, we institute your Grace
To be our Regent in these parts of France:
And, good my Lord of Somerset, unite
Your troops of horsemen with his bands of foot:
And like true subjects, sons of your progenitors,
Go cheerfully together and digest
Your angry choler on your enemies.
Ourself, my Lord Protector, will retire to Calais;
From thence to England, where we hope 'ere long
To be presented with your victories.
(*Exit* KING HENRY, GLOUCESTER, SOMERSET, BASSET,
SUFFOLK. *Left, a small disgruntled group arm themselves.*
YORK, VERNON, WARWICK *not arming but leaving them to
follow* KING HENRY. *Left also, old* EXETER.)

EXETER: My Lord of York, I promise you the King
Prettily, methought, did play the orator.

YORK: And so he did; but yet I like it not,
In that he wears the badge of Somerset.
(*Squires and servants arming* YORK; *his sergeants and men at
arms attend.*)

WARWICK: Tush, that was but his fancy; blame him not.

EXETER: I dare presume, sweet Prince, he thought no harm.

YORK: And if I wist he did – but let it rest;
Other affairs must now be managed.
(*Exit* YORK. *Exit* WARWICK *after* KING HENRY.)

EXETER: Well didst thou, Richard, to suppress thy voice;
For, had the passions of thy heart burst out . . .
(*Enter English army to* EXETER.)

SCENE 14

Bordeaux. Field of Battle. Trumpeter.

TALBOT: Bastard of Orleans, General of Bordeaux,
English John Talbot bravely calls you forth,
Servant in arms to Harry King of England;

And thus he would: Open your city gates,
Be humble to us, call my sovereign yours
And do him homage as obedient subjects,
And I'll withdraw me and my bloody power;
But if you frown upon this proffer'd peace,
You tempt the fury of my three attendants,
Lean Famine, quartering Steel, and climbing Fire.
(*Enter* BASTARD OF ORLEANS.)

BASTARD: Thou ominous and fearful owl of death,
Our nation's terror and their bloody scourge!
The period of thy tyranny approacheth.
On us thou canst not enter but by death;
For, I protest, we are well fortified,
If thou retire, the Dauphin, well appointed,
Stands with the snares of war to tangle thee;
On either hand thee there are squadrons pitch'd
To wall thee from the liberty of flight;
And no way canst thou turn thee for redress
But Death doth front thee with apparent spoil,
And pale Destruction meets thee in the face.
Hark! Hark! the Dauphin's drum, a warning bell.
Sings heavy music to thy timorous soul.
And mine shall ring thy dire departure out.
(TALBOT *with his battle group. A standard, archers, men at arms.*)

TALBOT: He fables not; I hear the enemy.
Out, some light horsemen, and peruse their wings.
(WATKINS *goes with the message. Music. The fight intensifying.* TALBOT *warns:*)
O, negligent and heedless discipline!
How we are park'd and bounded in a pale –
A little herd of England's timorous deer,
Maz'd with a yelping kennel of French curs!
(*An order written. Given to* EXETER.)
My Lord of Exeter, though your martial counsel
Means much to me, deliver me this urgent plea.
(*The order given. Exit* EXETER. *A great roar goes up from the French, an oath.*)

WATKINS: Ten thousand French have ta'en the sacrament

To rive their dangerous artillery
Upon no Christian soul but English Talbot.
(*Then a terrible din. The shrieking and unnatural din they have
withstood before.*)
The witch! The witch!
(*Exit* WATKINS.)

TALBOT: If we be English deer, be then in blood;
Not rascal-like to fall down with a pinch,
But rather, moody-mad and desperate stags,
Turn on the bloody hounds with heads of steel
And make the cowards stand aloof at bay:
Sell every man his life as dear as mine,
And they shall find dear deer of us, my friends.
God and Saint George, Talbot and England's right,
Prosper our colours in this dangerous fight!
(*The din reaches its crescendo then stops.*)

SCENE 15

Gascony. Enter YORK.

YORK: A plague upon that villain Somerset
That thus delays my promised supply
Of horsemen that were levied for this siege!
Renowned Talbot doth expect my aid,
And I am louted by a traitor villain.
(*Enter* EXETER, *exhausted, bloodied.*)

EXETER: Spur to the rescue of noble Talbot,
Who now is girdled with a waist of iron,
And hemm'd about with grim destruction.
To Bordeaux, warlike Duke! Else farewell, Talbot.
(YORK *holds up* EXETER, *reads the despatch, hand out for
wine, a servant instantly providing for both nobles. Enter,
opposite,* SOMERSET. *Enter* WATKINS *with despatch. Read
by* SOMERSET.)

SOMERSET: It is too late; I cannot send them now:
This expedition was by York and Talbot
Too rashly plotted: the over-daring Talbot
Hath sullied all his gloss of former honour.

York set him on to fight and die in shame
That, Talbot dead, great York might bear the name.
(YORK *throws down the despatch*.)
YORK: O God, that Somerset were in Talbot's place!
So should we save a valiant gentleman
By forfeiting a traitor and a coward.
EXETER: O, send some succour to the distress'd lord!
YORK: He dies, we lose; I break my warlike word;
We mourn, France smiles; we lose, they daily get —
All long of this vile traitor Somerset.
Away, vexation almost stops my breath.
(SOMERSET *throws down the despatch*.)
Exeter, farewell; no more my fortune can
But curse the cause I cannot aid the man.
(*Shrieking noise, the* TALBOT *group staggers, droops, then still.*
WATKINS *towards* YORK.)
Maine, Blois, Poictiers, and Tours, are won away,
Long all of Somerset and his delay.
(*Exit* YORK. EXETER *towards* SOMERSET.)
SOMERSET: How now, good Exeter! whither were you sent?
EXETER: Whither, young lord! From bought and sold Lord
Talbot,
Who, ring'd about with bold adversity,
Cries out for fresh young York and Somerset.
SOMERSET: York set him on; York should have sent him aid.
EXETER: And York as fast upon your Grace exclaims,
Swearing that you withhold his levied horse,
Collected for this expedition.
SOMERSET: York lies; he might have sent and had the horse:
I owe him little duty, and less love,
And take foul scorn to fawn on him by sending.
EXETER: The fraud of England, not the force of France,
Hath now entrapp'd the noble-minded Talbot:
Never to England shall he bear his life,
But dies betray'd to fortune by your strife.
SOMERSET: If he be dead, brave Talbot, then adieu!
(*Exit* SOMERSET.)
EXETER: His fame lives in the world, his shame in you.
(*Exit* EXETER.)

36

WATKINS: Thus, while the vulture of sedition
    Feeds in the bosom of such great commanders,
    Sleeping neglection doth betray to loss
    The conquest of our scarce-cold conqueror,
    That ever-living man of memory,
    Henry the Fifth. Whiles they each other cross,
    Lives, honours, lands, and all, hurry to loss.

SCENE 16

The English camp near Bordeaux. A shout from off: 'A Talbot!'

JOHN TALBOT: A Talbot!
GROUP: A Talbot!
    (*Enter* JOHN TALBOT *through the French.*)
TALBOT: O young John Talbot, I did send for thee
    To tutor thee in stratagems of war . . .
    (TALBOT *out of the group to greet his son. A ragged cheer.*)
    That Talbot's name might be in thee reviv'd.
    Now thou art come unto a feast of death,
    A terrible and unavoided danger;
    Therefore, dear boy, mount on my swiftest horse,
    And I'll direct thee how thou shalt escape
    By sudden flight. Come, dally not, be gone.
JOHN TALBOT: Is my name Talbot? and am I your son?
    And shall I fly?
TALBOT: Fly, to revenge my death if I be slain.
JOHN TALBOT: He that flies so will ne'er return again.
TALBOT: Shall all thy mother's hopes lie in one tomb?
JOHN TALBOT: Ay, rather than I'll shame my mother's womb.
TALBOT: Part of thy father may be sav'd in thee.
JOHN TALBOT: No part of him but will be sham'd in me.
TALBOT: Thou never hadst renown, nor canst not lose it.
JOHN TALBOT: Yes, your renowned name: shall flight abuse it?
TALBOT: Thy father's charge shall clear thee from that stain.
JOHN TALBOT: You cannot witness for me, being slain.
    If death be so apparent, then both fly.
TALBOT: And leave my followers here to fight and die?

My age was never tainted with such shame.
JOHN TALBOT: And shall my youth be guilty of such blame?
No more can I be sever'd from your side
Than can yourself yourself in twain divide.
Stay, go, do what you will, the like do I;
For live I will not, if my father die.
TALBOT: Then here I take my leave of thee, fair son,
Born to eclipse thy life this afternoon.
Come, side by side, together live and die,
And soul with soul from France to heaven fly.
(*Into the group,* TALBOT *and his son at the standard.*)
JOHN TALBOT: Then talk no more of flight, it is no boot;
If son to Talbot, die at Talbot's foot.
(TALBOT *shouts:*)
TALBOT: Then follow thou thy desperate sire of Crete,
Thou Icarus; thy life to me is sweet:
If thou wilt fight, fight by thy father's side,
And, commendable prov'd, let's die in pride.
Saint George and victory! Fight soldiers, fight:
York and Somerset hath with Talbot broke their words,
And left us to the rage of France, their swords.
Saint George and victory!
ALL: Saint George and victory!
TALBOT: Where is my other life? Mine own is gone.
O, where's young Talbot? Where is valiant John?
Triumphant death, smear'd with captivity,
Young Talbot's valour makes me smile at thee.
When he perceiv'd me shrink and on my knee,
His bloody sword he brandish'd over me,
And like a hungry lion did commence
Rough deeds of rage and stern impatience;
But when my angry guardant stood alone,
Tendering my ruin and assail'd of none,
Dizzy-ey'd fury and great rage of heart
Suddenly made him from my side to start
Into the clust'ring battle of the French;
And in that sea of blood my boy did drench
His overmounting spirit; and there died
My Icarus, my blossom, in his pride.

(TALBOT *shrieks and gathers up his son.*)
Thou antic Death, which laugh'st us here to scorn,
Anon, from thy insulting tyranny,
Two Talbots winged through the lither sky,
In thy despite shall scape mortality.
Soldiers, adieu! I have what I would have,
Now my old arms are young John Talbot's grave.
(TALBOT *speared by the French. He dies.*)

SCENE 17

Enter singly, in awe, to whisper; CHARLES, ALENÇON,
BURGUNDY, *the* BASTARD OF ORLEANS, JOAN LA PUCELLE.

CHARLES: Had York and Somerset brought rescue in,
    We should have found a bloody day of this.
BURGUNDY: Is Talbot slain – the Frenchmen's only Scourge,
    Our kingdom's Terror and black Nemesis?
BASTARD: Hew them to pieces, hack their bones asunder,
    Whose life was England's glory, Gallia's wonder.
CHARLES: O no, forbear! For that which we have fled
    During the life, let us not wrong it dead.
    (*Enter* MESSENGER *to* ALENÇON.)
    What tidings send our scouts?
ALENÇON: The English army, that divided was
    Into two parties, is now conjoin'd in one,
    And means to give you battle presently.
CHARLES: Somewhat too sudden, sirs, the warning is;
    But we will presently provide for them.
BURGUNDY: I trust the ghost of Talbot is not there.
CHARLES: Now he is gone, my lord, you need not fear.
PUCELLE: Of all base passions, fear is most accurs'd.
    Command the conquest, Charles, it shall be thine.
CHARLES: Then on, my lords; and France be fortunate.
    (*Exeunt all.*)

Before Angiers. JOAN LA PUCELLE.

PUCELLE: The Regent conquers and the Frenchmen fly.
 Now help, ye charming spells and periapts;
 Now, ye familiar spirits that are cull'd
 Out of the powerful regions under earth.
 Help me this once, that France may get the field.
 O, hold me not with silence over-long!
 Where I was wont to feed you with my blood,
 I'll lop a member off and give it you
 So you do condescend to help me now.
 No hope to have redress? My body shall
 Pay recompense if you will grant my suit.
 Cannot my body nor blood-sacrifice
 Entreat you to your wonted furtherance?
 Then take my soul; my body, soul and all.
 See! they forsake me. Now the time is come
 That France must vail her lofty-plumed crest
 And let her head fall into England's lap.
 (*Enter* YORK *with nets.*)
YORK: Damsel of France, I think I have you fast.
 (*Enter* SOMERSET *with nets.*)
 Unchain your spirits now with spelling charms,
 And try if they can gain your liberty.
SOMERSET: See how the ugly witch doth bend her brows,
 As if, with Circe, she would change my shape!
PUCELLE: Chang'd to a worser shape thou canst not be.
YORK: O, Charles the Dauphin is a proper man:
 No shape but his can please your dainty eye.
PUCELLE: A plaguing mischief light on Charles and thee!
 And may ye both be suddenly surpris'd
 By bloody hands, in sleeping on your beds!
YORK: Fell banning hag, enchantress, hold thy tongue!
PUCELLE: I prithee, give me leave to curse awhile.
YORK: Curse, miscreant, when thou comest to the stake!
SOMERSET: Take her away, for she hath liv'd too long,
 To fill the world with vicious qualities.

(PUCELLE *dragged, screaming. Soldiers strip her and tie her to stake.*)

WARWICK: And hark ye, sirs, because she is a maid,
Spare for no faggots, let there be enow:
Place barrels of pitch upon the fatal stake,
So that her torture may be shortened.
(*A red cross is painted on* PUCELLE.)

PUCELLE: I am with child, ye bloody homicides;
Murder not then the fruit within my womb,
Although ye hale me to a violent death.

YORK: Now heaven forfend!
(*He crosses himself. As does the entire army.*)
The holy maid with child!

WARWICK: The greatest miracle that e'er ye wrought!
Well, go to; we will have no bastards live,
Especially since Charles but father it.

PUCELLE: You are deceiv'd; my child is none of his:
It was Alençon that enjoy'd my love.
(*The army sits, exhausted from fighting but now enlivened by
the spectacle of the wretched* PUCELLE. *They jeer each
utterance.* WATKINS *starts to perform, a nod from* YORK *after
his first carefully timed interjection:*)

WATKINS: Alençon!
Alençon! that notorious Machiavel!
It dies and if it had a thousand lives.

PUCELLE: O, give me leave, I have deluded you:
'Twas neither Charles, nor yet the Duke I nam'd,
But Reignier, King of Naples, that prevail'd.

WATKINS: A married man! that's most intolerable.
(*The nobles, amused, withdrawing, hands out; wine, food,
scurrying servants from the mound of dead.*)

VERNON: Why, here's a girl!

WATKINS: I think she knows not well —

BASSET: There were so many — whom she may accuse.
(*Stakes brought, faggots set up.*)

WATKINS: And yet, forsooth, she is a virgin pure!
(YORK *puts a stop to the jeering.*)

YORK: Strumpet, thy words condemn thy brat and thee:
Use no entreaty, for it is in vain.

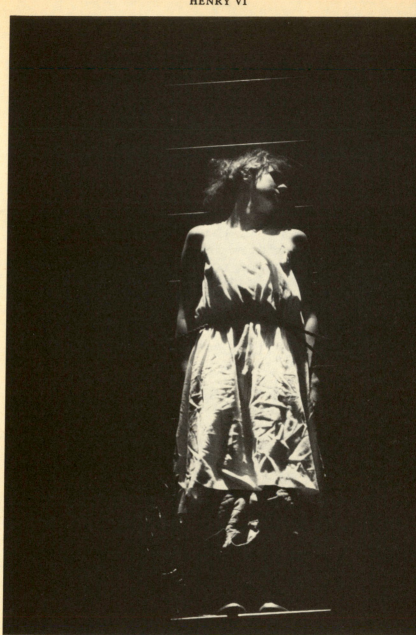

(PUCELLE *at the stake, the flames lick up, she is on the mound*
of bodies formed by TALBOT *and his group; she writhes, she*
screams:)

PUCELLE: I never had to do with wicked spirits;
    But you, that are polluted with your lusts,
    Stain'd with the guiltless blood of innocents,
    Corrupt and tainted with a thousand vices,
    Because you want the grace that others have,
    You judge it straight a thing impossible
    To compass wonders but by help of devils.
    No, misconceived Joan of Arc hath been
    A virgin from her tender infancy,
    Chaste and immaculate in very thought;
    Whose maiden blood, thus rigorously effus'd
    Will cry for vengeance at the gates of heaven.

YORK: Break thou in pieces and consume to ashes,
    Thou foul accursed minister of hell!
    Joan grilled!!
    Sceaboles! Arbaron! Elohi!
    Elmigith! Herenobulcule!
    Methe! Baluth!
    Ferete!
    Bacuhaba! Guvarin"
    By the empire which ye exert over us,
    Fulfil this work that I may pass invisible
    To whom I wish!

WATKINS: Fear him who was immolated in Isaac
    Sold in Joseph
    Slain in the lamb, fear him,
    Fear him whom was crucified in man!
    (*He thrusts the cross at her.*)
    Fear him who was triumphant over hell.
    (*As* PUCELLE *touches the cross she writhes and dies and the*
    flames and smoke leap up.)

SCENE 19

London. The palace.
Enter KING HENRY *and* GLOUCESTER.

KING HENRY: Have you perus'd the letters from the Pope,
    The Emperor, and the Earl of Armagnac?
GLOUCESTER: I have, my lord; and their intent is this:
    They humbly sue unto your Excellence
    To have a godly peace concluded of
    Between the realms of England and of France.
KING HENRY: How doth your Grace affect their motion?
GLOUCESTER: Well, my good lord, and as the only means
    To stop effusion of our Christian blood
    And stablish quietness on every side.
KING HENRY: Ay, marry, uncle, for I always thought
    It was both impious and unnatural
    That such immanity and bloody strife
    Should reign among professors of one faith.
GLOUCESTER: Beside, my lord, the sooner to effect
    And surer bind this knot of amity,
    The Earl of Armagnac, near knit to Charles,
    A man of great authority in France,
    Proffers his only daughter to your Grace
    In marriage, with a large and sumptuous dowry.
KING HENRY: Marriage, uncle! Alas, my years are young!
    And fitter is my study and my books
    Than wanton dalliance with a paramour.
    Yet call th' ambassadors, and, as you please,
    I shall be well content with any choice
    Tends to God's glory and my country's weal.
GLOUCESTER: I shall inform the Pope, Charles and the Earl
    As, liking of the lady's virtuous gifts,
    Her beauty, and the value of her dower,
    You do intend she shall be England's Queen.
KING HENRY: Bear her this jewel, pledge of my affection.
    (*Exit.*)

SCENE 20

Camp of the Duke of York in Anjou.
Enter CARDINAL BEAUFORT (*formerly Bishop of Winchester*),
with LEGATE, *to* YORK.

44

CARDINAL BEAUFORT: Lord Regent, I do greet your
                                    Excellence
 With letters of commission from the King.
 For know, my lords, the states of Christendom,
 Mov'd with remorse of these outrageous broils,
 Have earnestly implor'd a general peace
 Betwixt our nation and the aspiring French.
YORK: Is all our travail turn'd to this effect?
 After the slaughter of so many peers
 So many captains, gentlemen, and soldiers,
 That in this quarrel have been overthrown
 And sold their bodies for their country's benefit,
 Shall we at last conclude effeminate peace?
 O, Warwick, Warwick! I foresee with grief
 The utter loss of all the realm of France.
WARWICK: Be patient, York: if we conclude a peace,
 It shall be with such strict and several covenants
 As little shall the Frenchmen gain thereby.
 (SOMERSET *at the side of* CARDINAL BEAUFORT, BASSET
 *joining him. The united army dividing into white and red rose
 again.* YORK, *in despair:*)
YORK: So, now dismiss your army when ye please;
 Hang up your ensigns, let your drums be still,
 For here we entertain a solemn peace.
 (*Exeunt all except* CARDINAL BEAUFORT, EXETER *and*
 LEGATE.)
CARDINAL BEAUFORT: Stay, my Lord Legate; you shall first
                                                receive
 The sum of money which I promised
 Should be deliver'd to his Holiness
 For clothing me in these grave ornaments.
 (*Exit* CARDINAL BEAUFORT *and* LEGATE.)
EXETER: What! is my Lord of Winchester install'd
 And call'd unto a cardinal's degree?
 Then I perceive that will be verified
 Henry the Fifth did sometime prophesy:
 'If once he come to be a cardinal,
 He'll make his cap co-equal with the crown.'
 (*Exit* EXETER.)

Enter MARGARET. *Enter* SUFFOLK *to watch her.*

SUFFOLK: O fairest beauty, do not fear nor fly!
　　For I will touch thee but with reverent hands,
　　And lay them gently on thy tender side.
　　I kiss these fingers for eternal peace.
　　Who art thou, say, that I may honour thee?
MARGARET: Margaret my name, and daughter to a king,
　　The king of Naples – whosoe'er thou art.
SUFFOLK: An earl I am, and Suffolk am I call'd.
　　Be not offended, nature's miracle,
　　Thou art allotted to be ta'en by me:
　　So doth the swan her downy cygnets save,
　　Keeping them prisoner underneath her wings.
　　Yet, if this servile usage once offend,
　　Go and be free again as Suffolk's friend.
　　(*She is going.*)
　　O, stay! – I have no power to let her pass;
　　Fain would I woo her, yet I dare not speak.
MARGARET: Say, Earl of Suffolk, if thy name be so,
　　What ransom must I pay before I pass?
SUFFOLK: How canst thou tell she will deny thy suit,
　　Before thou make a trial of her love?
MARGARET: Why speak'st thou not? What ransom must I pay?
SUFFOLK: She's beautiful, and therefore to be woo'd;
　　She is a woman, therefore to be won.
MARGARET: Wilt thou accept of ransom, yea or no?
SUFFOLK: Fond man, remember that thou hast a wife;
　　Then how can Margaret be thy paramour?
MARGARET: He talks at random; sure, the man is mad.
SUFFOLK: And yet a dispensation may be had.
MARGARET: And yet I would that you would answer me.
SUFFOLK: I'll win this Lady Margaret. For whom?
　　Why, for my king! Tush, that's a wooden thing!
MARGARET: He talks of wood: it is some carpenter.
SUFFOLK: Yet so my fancy may be satisfied,
　　And peace establish'd between these realms.

Henry is youthful and will quickly yield. –
Lady, vouchsafe to listen what I say.
MARGARET: Perhaps I shall be rescu'd by the French;
And then I need not crave his courtesy.
SUFFOLK: Sweet madam, give me hearing in a cause –
MARGARET: Tush, women have been captivate ere now.
SUFFOLK: Lady, wherefore talk you so?
MARGARET: I cry you mercy, 'tis but quid for quo.
SUFFOLK: Say, gentle Princess, would you not suppose
Your bondage happy, to be made a queen?
MARGARET: To be a queen in bondage is more vile
Than is a slave in base servility;
For princes should be free.
SUFFOLK: And so shall you.
I'll undertake to make thee Henry's queen,
To put a golden sceptre in thy hand
And set a precious crown upon thy head,
If thou wilt condescend to be my –
MARGARET: What?
SUFFOLK: His love.
MARGARET: I am unworthy to be Henry's wife.
    (*Enter* REIGNIER.)
SUFFOLK: See, Reignier, see, thy daughter prisoner!
REIGNIER: To whom?
SUFFOLK: To me.
REIGNIER: Suffolk, what remedy?
I am a soldier and unapt to weep
Or to exclaim on fortune's fickleness.
SUFFOLK: Consent, and for thy honour give consent,
Thy daughter shall be wedded to my king.
REIGNIER: Upon condition I may quietly
Enjoy mine own, the country Maine, and Anjou,
Free from oppression or the stroke of war,
My daughter shall be Henry's, if he please.
SUFFOLK: Regnier of France, I give thee kingly thanks,
Because this is in traffic of a king.
REIGNIER: I do embrace thee, as I would embrace
The Christian prince, King Henry, were he here.
SUFFOLK: So farewell, Reignier: set this diamond safe

In golden palaces, as it becomes.
Farewell, sweet maid; but hark you, Margaret:
No princely commendations to my king?

MARGARET: Such commendations as becomes a maid,
A virgin, and his servant, say to him.

SUFFOLK: Words sweetly plac'd and modestly directed;
But, madam, I must trouble you again:
No loving token to his Majesty?

MARGARET: Yes, my good lord; a pure unspotted heart,
Never yet taint with love, I send the King.

SUFFOLK: And this withal.

(SUFFOLK *kisses her*.)

MARGARET: That for thyself: I will not so presume
To send such foolish tokens to a king.

(*Exit* REIGNIER *and* MARGARET.)

SUFFOLK: O, wert thou for myself! But, Suffolk, stay;
Thou may'st not wander in that labyrinth:
There Minotaurs and ugly treasons lurk.
Solicit Henry with her wondrous praise.
Bethink thee on her virtues that surmount,
And natural graces that extinguish art;
That, when thou com'st to kneel at Henry's feet,
Thou may'st bereave him of his wits with wonder.
Thus Suffolk shall prevail, and thus he goes;
Margaret shall now be Queen, and rule the King;
But I will rule both her, the King, and realm.

(*Enter the English army to* SUFFOLK. *Flourish and solemn music. The English leave France.*)

ACT TWO

SCENE I

London. Garden of the royal palace.
Enter HENRY *and* SUFFOLK.

KING HENRY: Your wondrous rare description, noble Earl,
    Of beauteous Margaret hath astonish'd me.
SUFFOLK: Yet, what is more, she is not so divine,
    So full replete with choice of all delights,
    But with as humble lowliness of mind,
    She is content to be at your command;
    Command, I mean, of virtuous chaste intents,
    To love, and honour Henry as her lord.
KING HENRY: And otherwise will Henry ne'er presume.
    Therefore, my Lord Protector, give consent
    That Margaret may be England's royal Queen.
GLOUCESTER: So should I give consent to flatter sin,
    You know, my lord, your Highness is betroth'd
    Unto another lady of esteem.
SUFFOLK: A poor earl's daughter in unequal odds.
GLOUCESTER: Why what, I pray, is Margaret more than that?
SUFFOLK: Yes, my lord, her father is a king
    The King of Naples and Jerusalem;
    And of such great authority in France
    As his alliance will confirm our peace.
GLOUCESTER: And so the Earl of Armagnac may do.
EXETER: Beside, his wealth doth warrant a liberal dower.
SUFFOLK: A dower, my lords!
    (KING HENRY *walks apart again.*)
                        Disgrace not so your king,
    That he should be so abject, base, and poor,
    To choose for wealth and not for perfect love.
    Whom should we match with Henry, being a king,
    But Margaret, that is daughter to a king?
KING HENRY: Whether it be through force of your report,
    My noble Lord of Suffolk, or for that
    My tender youth was never yet attaint

With any passion of inflaming love,
I cannot tell; but this I am assur'd,
I feel such sharp dissension in my breast,
Such fierce alarums both of hope and fear,
As I am sick with working of my thoughts.
Go therefore, Suffolk, bring her to our presence.
(*Exit* SUFFOLK.)
And you, good uncle, banish all offence;
If you do censure me by what you were,
Not what you are, I know it will excuse
This sudden execution of my will.
(*Re-enter* SUFFOLK *and* MARGARET.)

SUFFOLK: Before your high imperial Majesty,
I humbly now upon my bended knee,
In sight of England and her lordly peers,
Deliver up the lady Margaret
The happiest gift that ever marquess gave,
The fairest queen that ever king receiv'd.

KING HENRY: Suffolk arise. Welcome, Queen Margaret;
I can express no kinder sign of love
Than this kind kiss. O Lord, that lends me life,
Lend me a heart replete with thankfulness!
For thou hast given me in this beauteous face
A world of earthly blessings to my soul,
If sympathy of love unite our thoughts.

QUEEN MARGARET: Great King of England, and my gracious
lord,
The mutual conference that my mind hath had
By day, by night, waking, and in my dreams,
In courtly company, or at my beads,
With you mine alderliefest sovereign,
Makes me the bolder to salute my king,
With ruder terms, such as my wit affords,
And over joy of heart doth minister.

KING HENRY: Her sight did ravish, but her grace in speech,
Her words y-clad with wisdom's majesty,
Makes me from wond'ring, fall to weeping joys,
Such is the fulness of my heart's content.
Lords, and with one cheerful voice welcome my love.

SUFFOLK: Long live Queen Margaret, England's happiness!

ALL: Long live Queen Margaret, England's happiness!

QUEEN MARGARET: We thank you all.

SUFFOLK: My Lord Protector, so it please your Grace,
Here are the articles of contracted peace.

(GLOUCESTER *reads:*)

GLOUCESTER: 'Imprimus, It is agreed between the French
King Charles, and William de la Pole, Marquess of Suffolk,
ambassador for Henry King of England, That the said
Henry shall espouse the Lady Margaret, daughter unto
Reignier King of Naples, Sicilia, and Jerusalem, and crown
her Queen of England, ere the thirtieth of May next
ensuing. Item, That the duchy of Anjou and the county of
Maine shall be releas'd and deliver'd to the King her father' –

KING HENRY: Uncle, how now!

GLOUCESTER: Pardon me, gracious Lord;
Some sudden qualm hath struck me at the heart
And dimm'd mine eyes, that I can read no further.

KING HENRY: Uncle of Winchester, I pray read on.

CARDINAL BEAUFORT: 'Item, It is further agreed between
them, That the duchies of Anjou and Maine shall be
releas'd and deliver'd to the King her father, and she sent
over of the King of England's own proper cost and charges,
without having any dowry.'

KING HENRY: They please us well.
Lord Marquess, kneel down: we here create thee
First Duke of Suffolk, and gird thee with the sword.
Cousin of York, we here discharge your Grace
From being Regent in the parts of France,
Till term of eighteen months be full expir'd.
We thank you all for this great favour done,
In entertainment of our princely Queen.
Come, let us in, and with all speed provide
To see her coronation be perform'd.

(*Exeunt* KING HENRY, QUEEN MARGARET, *and* SUFFOLK.
Manet the rest.)

GLOUCESTER: Brave Peers of England, pillars of the state,
To you Duke Humphrey must unload his grief –
Your grief, the common grief of the land.

What! did my brother Henry spend his youth,
His valour, coin, and people, in the wars?
To conquer France, his true inheritance?
And did my brother Bedford toil his wits,
To keep by policy what Henry got?
Have you, brave York, Somerset and Warwick,
Receiv'd deep scars in France and Normandy?
Or hath the Cardinal here and myself
Studied so long, sat in the Council House
Early and late, debating to and fro
How France and Frenchmen might be kept in awe?
And shall these labours and these honours die?
O peers of England! Shameful is this league,
Fatal this marriage, cancelling your fame,
Undoing all, as all had never been!

CARDINAL BEAUFORT: My lord, what means this passionate
                                                discourse?
Why France, 'tis ours; and we will keep it still.

GLOUCESTER: Ay, Beaufort, we will keep it, if we can;
But now it is impossible we should.

WARWICK: Suffolk, the new-made duke that rules the roast,
Hath given the duchy of Anjou and Maine
Unto her father, the poor King Reignier,
Who with will and main gave a bastard to the Maid.

GLOUCESTER: A proper jest, and never heard before,
That Suffolk should demand a whole fifteenth
For costs and charges in transporting her!
She should have stayed in France, and starv'd in France,
Before —

CARDINAL BEAUFORT: My Lord of Gloucester, now ye grow
                                                too hot:
It was the pleasure of my lord the King.

GLOUCESTER: My Lord of Winchester, I know your mind:
'Tis not my speeches that you do mislike
But 'tis my presence that doth trouble thee.
Rancour will out: proud prelate, in thy face
I see thy fury. If I longer stay
We shall begin our ancient bickerings.
My lords, farewell; and say, when I am gone,

I prophesied France will be lost ere long.
(*Exit* GLOUCESTER.)
CARDINAL BEAUFORT: So, there goes our Protector in a rage.
'Tis known to you he is mine enemy;
Nay, more, an enemy unto you all.
EXETER: I never saw but Humphrey, Duke of Gloucester,
Did bear him like a noble gentleman.
The common people favour him,
Calling him, 'Humphrey, the good Duke of Gloucester',
Clapping their hands, and crying with loud voice,
'Jesu maintain your royal Excellence!'
And 'God preserve the good Duke Humphrey!'
CARDINAL BEAUFORT: I fear me, lords, for all this flattering
gloss,
He will be found a dangerous Protector.
Consider, lords, he is the next of blood,
And heir apparent to the English crown.
SOMERSET: Why should he then protect our sovereign,
He being of age to govern of himself?
CARDINAL BEAUFORT: Look to it, lords: let not his smoothing
words
Bewitch your hearts; be wise and circumspect.
(*Exit* CARDINAL BEAUFORT.)
SOMERSET: Yet let us watch the haughty Cardinal:
If Gloucester be displac'd, he'll be Protector.
YORK: Or thou, or I?
(*Exit* SOMERSET, EXETER *and lords.*)
WARWICK: My Lord of York –
Thy late exploits done in the heart of France,
When thou wert Regent for our sovereign,
Have made thee fear'd and honour'd of the people.
Join we together for the public good,
In what we can, to bridle and suppress
The pride of Suffolk and the Cardinal.
And, as we may, cherish Duke Humphrey's deeds,
While they do tend the profit of the land.
So God help Warwick, as he loves the land,
And common profit of his country!
YORK: And so says York – for he has greater cause.

WARWICK: Then let's make haste and look unto the main.
YORK: Unto the main! O Warwick, Maine is lost!
(*Exit* WARWICK.)
So York must sit and fret and bite his tongue
While his own lands are bargain'd for and sold.
Anjou and Maine both given to the French!
The peers agreed, and Henry was well pleas'd
To change two dukedoms for a duke's fair daughter.
Cold news for me, for I had hope of France,
Even as I have of fertile England's soil.
A day will come when York shall claim his own;
And therefore I will take the Nevil's part
And make show of love to proud Duke Humphrey,
And when I spy advantage, claim the crown,
For that's the golden mark I seek to hit.
Then, York, be still awhile, till time do serve:
Watch thou, and wake when others be asleep,
To pry into the secrets of the state;
Till Henry surfeit in the joys of love,
With his new bride and England's dear-bought queen,
And Humphrey with the peers be fall'n at jars:
Then will I raise aloft the milk-white rose,
With whose sweet smell the air shall be perfum'd,
And in my standard bear the arms of York,
To grapple with the house of Lancaster;
And force perforce I'll make him yield the crown,
Whose bookish rule hath pull'd fair England down.
(*Exit* YORK.)

SCENE 2

The Duke of Gloucester's house.
Enter GLOUCESTER *and* ELEANOR.

ELEANOR: Why droops my lord, like over-ripen'd corn,
Hanging the head at Ceres' plenteous load?
Why are thine eyes fix'd to the sullen earth,
Gazing on that which seems to dim thy sight?
What seest thou there? King Henry's diadem,

Enchas'd with all the honours of the world?
If so, gaze on, and grovel on thy face,
Until thy head be circled with the same.
Put forth thy hand, reach at the glorious gold.
GLOUCESTER: O Nell, sweet Nell, if thou dost love thy lord,
Banish the canker of ambitious thoughts!
ELEANOR: But list to me, my Humphrey, my sweet duke:
I dreamt last night I sat in majesty
In the cathedral church of Westminster,
And in that chair where kings and queens are crown'd;
Where Henry and Dame Margaret kneel'd to me,
And on my head did set the diadem.
GLOUCESTER: Nay, Eleanor, then must I chide outright:
Art thou not second woman in the realm,
And the Protector's wife, belov'd of him?
And wilt thou still be hammering treachery,
To tumble down thy husband and thyself
From top of Honour to Disgrace's feet?
Away from me, and let me hear no more!
ELEANOR: What, what, my lord! Are you so choleric
With Eleanor, for telling but her dream?
Next time I'll keep my dreams unto myself,
And not be check'd.
GLOUCESTER: Nay, be not angry, I am pleas'd again.
(*Enter* MESSENGER.)
MESSENGER: My Lord Protector, 'tis his Highness' pleasure,
You do prepare to ride unto Saint Albans,
Where as the King and Queen do mean to hawk.
GLOUCESTER: I go. Come, Nell, wilt ride with me?
ELEANOR: Yes, my good lord, I'll follow presently.
(*Exit* GLOUCESTER *and* MESSENGER.)
Follow I must; I cannot go before,
While Gloucester bears this base and humble mind.
Were I a man, a duke, and next of blood,
I would remove these tedious stumbling-blocks,
And smooth my way upon their headless necks;
And, being a woman, I will not be slack
To play my part in Fortune's pageant.
Where are you there, Sir John? nay, fear not, man,

We are alone; here's none but thee, and I.
(*Enter* HUME.)
HUME: Jesu preserve your royal Majesty!
ELEANOR: What say'st thou, man? Hast thou as yet conferr'd
    With Margery Jourdain, the cunning witch,
    With Roger Bolingbroke, the conjurer?
HUME: This they have promis'd me, to show your Highness
    A spirit rais'd from depth of under ground,
    That shall make answer to such questions
    As by your Grace shall be propounded him.
ELEANOR: Here, Hume, take this reward; make merry, man,
    With thy confederates in this weighty cause.
    (*Exit* ELEANOR.)
HUME: Dame Eleanor gives gold to bring the witch:
    Gold cannot come amiss, were she a devil.
    Yet have I gold flies from another coast:
    I dare not say from the rich Cardinal
    And from the great and new-made Duke of Suffolk;
    Yet I do find it so; and thus, I fear, at last
    Hume's knavery will be the Duchess' wrack,
    And her attainture will be Humphrey's fall.
    Sort how it will, I shall have gold for all.
    (*Exit.*)

SCENE 3

The palace.
Enter KING HENRY, QUEEN MARGARET, GLOUCESTER,
CARDINAL BEAUFORT, YORK, SOMERSET, SALISBURY,
WARWICK, SUFFOLK *and* ELEANOR.

KING HENRY: For my part, noble lords, I care not which;
    Or Somerset or York, all's one to me.
YORK: If York have ill demean'd himself in France,
    Then let him be denay'd the regentship.
SOMERSET: If Somerset be unworthy of the place,
    Let York be regent; I will yield to him.
SUFFOLK: Before we make election, give me leave
    To show some reason, of no little force,

That York is most unmeet of any man.
YORK: I'll tell thee, Suffolk, why I am unmeet:
First, for I cannot flatter thee in pride;
Next, if I be appointed for the place,
My Lord of Somerset will keep me here,
Without discharge, money, or furniture,
Till France be won into the Dauphin's hands.
Last time I danc'd attendance on his will
Till Paris was besieg'd, famin'd and lost.
WARWICK: That can I witness; and a fouler fact
Did never traitor in the land commit.
SUFFOLK: Peace, headstrong Warwick!
WARWICK: Image of Pride, why should I hold my peace?
GLOUCESTER: Hold, my lords, and show good reason, Suffolk,
Why Somerset should be preferr'd in this.
QUEEN MARGARET: Because the king, forsooth, will have it so.
GLOUCESTER: Then let Somerset be Regent o'er the French,
But, madam, the king is old enough himself
To give his censure. These are no women's matters.
QUEEN MARGARET: If he be old enough, what needs your
                                  Grace
To be Protector of his Excellence?
GLOUCESTER: Madam, I am Protector of the realm,
And at his pleasure will resign my place.
SUFFOLK: Resign it then, and leave thine insolence.
Since thou wert king – as who is king but thou? –
The commonwealth hath daily run to wrack;
The Dauphin hath prevail'd beyond the seas;
And all the peers and nobles of the realm
Have been as bondmen to thy sovereignty.
CARDINAL BEAUFORT: The commons hast thou rack'd; the
                                  clergy's bags
Are lank and lean with thy extortions.
SOMERSET: Thy sumptuous buildings and thy wife's attire
Have cost a mass of public treasury.
CARDINAL BEAUFORT: Thy cruelty in execution
Upon offenders hath exceeded law,
And left thee to the mercy of the law.
QUEEN MARGARET: Thy sale of offices and towns in France,

If they were known, as the suspect is great,
Would make thee quickly hop without thy head.

GLOUCESTER: I came to talk of commonwealth affairs.
As for your spiteful false objections,
Prove them, and I lie open to the law:
But God in mercy so deal with my soul
As I in duty love my king and country!
Farewell, my Lords.
(*Exit.*)

KING HENRY: Oh, how irksome is this music to my heart!
When such strings jar, what hope of harmony?
(*Exit.*)

QUEEN MARGARET: My Lord of Suffolk, say, is this the guise,
Is this the government of Britain's isle?
What! shall King Henry be a pupil still
Under the surly Gloucester's governance?
Am I a queen in title and in style,
And must be made a subject to a duke?
I tell thee, Pole, when in the city Tours
Thou ran'st a tilt in honour of my love,
And stol'st away the ladies' hearts of France,
I thought King Henry had resembled thee
In courage, courtship, and proportion:
But all his mind is bent to holiness,
His study is his tilt-yard, and his loves
Are brazen images of canoniz'd saints.
I would the college of the Cardinals
Would choose him Pope, and carry him to Rome,
And set the triple crown upon his head;
That were a state fit for his holiness.

SUFFOLK: Madam, be patient; as I was cause
Your Highness came to England, so will I
In England work your Grace's full content.

QUEEN MARGARET: Beside the haughty Protector, have we
Beaufort,
The imperious churchman; Somerset,
And grumbling York; and not the least of these
But can do more in England than the King.

SUFFOLK: And he of these that can do most of all

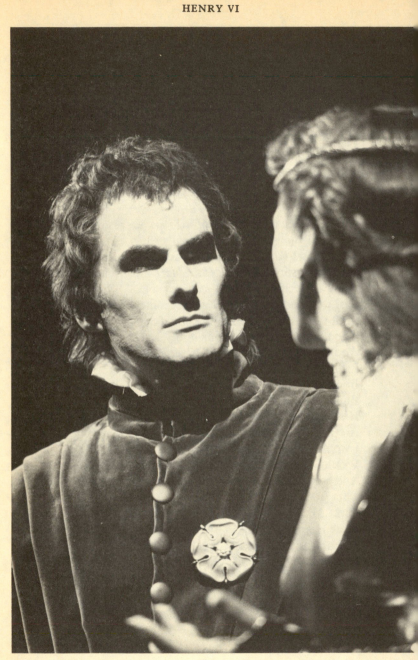

Cannot do more in England that the Nevils.
My Lord of Warwick is no simple peer.
QUEEN MARGARET: Not all these lords do vex me half so
                                                    much
    As that proud dame, the Lord Protector's wife:
    She sweeps it through the court with troops of ladies,
    More like an empress than Duke Humphrey's wife.
    Strangers in court do take her for the queen.
    Shall I not live to be aveng'd on her?
    Contemptuous base-born callet as she is.
SUFFOLK: Madam, myself have lim'd a bush for her,
    And plac'd a quire of such enticing birds
    That she will light to listen to their lays,
    And never mount to trouble you again.
    So, let her rest: and, madam, list to me:
    Although we fancy not the Cardinal,
    Yet must we join with him and with the lords
    Till we have brought Duke Humphrey in disgrace.
    So, one by one, we'll weed them all at last,
    And you yourself shall steer the happy helm.
    (*Exit* QUEEN MARGARET *and* SUFFOLK.)
YORK: Now, my good Lord Warwick, give me leave,
    Being alone, to satisfy myself,
    In craving your opinion of my title,
    Which is infallible, to England's crown.
WARWICK: My lord, break off. I know your mind in full.
    And in this private plot I'll be the first
    That shall salute our rightful sovereign
    With honour of his birthright to the crown.
YORK: I thank thee, Warwick. I am not your king
    Till I be crown'd and that my sword be stain'd
    With heart-blood of the house of Lancaster;
    And that's not suddenly to be perform'd
    But with advice and silent secrecy.
    Do you as I do in these dangerous days,
    Wink at the Duke of Suffolk's insolence,
    At Beaufort's pride, at Somerset's ambition.
    Till they have snar'd the shepherd of the flock,
    That virtuous prince, the good Duke Humphrey:

61

'Tis that they seek; and they, in seeking that,
Shall find their deaths, if York can prophesy.

WARWICK: My heart assures me, that the Earl of Warwick
Shall one day make the Duke of York a king.

YORK: And, Nevil, this I do assure myself;
Richard shall live to make the Earl of Warwick
The greatest man in England but the king.
(*Exit* WARWICK *and* YORK.)

SCENE 4

Gloucester's garden.
Enter BOLINGBROKE, MARGERY JOURDAIN *and* SOUTHWELL.
Enter HUME *and* ELEANOR.

HUME: Come, my masters; the Duchess, I tell you, expects
performance of your promises.

BOLINGBROKE: Master Hume, we are therefore provided.

MARGERY JOURDAIN: Then, Roger Bolingbroke, about thy
task
And frame a circle here upon the earth,
Whilst I do whisper with the devils below
And conjure them for to obey our will.

BOLINGBROKE: Mother Jourdain, be you prostrate, and grovel
on the earth; John Southwell, read you; and let us to work.

ELEANOR: Well said, my masters; and welcome all to this gear,
the sooner the better.

BOLINGBROKE: Patience, good lady; wizards know their times.

SOUTHWELL: Diavolo che sei capo
Di tutti i diavoli!

MARGERY JOURDAIN: Eorthe the onbere eallum hier mihtum
ond maegenum!

HUME: Quod superius, sicut inferius!

BOLINGBROKE: Metatron, Melekh, Beroth, Noth,
Vennibeth, Mach and all ye, conjure te –
(MARGERY JOURDAIN *sits up suddenly, as if transfixed.*)

MARGERY JOURDAIN: Adsum. Asnath!
By the eternal God, whose name and power
Thou tremblest at, answer that I shall ask.

62

Ask what thou wilt.

(ELEANOR *whispers to* HUME, *who whispers to*
BOLINGBROKE, *who asks:*)

BOLINGBROKE: First, of the King, what shall of him become?

MARGERY JOURDAIN: The duke yet lives that Henry shall
depose;
But him outlive, and die a violent death.

BOLINGBROKE: What fate awaits the Duke of Suffolk?

MARGERY JOURDAIN: By water shall he die and take his end.

BOLINGBROKE: What shall betide the Duke of Somerset?

(*Enter* SUFFOLK *with falconers, unseen.*)

MARGERY JOURDAIN: Let him shun castles.

ELEANOR: What dost thou prophesy of Gloucester's house?

MARGERY JOURDAIN: Why, Gloucester shall be king,
Gloucester king.
Have done, for more I hardly can endure.

BOLINGBROKE: Descend to darkness and the burning lake:
False fiend, avoid!

(MARGERY JOURDAIN *shaking, now a small empty creature.*
ELEANOR *stunned. Enter* SUFFOLK *and soldiers.*)

SUFFOLK: Lay hands upon these traitors and their trash.
What! madam, are you there? The king and commonwealth
Are deeply indebted for this piece of pains:
My Lord Protector will, I doubt it not,
See you well guerdon'd for these good deserts.
Away with them! Let them be clapp'd up close,
And kept asunder —

SCENE 5

Saint Albans.
Enter KING HENRY, QUEEN MARGARET, GLOUCESTER,
CARDINAL BEAUFORT *and* EXETER, *with falconers hallowing.*

QUEEN MARGARET: Believe me, lords, for flying at the brook,
I saw not better sport these seven years' day:
Yet, by your leave, the wind was very high,
And, ten to one, old Joan had not gone out.

KING HENRY: But what a point, my lord, your falcon made,

And what a pitch she flew above the rest!
To see how God in all his creatures works!
Yea, man and birds are fain of climbing high.
(*Enter the* MAYOR.)

ALL: A miracle! A miracle!

GLOUCESTER: What means this noise?

MAYOR: A miracle!

GLOUCESTER: Fellow, what miracle?

MAYOR: Forsooth, a blind man at Saint Alban's shrine,
Within this half-hour hath receiv'd his sight;
A man that ne'er saw in his life before.

KING HENRY: Now, God be prais'd, that to believing souls
Gives light in darkness, comfort in despair!

SIMPCOX: Born blind –

SIMPCOX'S WIFE: A miracle.

GLOUCESTER: Stand by, my masters; bring him near the King;
His Highness' pleasure is to talk with him.

KING HENRY: Good fellow, tell us here the circumstance,
That we for thee may glorify the Lord.

SIMPCOX: Born blind, and 't please your Grace.

SIMPCOX'S WIFE: Ay, indeed, was he.

WARWICK: What woman is this?

SIMPCOX'S WIFE: His wife, and 't like your worship.

GLOUCESTER: Hadst thou been his mother, that could'st have
better told.

KING HENRY: Where wert thou born?

SIMPCOX: At Berwick in the north, and 't like your Grace.

KING HENRY: Poor soul! God's goodness hath been great to
thee.

QUEEN MARGARET: Say, good fellow, cam'st thou here by
chance,
Or of devotion, to his holy shrine?

SIMPCOX: God knows, of pure devotion; being call'd
A hundred times and oft'ner in my sleep,
By good Saint Alban; who said, 'Simon, come;
Come, offer at my shrine, and I will help thee.'
(*His* WIFE *says it at the same time as him. And then says:*)

SIMPCOX'S WIFE: Most true, forsooth; and many time and oft
Myself have heard a voice to call him so.

CARDINAL BEAUFORT: What! art thou lame?
SIMPCOX: A fall of a tree.
SIMPCOX'S WIFE: A plum tree, master.
GLOUCESTER: How long hast thou
    been blind?
SIMPCOX: O! born so, master.
GLOUCESTER: What! and would'st climb a tree?
SIMPCOX: Alas! good master, my wife desir'd some damsons,
    And made me climb with danger of my life.
GLOUCESTER: Let me see thy eyes: wink now: now open them.
    In my opinion yet thou see'st not well.
SIMPCOX: Yes, master, clear as day, I thank God and Saint
    Alban.
GLOUCESTER: Say'st thou me so? What colour is this cloak of?
SIMPCOX: Red, master; red as blood.
GLOUCESTER: Why, that's well said. What colour is my gown
    of?
SIMPCOX: Black, forsooth; coal-black as jet.
KING HENRY: Why then, thou know'st what colour jet is of?
WARWICK: And yet, I think, jet he never did see.
GLOUCESTER: Tell me, sirrah, what's thy name?
SIMPCOX: Saunder Simpcox, and if it please you, master.
GLOUCESTER: Then Saunder, sit thou there, the lying'st knave
                        in Christendom.
    Sight may distinguish colours; but suddenly
    To nominate them all, it is impossible.
    Saint Alban here hath done a miracle;
    And would ye not think his cunning to be great,
    That could restore a cripple to his legs?
SIMPCOX: O master, that you could!
GLOUCESTER: Well, sirrah, if you mean to save yourself
    From whipping, leap me over this stool and run.
SIMPCOX: Alas! master, I am not able to stand alone:
    You go about to torture me in vain.
GLOUCESTER: Well, sirrah, we must have you find your legs.
BASSET: Come on, sirrah, off with your doublet quickly.
SIMPCOX: Alas! master, what shall I do?
    (GLOUCESTER *whips him. He shudders once and gasps:*)
    I am not able to stand.

VERNON: Whip him till he leap over that same stool.
> (GLOUCESTER *whips him again and he leaps up and over the stool and is gone. Exit* SIMPCOX.)

ALL: A miracle!

KING HENRY: O God! seest Thou this, and bearest so long?

QUEEN MARGARET: It made me laugh to see the villain run.

GLOUCESTER: Follow the knave; and take this drab away.
> (SIMPCOX'S WIFE *spits out angrily:*)

SIMPCOX'S WIFE: Alas! sir, we did it for pure need.

GLOUCESTER: Let them be whipp'd through every market
> town,
> Till they come to Berwick, from whence they came.
> (*Enter* SUFFOLK.)

KING HENRY: What tidings from the Duke of Suffolk?

SUFFOLK: Such as my heart doth tremble to unfold:
> A sort of naughty persons, lewdly bent,
> Under the countenance and confederacy
> Of Lady Eleanor, the Protector's wife,
> Have practis'd dangerously against your state,
> Dealing with witches and with conjurers:
> Whom we have apprehended in the fact;
> Raising up wicked spirits from under ground,
> Demanding of King Henry's life and death.

KING HENRY: O God! what mischiefs work the wicked ones,
> Heaping confusion on their own heads thereby!

QUEEN MARGARET: Gloucester, see here the tainture of thy
> nest,
> And look thyself be faultless, thou wert best.

GLOUCESTER: Madam, for myself, to heaven I do appeal,
> How I have lov'd my King and commonweal;
> And, for my wife, I know not how it stands.
> Noble she is, but if she have forgot
> Honour and virtue, and convers'd with such
> As, like to pitch, defile nobility;
> I banish her my bed and company,
> And give her as a prey to law and shame,
> Than hath dishonour'd Gloucester's honest name.
> Mine eyes are full of tears, my heart of grief.
> I beseech your Majesty, give me leave to go;

Sorrow would solace and mine age would ease.
KING HENRY: Stay Humphrey, Duke of Gloucester: ere thou
go,

Give up thy staff: Henry will to himself
Protector be; and God shall be my hope,
My stay, my guide, and lantern to my feet.
And go in peace, Humphrey, no less belov'd
Than when thou wert Protector to thy King.

GLOUCESTER: My staff? here, noble Henry, is my staff:
As willingly do I the same resign
As erst thy father Henry made it mine;
And even as willingly at thy feet I leave it
As others would ambitiously receive it.
Farewell, good king! when I am dead and gone,
May honourable peace attend thy throne.
(*Exit.*)

QUEEN MARGARET: Why, now is Henry King, and Margaret
Queen;

This staff of office raught; there let it stand,
Where is best fits to be, in Henry's hand.

KING HENRY: Well, for this night we will repose us here:
Tomorrow toward London back again,
To look into this business thoroughly,
And call these foul offenders to their answers,
And poise the cause in Justice' equal scales,
Whose beam stands sure, whose rightful cause prevails.
(*Flourish. Exeunt.*)

SCENE 6

The abbey at Bury St Edmunds.
Sennet. Enter KING HENRY, QUEEN MARGARET, CARDINAL
BEAUFORT, YORK, SALISBURY, *and* WARWICK *to the*
Parliament.

KING HENRY: I muse my Lord of Gloucester is not come:
'Tis not his wont to be the hindmost man.

QUEEN MARGARET: Can you see? or will ye not observe

The strangeness of his alter'd countenance?
With what a majesty he bears himself,
How insolent of late he is become,
How proud, how peremptory, and unlike himself?
Small curs are not regarded when they grin,
But great men tremble when the lion roars;
And Humphrey is no little man in England.
First note that he is near you in descent,
And should you fall, he is the next will mount.
By flattery hath he won the commons' hearts,
And when he please to make commotion,
'Tis to be fear'd they all will follow him.
Now 'tis the spring, and weeds are shallow-rooted;
Suffer them now, and they'll o'ergrow the garden,
And choke the herbs for want of husbandry.
The reverent care I bear unto my lord
Made me collect these dangers in the Duke.
My Lords of Suffolk, Winchester and York,
Reprove my allegation if you can;
Or else conclude my words effectual.

SUFFOLK: Well hath your Highness seen into this duke;
The duchess by his subornation
Upon my life, began her devilish practices:
Smooth runs the water where the brook is deep,
And in his simple show he harbours treason.

CARDINAL BEAUFORT: Did he not, contrary to form of law,
Devise strange deaths for small offences done?

YORK: And did he not, in his Protectorship,
Levy great sums of money through the realm
For soldiers' pay in France, and never sent it?

KING HENRY: My lords, at once: the care you have of us
Is worthy praise; but shall I speak my conscience,
Our kinsman Gloucester is an innocent
From meaning treason to our royal person,
As is the sucking lamb or harmless dove.
(*Enter* SOMERSET.)

SOMERSET: All health unto my gracious sovereign!

KING HENRY: Welcome, Lord Somerset. What news from
France?

SOMERSET: That all your interest in those territories
    Is utterly bereft you: all is lost.
KING HENRY: Cold news, Lord Somerset: but God's will be
    done!
(*Enter* GLOUCESTER.)
GLOUCESTER: All happiness unto my lord the King!
    Pardon, my liege, that I have stay'd so long.
SUFFOLK: Nay, Gloucester, know that thou art come too soon,
    Unless thou wert more loyal than thou art.
    I do arrest thee of high treason here.
GLOUCESTER: Well, Suffolk's Duke, thou shalt not see me
                          blush.
    The purest spring is not so free from mud
    As I am clear from treason to my sovereign.
    Who can accuse me? Wherein am I guilty?
YORK: 'Tis thought, my lord, that you took bribes of France,
    And, being Protector, stay'd the soldiers' pay;
    By means whereof his Highness hath lost France.
GLOUCESTER: Is it but thought so? What are they that think it?
    I never robb'd the soldiers of their pay,
    Nor ever had one penny bribe from France.
    So help me God, as I have watch'd the night,
    Ay, night by night, in studying good for England!
YORK: In your Protectorship you did devise
    Strange tortures for offenders, never heard of,
    That England was defam'd by tyranny.
GLOUCESTER: Why, 'tis well known that, whiles I was
                      Protector,
    Pity was all the fault that was in me.
SUFFOLK: My lord, these faults are easy, quickly answer'd;
    But mightier crimes are laid unto your charge,
    Whereof you cannot easily purge yourself.
    I do arrest you in his Highness' name.
KING HENRY: My Lord of Gloucester, 'tis my special hope
    That you will clear yourself from all suspect:
    My conscience tells me you are innocent.
GLOUCESTER: Ah! gracious lord, these days are dangerous:
    Virtue is chok'd with foul Ambition,
    And Charity chas'd hence by Rancour's hand.

I know their complot is to have my life;
And if my death might make this island happy,
I would expend it with all willingness.
But mine is made the prologue to their play;
For thousands more, that yet suspect no peril,
Will not conclude their plotted tragedy.
Beaufort's red sparkling eyes blab his heart's malice,
And Suffolk's cloudy brow his stormy hate;
And dogged York, that reaches at the moon,
Whose overweening arm I have pluck'd back,
By false accuse doth level at my life.
And you, my sovereign lady, with the rest,
And with your best endeavour have stirr'd up
My liefest liege to be mine enemy.
Ay, all of you have laid your heads together –
Myself had notice of your conventicles –
And all to make away my guiltless life.

CARDINAL BEAUFORT: My liege, his railing is intolerable.

SUFFOLK: Hath he not twit our sovereign lady here
With ignominious words, though clerkly couch'd?

QUEEN MARGARET: But I can give the loser leave to chide.

CARDINAL BEAUFORT: Sirs, take away the Duke, and guard
him sure.

GLOUCESTER: Ah! thus King Henry throws away his crutch
Before his legs be firm to bear his body.
Thus is the shepherd beaten from thy side,
And wolves are gnarling who shall gnaw thee first.
Ah! that my fear were false; ah! that it were;
For, good King Henry, thy decay I fear.
(*Exit* GLOUCESTER.)

KING HENRY: My lords, what to your wisdoms seemeth best,
Do, or undo, as if ourself were here.

QUEEN MARGARET: What! will your Highness leave the
Parliament?

KING HENRY: Ay, Margaret; my heart is drown'd with grief,
Whose flood begins to flow within mine eyes:
Ah! uncle Humphrey, in thy face I see
The map of Honour, Truth, and Loyalty;
And yet, good Humphrey, is the hour to come

71

That e'er I prov'd thee false, or fear'd thy faith.
What low'ring star now envies thy estate,
That these great lords, and Margaret our Queen,
Do seek subversion of thy harmless life?
Thou never didst them wrong, nor no man wrong;
And as the butcher takes away the calf,
And binds the wretch, and beats it when it strains,
Bearing it to the bloody slaughter-house;
Even so, remorseless, have they borne him hence;
And as the dam runs lowing up and down,
Looking the way her harmless young one went,
And can do nought but wail her darling's loss;
Even so myself bewails good Gloucester's case
With sad unhelpful tears, and with dimm'd eyes
Look after him, and cannot do him good;
So mighty are his vowed enemies.
His fortunes I will weep; and 'twixt each groan
Say, 'Who's a traitor? Gloucester he is none.'
(*Exeunt all but* QUEEN MARGARET, CARDINAL BEAUFORT,
SUFFOLK *and* YORK. SOMERSET *remains apart.*)

QUEEN MARGARET: Free lords, cold snow melts with the sun's
                                    hot beams.
Henry my lord is cold in great affairs,
Too full of foolish pity; and Gloucester's show
Beguiles him as the mournful crocodile
With sorrow snares relenting passengers;
This Gloucester should be quickly rid the world,
To rid us from the fear we have of him.

CARDINAL BEAUFORT: That he should die is worthy policy;
But yet we want a colour for his death.
'Tis meet he be condemn'd by course of law.

SUFFOLK: But in my mind that were no policy:
The King will labour still to save his life;
The commons haply rise to save his life;
Let us not stand on quillets how to slay him.

QUEEN MARGARET: Thrice-noble Suffolk, 'tis resolutely
spoke.

SUFFOLK: Not resolute, except so much were done;
And to preserve my sovereign from his foe,

Say but the word and I will be his priest.

CARDINAL BEAUFORT: But I would have him dead, my Lord of
                                       Suffolk,

    Ere you can take due orders for a priest:

    Say you consent –

SUFFOLK: Here is my hand –

CARDINAL BEAUFORT: I'll provide his executioner.

SUFFOLK: – the deed is worthy doing.

QUEEN MARGARET: And so say I.

YORK: And I: and now we three have spoken it,

    It skills not greatly who impugns our doom,

    (*Enter* POST.)

POST: Great lords, from Ireland am I come amain.

    Th' uncivil Irish rebels are in arms

    And temper clay with blood of Englishmen:

    Send succour, lords, and stop the rage betime –

CARDINAL BEAUFORT: A breach that craves a quick expedient
                                      stop!

    My Lord of York, try what your fortune is.

    To Ireland will you lead a band of men.

YORK: Let Somerset be sent as Regent thither.

    'Tis meet that lucky ruler be employ'd;

    Witness the fortune he hath had in France.

SOMERSET: If York, with all his far-fet policy,

    Had been the Regent there instead of me,

    He never would have stay'd in France so long.

YORK: Show me one scar character'd on thy skin:

    Men's flesh preserv'd so whole do seldom win.

CARDINAL BEAUFORT: Then, noble York, take thou this task
                                   in hand,

    Then try your hap against the Irishmen.

YORK: I will, my lord, so please his Majesty.

SUFFOLK: Why, our authority is his consent –

YORK: I am content: provide me soldiers –

SUFFOLK: I'll see it truly done, my Lord of York.

    (*Exeunt all except* YORK.)

YORK: Now, York, or never, steel thy fearful thoughts,

    And change misdoubt to resolution:

    Be that thou hop'st to be or what thou art

Resign to death; it is not worth th' enjoying.
(*Exit* YORK.)

SCENE 7

A hall of justice.
Enter ELEANOR, HUME, BOLINGBROKE, SOUTHWELL,
SUFFOLK, MARGERY JOURDAIN *and* CARDINAL BEAUFORT.

CARDINAL BEAUFORT: Receive the sentence of the law for sins
Such as by God's book are adjudg'd to death.
The witch in Smithfield shall be burn'd to ashes.
And you three shall be strangled on the gallows.
HUME: My lord!
(HUME *is beaten back.*)
CARDINAL BEAUFORT: You, madam, for you are more nobly
born,
Despoiled of your honour in your life,
Shall, after three days' open penance done,
Live in your country here in banishment.
ELEANOR: Welcome is banishment; welcome were my death.
(*Enter* GLOUCESTER.)
Come you, my lord, to see my open shame?
Now thou dost penance too. Look how they gaze!
Ah! Gloucester, hide thee from their hateful looks,
And, in thy closet pent up, rue my shame,
And ban thine enemies, both mine and thine.
GLOUCESTER: Ah! Nell, forbear: thou aimest all awry;
I must offend before I be attainted;
They still cannot procure me any scathe,
So long as I am loyal, true, and crimeless.
Be patient, gentle Nell; forget this grief.
ELEANOR: Ah! Gloucester, teach me to forget myself.
Now dark shall be my light, and night my day;
To think upon my pomp shall be my hell.
GLOUCESTER: Eleanor, the law, thou seest, hath judged thee:
I cannot justify whom the law condemns.
Sort thy heart to patience, gentle Nell.
Thy greatest help is quiet.

ELEANOR: What! gone, my lord, and bid me not farewell.
GLOUCESTER: Witness my tears, I cannot stay to speak.
   (*Exit* GLOUCESTER.)
ELEANOR: Art thou gone too? All comfort go with thee!
   For none abides with me: my joy is death;
   (*A shout and roar of flame as the witch is burned.*)
   Death, at whose name I oft have been afeard,
   Because I wish'd this world's eternity.
   (*Exit* ELEANOR.)
HUME: My Lord of Suffolk –
   (*Exit* SUFFOLK.)
MARGERY JOURDAIN: Cheros! Maitor! Tangedum!
   Transedim! Suvantos! Abelois! Bored!
   Belemuth! Castumi! Dabuel!
   Fulfil this work, that I may pass invisible
   To whom I wish!
BOLINGBROKE: Almiras, master of invisibility,
   I conjure thee and thy ministers –
HUME: My Lord Cardinal –
   (*Exit* CARDINAL BEAUFORT. *The prisoners are hanged.*
   Exeunt all except YORK.)
YORK: Let pale-fac'd fear keep with the mean-born man,
   And find no harbour in a royal heart.
   Faster than spring-time showers comes thought on thought,
   And not a thought but thinks on dignity.
   My brain, more busy than the labouring spider,
   Weaves tedious snares to trap mine enemies.
   Well, nobles, well; 'tis politicly done,
   To send me packing with an host of men:
   I fear me you but warm the starved snake,
   Who, cherish'd in your breasts, will sting your hearts.
   'Twas men I lack'd, and you will give them me:
   I take it kindly; yet be well assur'd
   You put sharp weapons in a madman's hands.
   Whiles I in Ireland nourish a mighty band,
   I will stir up in England some black storm
   Shall blow ten thousand souls to heaven, or hell;
   And this fell tempest shall not cease to rage
   Until the golden circuit on my head,

Like to the glorious sun's transparent beams,
Do calm the fury of this mad-bred flaw.
And, for a minister of my intent,
I have seduc'd a headstrong Kentishman,
John Cade of Ashford,
To make commotion as full well he can.
In Ireland have I seen this stubborn Cade
Oppose himself against a troop of kerns,
And fought so long, till that his thighs with darts
Were almost like a sharp-quill'd porpentine:
This devil here shall be my substitute;
By this I shall perceive the commons' mind,
How they affect the house and claim of York.
Say he be taken, rack'd, and tortured,
I know no pain they can inflict upon him
Will make him say I mov'd him to those arms.
Say that he thrive, as 'tis great like he will,
Why, then from Ireland come I with my strength,
And reap the harvest which that rascal sow'd;
For Humphrey being dead, as he shall be,
And Henry put apart, the next for me.
(*Exit* YORK.)

SCENE 8

Cardinal Beaufort's house.
Enter two MURDERERS.

FIRST MURDERER: Run to my Lord of Suffolk; let him know
  We have dispatched the Duke, as he commanded.
SECOND MURDERER: Would that it were to do! O, what have
                              we done?
  Did'st ever hear a man so penitent?
  (*Enter* SUFFOLK.)
  Here comes my lord.
SUFFOLK: Now, sirs, have you dispatched this thing?
FIRST MURDERER: Ay, my good lord, he's dead.
SUFFOLK: Why, that's well said. Go, get you to my house;
  The King and all the peers are here at hand.

(*Exit* MURDERERS. *Enter* KING HENRY, QUEEN
MARGARET, CARDINAL BEAUFORT, WARWICK *and others*,
SOMERSET *and* EXETER.)

KING HENRY: Go, call our uncle to our presence straight;
Say we intend to try his Grace today,
If he be guilty, as 'tis published.

SUFFOLK: I'll call him presently, my noble lord.
(*Exit*.)

KING HENRY: Lords, take your places; and, I pray you all,
Proceed no straiter 'gainst our uncle Gloucester
Than from true evidence, of good esteem,
He be approv'd in practice culpable.

QUEEN MARGARET: God forbid any malice should prevail.
Pray God he may acquit him of suspicion!

KING HENRY: I thank thee, Meg; these words content me
much.

(*Enter* SUFFOLK.)
How now! Why lookest thou so pale? Why tremblest thou?
Where is our uncle? What's the matter, Suffolk?

SUFFOLK: Dead in his bed, my lord; Gloucester is dead.

QUEEN MARGARET: Marry, God forfend!

CARDINAL BEAUFORT: God's secret judgment: I did dream
tonight
The Duke was dumb and could not speak a word.
(KING HENRY *swoons*.)

QUEEN MARGARET: How fares my lord? Help, lords! The King
is dead.
Run, go, help, help! O, Henry, ope thine eyes!

SUFFOLK: He doth revive again: madam, be patient.

KING HENRY: O heavenly God!

QUEEN MARGARET: How fares my gracious lord?

SUFFOLK: Comfort, my sovereign! Gracious Henry, comfort!

KING HENRY: What, doth my Lord of Suffolk comfort me?
Came he right now to sing a raven's note,
Whose dismal tune bereft my vital powers,
And thinks he that the chirping of a wren,
By crying comfort from a hollow breast,
Can chase away the first-conceived sound?
Lay not thy hands on me; forbear, I say;

Their touch affrights me as a serpent's sting.
Upon thy eyeballs murderous Tyranny
Sits in grim majesty to fright the world.

QUEEN MARGARET: Why do you rate my Lord of Suffolk thus?
Although the Duke was enemy to him,
Yet he, most Christian-like, laments his death:
What know I how the world may deem of me?
It may be judg'd I made the Duke away;
For it is known we were but hollow friends.
So shall my name with Slander's tongue be wounded.

KING HENRY: Ah! woe is me for Gloucester, wretched man.

QUEEN MARGARET: Be woe for me, more wretched than he is.
What, dost thou turn away and hide thy face?
I am no loathsome leper; look on me.
Is all thy comfort shut in Gloucester's tomb?
Erect his statue and worship it,
And make my image but an alehouse sign.
Was I for this nigh wreck'd upon the sea,
And twice by awkward wind from England's bank
Drove back again unto my native clime?
What boded this, but well forewarning wind
Did seem to say, 'Seek not scorpion's nest,
Nor set no footing on this unkind shore'?
What! art thou, like the adder, waxen deaf?
Be poisonous too, and kill thy forlorn Queen.

WARWICK: It is reported, mighty sovereign,
That good Duke Humphrey traitorously is murder'd
By Suffolk and the Cardinal Beaufort's means.
The commons, like an angry hive of bees
That want their leader, scatter up and down,
And care not who, they sting in his revenge.
Myself have calm'd their spleenful mutiny,
Until they hear the order of his death.

KING HENRY: That he is dead, good Warwick, 'tis too true;
But how he died God knows, not Henry.
Enter his chamber, view his breathless corpse,
And comment then upon his sudden death.

WARWICK: That shall I do, my liege. Stay, Exeter,
With the rude multitude till I return.

(*Exit* WARWICK, *then* EXETER *and the commons.*)

KING HENRY: O Thou that judgest all things, stay my
thoughts –
My thoughts that labour to persuade my soul
Some violent hands were laid on Humphrey's life.
If my suspect be false, forgive me, God,
For judgment only doth belong to Thee.

(*Enter* WARWICK *with* GLOUCESTER's *body.*)

WARWICK: Come hither, gracious sovereign, view this body.

KING HENRY: That is to see how deep my grave is made;
For with this soul fled all my worldly solace,
For, seeing him, I see my life in death.

WARWICK: As surely as my soul intends to live,
I do believe that violent hands were laid
Upon the life of this thrice-famed duke.

SUFFOLK: What instances gives Lord Warwick for his vow?

WARWICK: But see, his face is black and full of blood,
His eyeballs further out than when he liv'd,
Staring full ghastly like a strangled man;
His hair uprear'd, his nostrils stretch'd with struggling;
His hands abroad display'd, as one that grasp'd
And tugg'd for life, and was by strength subdued.
Look, on the sheets his hair, you see, is sticking;
It cannot be but he was murder'd here.

SUFFOLK: Why, Warwick, who should do the Duke to death?
Myself and Beaufort had him in protection;
And we, I hope, sir, are no murderers.

WARWICK: But both of you were vow'd Duke Humphrey's
foes,
And you, forsooth, had the good Duke to keep.

QUEEN MARGARET: Then you, belike, suspect these noblemen
As guilty of Duke Humphrey's timeless death.

(*Exit* CARDINAL BEAUFORT.)

WARWICK: Who finds the heifer dead and bleeding fresh,
And sees fast by a butcher with an axe,
But will suspect 'twas he that made the slaughter?

QUEEN MARGARET: Are you the butcher, Suffolk? Where's
your knife?

WARWICK: Madam, be still, with reverence may I say;

For every word you speak in his behalf
Is slander to your royal dignity.

SUFFOLK: I wear no knife to slaughter sleeping men,
    Say, if thou dar'st, proud Lord of Warwickshire,
    That I am faulty in Duke Humphrey's death.

WARWICK: What dares not Warwick, if false Suffolk dare him?
    And that my sovereign's presence makes me mild,
    I would, false coward send thy soul to hell,
    Pernicious blood-sucker of sleeping men!

KING HENRY: Why, how now, lords! your wrathful weapons
                                         drawn
    Here in our presence! Dare you be so bold?

EXETER: Dread lord, the commons sends you word by me,
    Unless Lord Suffolk straight be done to death,
    Or banish'd fair England's territories,
    They will by violence tear him from your palace.
    They say, by him the good Duke Humphrey died;
    They say, in him they fear your Highness' death;
    And mere instinct of love and loyalty
    Makes them thus forward in his banishment

KING HENRY: Go, Exeter, and tell them all from me,
    I thank them for their tender loving care;
    And had I not been cited so by them,
    Yet did I purpose as they do entreat;
    For sure, my thoughts do hourly prophesy
    Mischance unto my state by Suffolk's means:
    And therefore by His Majesty I swear,
    Whose far unworthy deputy I am,
    He shall not breathe infection in this air
    But three days longer, on the pain of death.
    (*Exit* EXETER.)

QUEEN MARGARET: O Henry, let me plead for gentle Suffolk!

KING HENRY: Ungentle Queen, to call him gentle Suffolk!
    No more, I say; if thou dost plead for him
    Thou wilt but add increase unto my wrath.
    Had I but said, I would have kept my word;
    But when I swear, it is irrevocable.
    (*To* SUFFOLK:)
    If after three days' space thou here be'st found

On any ground that I am ruler of,
The world shall not be ransom for thy life.
Come, Warwick, come, good Warwick, go with me;
I have great matters to impart to thee.
(*Exeunt all but* QUEEN MARGARET *and* SUFFOLK.)

QUEEN MARGARET: Mischance and Sorrow go along with you!
There's two of you; the devil make a third!
And threefold Vengeance tend upon your steps!

SUFFOLK: Cease, gentle queen, these execrations,
And let thy Suffolk take his heavy leave.

QUEEN MARGARET: Fie, coward woman and soft-hearted
             wretch!
Hast thou not spirit to curse thine enemy?

SUFFOLK: A plague upon them! Wherefore should I curse
             them?
My tongue should stumble in mine earnest words;
And even now my burden'd heart would break
Should I not curse them. Poison be their drink!
Gall, worse than gall, the daintiest that they taste!
Their softest touch as smart as lizards' stings!
Their music frightful as the serpent's hiss,
And boding screech-owls make the consort full!
All the foul terrors in dark-seated hell –

QUEEN MARGARET: Enough, sweet Suffolk; thou torments
thyself.

SUFFOLK: You bade me ban, and will you bid me leave?
Now, by the ground that I am banished from,
Well could I curse away a winter's night,
Though standing naked on a mountain top,
Where biting cold would never let grass grow,
And think it but a minute spent in sport.

QUEEN MARGARET: O! let me entreat thee cease. Give me thy
             hand,
That I may dew it with my mournful tears;
Nor let the rain of heaven wet this place,
To wash away my woeful monuments.
So, get thee gone, that I may know my grief;
'Tis but surmis'd whiles thou art standing by.
Go; speak not to me; even now be gone.

O! go not yet. Even thus two friends condemn'd
Embrace and kiss and take ten thousand leaves,
Loather a hundred times to part than die.
Yet now farewell; and farewell life with thee.
SUFFOLK: Thus is poor Suffolk ten times banished,
Once by the King, and three times thrice by thee.
'Tis not the land I care for, wert thou thence;
For where thou art, there is the world itself,
With every several pleasure in the world,
And where thou art not, desolation.
(*Enter* EXETER.)
QUEEN MARGARET: Whither goes Exeter? What news, I
prithee?
EXETER: To signify unto his Majesty
My brother Beaufort is at point of death;
For suddenly a grievous sickness took him,
That makes him gasp, and stare, and catch the air,
Blaspheming God, and cursing men on earth.
Sometimes he talks as if Duke Humphrey's ghost
Were by his side; sometime he calls the King,
And whispers to his pillow, as to him,
The secrets of his overcharged soul.
QUEEN MARGARET: Go, tell this heavy message to the King.
(*Exit* EXETER.)
Now get thee hence; the King, thou know'st, is coming;
If thou be found by me thou art but dead.
SUFFOLK: If I depart from thee I cannot live;
And in thy sight to die, what were it else
But like a pleasant slumber in thy lap?
To die by thee were but to die in jest;
From thee to die were torture more than death.
O! let me stay, befall what may befall.
To have thee with thy lips to stop my mouth.
QUEEN MARGARET: To France, sweet Suffolk! Let me hear
from thee;
For wheresoe'er thou art in this world's globe,
I'll have an Iris that shall find thee out.
Away!
SUFFOLK: I go.

QUEEN MARGARET: And take my heart with thee.
SUFFOLK: A jewel, lock'd into the woefull'st cask
That ever did contain a thing of worth.
Even as a splitted bark so sunder we:
This way fall I to death.
QUEEN MARGARET: This way for me.
(*Exeunt in opposite directions*.)

SCENE 9

A bedchamber.
Enter KING HENRY, EXETER *and* WARWICK *to* CARDINAL
BEAUFORT *in bed.*

KING HENRY: How fares my lord? Speak, Beaufort, to thy
sovereign.
CARDINAL BEAUFORT: If thou be'st death, I'll give thee
England's treasure,
Enough to purchase such another island,
So thou wilt let me live, and feel no pain.
WARWICK: Beaufort, it is thy sovereign speaks to thee.
CARDINAL BEAUFORT: Bring me unto my trial when you will.
Died he not in his bed? Where should he die?
O, torture me no more! I will confess.
Alive again? Then show me where he is:
I'll give a thousand pound to look upon him.
He hath no eyes, the dust hath blinded them.
Comb down his hair! look! it stands upright,
Like lime-twigs set to catch my winged soul.
KING HENRY: O thou eternal Mover of the heavens!
Look with a gentle eye upon this wretch;
And from his bosom purge this black despair.
WARWICK: See how the pangs of death do make him grin!
EXETER: Disturb him not; let him pass peaceably.
KING HENRY: Peace to his soul! if God's good pleasure be.
Lord Cardinal, if thou think'st on heaven's bliss,
Hold up thy hand, make signal of thy hope.
(CARDINAL BEAUFORT *dies*.)
He dies, and makes no sign. O God, forgive him!

WARWICK: So bad a death argues a monstrous life.
KING HENRY: Forbear to judge, for we are sinners all.
  (*Enter* QUEEN MARGARET *with* SUFFOLK'*s head*.)
QUEEN MARGARET: Ah! barbarous villains! Hath this lovely
                                                    face
    Rul'd like a wandering planet over me,
    And could it not enforce them to relent,
    That were unworthy to behold the same?
    O! my sweet Suffolk!
    Oft have I heard that grief softens the mind,
    And makes it fearful and degenerate;
    Think therefore on revenge, and cease to weep.
    Here may his head lie on my throbbing breast;
    But where's the body that I should embrace?
KING HENRY: Close up his eyes, and draw the curtain close;
    And let us all to meditation.
    (*Exeunt omnes*.)

THE RISE OF
EDWARD IV

The Rise of Edward IV was first performed at the Royal Shakespeare Theatre, Stratford-upon-Avon, on 6 October 1988, and subsequently transferred to the Barbican Theatre, London, on 22 March 1989.

The cast was as follows:

For York

RICHARD PLANTAGENET, DUKE OF YORK	David Calder
EDWARD, EARL OF MARCH, *later* EDWARD IV	Ken Bones
GEORGE, *later* DUKE OF CLARENCE	David Morrissey
RICHARD, *later* DUKE OF GLOUCESTER	Anton Lesser
EDMUND, EARL OF RUTLAND	Jason Watkins
DUCHESS OF YORK	Marjorie Yates
RICHARD NEVILLE, EARL OF WARWICK	David Lyon
LADY ELIZABETH GREY	Joanne Pearce
ANTHONY WOODVILLE, LORD RIVERS	Edward Harbour
WILLIAM, LORD HASTINGS	Edward Peel
DUKE OF BUCKINGHAM	Oliver Cotton

For Lancaster

HENRY VI	Ralph Fiennes
QUEEN MARGARET	Penny Downie
EDWARD, PRINCE OF WALES	Lyndon Davies
JOHN BEAUFORT, DUKE OF SOMERSET	Tom Fahy
THOMAS BEAUFORT, DUKE OF EXETER	Nicholas Smith
LORD CLIFFORD	Roger Watkins
YOUNG CLIFFORD	Mark Hadfield

The rebels
JACK CADE   Oliver Cotton
DICK THE BUTCHER   Robert Demeger
SMITH THE WEAVER   Trevor Gordon

Directed by Adrian Noble
Designed by Bob Crowley
Lighting by Chris Parry
Music by Edward Gregson
Fight Director Malcolm Ranson
Sound by Paul Slocombe
Company voice work by Cicely Berry and Andrew Wade
Music Director Michael Tubbs
Assistant Director Stephen Rayne
Additional script work by Colin Chambers
Stage Manager Alison Owen
Photographs by Richard Mildenhall

CHARACTERS

KING HENRY VI
QUEEN MARGARET, his wife
EDWARD, PRINCE OF WALES, his son
EARL OF OXFORD
EARL OF WARWICK
DUKE OF BUCKINGHAM
DUKE OF EXETER
DUKE OF NORFOLK
DUKE OF SOMERSET
DUKE OF YORK
DUCHESS OF YORK, his wife
EDWARD, his son, *later* DUKE OF YORK and KING
   EDWARD IV
LADY ELIZABETH GREY, *later* Queen to Edward IV
GEORGE, his son, *later* DUKE OF CLARENCE
RICHARD, his son, *later* DUKE OF GLOUCESTER
EDMUND, EARL OF RUTLAND, his son
OLD CLIFFORD
YOUNG CLIFFORD, his son
SIR HUMPHREY STAFFORD
WILLIAM STAFFORD, his brother
BASSET, of Lancaster faction
EARL RIVERS, brother to Queen Elizabeth
LORD HASTINGS
HENRY, EARL OF RICHMOND
JACK CADE, a rebel
GEORGE BEVIS
DICK THE BUTCHER
JOHN HOLLAND
SMITH THE WEAVER
MICHAEL
CLERK, of Chatham
ALEXANDER IDEN, a Kentish gentleman
A SON that hath killed his father
A FATHER that hath killed his son
LEWIS XI, King of France
BONA, his sister
Lieutenant of the Tower, Soldiers, Messengers and Posts,
   Keepers, Watchmen

ACT ONE

SCENE I

Blackheath.
Enter GEORGE BEVIS *and* JOHN HOLLAND.

BEVIS: Come, and get thee a sword, though made of a lath; they
have been up these two days.

HOLLAND: They have the more need to sleep now then.

BEVIS: I tell thee, Jack Cade the clothier means to dress the
commonwealth, and turn it, and set a new nap upon it.

HOLLAND: So he had need, for 'tis threadbare. Well, I say, it was
never merry world in England, since gentlemen came up.

BEVIS: O miserable age! Virtue is not regarded in
handicraftsmen.

HOLLAND: The nobility think scorn to go in leather aprons.

BEVIS: Nay, more; the King's Council are no good workmen.

HOLLAND: True; and yet it is said, 'Labour in thy vocation':
which is as much to say, as 'Let the magistrates be
labouring men'; and therefore should we be magistrates.

BEVIS: Thou hast hit it; for there's no better sign of a brave
mind than a hard hand.
(*Drum. Enter* JACK CADE, DICK THE BUTCHER *and* SMITH
THE WEAVER, *with infinite numbers.*)

CADE: We John Cade, so term'd of our supposed father –

BUTCHER: Or rather, of stealing a cade of herrings.

CADE: For our enemies shall fall before us, inspir'd with the
spirit of putting down kings and princes – command
silence.

BUTCHER: Silence!

CADE: My father was a Mortimer –

BUTCHER: He was an honest man, and a good bricklayer.

CADE: My mother a Plantagenet –

BUTCHER: I knew her well; she was a midwife.

CADE: Therefore am I of an honourable house.

BUTCHER: Ay, by my faith, the field is honourable, and there
he was born, under a hedge.

93

CADE: Valiant I am.

WEAVER: A must needs, for beggary is valiant.

CADE: I am able to endure much.

BUTCHER: No question of that, for I have seen him whipp'd three market days together.

CADE: Be brave then; for your captain is brave, and vows reformation. There shall be in England, seven halfpenny loaves sold for a penny; and I will make it felony to drink small beer. All the realm shall be in common, and in Cheapside shall my palfrey go to grass. And when I am king, as king I will be –

ALL: God save your Majesty!

CADE: I thank you, good people – there shall be no money; all shall eat and drink on my score, and I will apparel them all in one livery, that they may agree like brothers, and worship me their lord.

BUTCHER: The first thing we do, let's kill all the lawyers.

CADE: Nay, that I mean to do. Is this not a lamentable thing, that of the skin of an innocent lamb should be made parchment? that parchment, being scribbled o'er, should undo a man? How now! Who's there?

(*Enter a* CLERK.)

WEAVER: The Clerk of Chatham: he can write and read.

CADE: O monstrous!

WEAVER: H'as a book in his pocket with red letters in 't.

CADE: Here's a villain. Come hither, sirrah, I must examine thee. What is thy name?

CLERK: Emmanuel.

CADE: Dost thou use to write thy name? Or hast thou a mark to thyself, like an honest plain-dealing man?

CLERK: Sir, I thank God I have been so well brought up that I can write my name.

CADE: He hath confess'd: away with him! Hang him with his pen and ink-horn about his neck.

(*Fight. Death of the* CLERK. *Enter* MICHAEL.)

MICHAEL: Where's our general?

CADE: Here I am, thou particular fellow.

MICHAEL: Fly, fly, fly! Sir Humphrey Stafford and his brother are hard by, with the King's forces.

CADE: Stand, villain, stand, or I'll fell thee down. He shall be
encounter'd with a man as good as himself. He is but a
knight, is a?

MICHAEL: No.

CADE: To equal him, I will make myself a knight presently.
Kneel down, John Mortimer. Rise up, Sir John Mortimer.
Is there any more of them that be knight?

MICHAEL: Aye, his brother.

CADE: Then, kneel down, Dick the butcher. Rise up, Sir Dick
the butcher. Now have at him!

(*Enter* SIR HUMPHREY STAFFORD *and* WILLIAM
STAFFORD *his brother*.)

SIR HUMPHREY STAFFORD: Rebellious hinds, the filth and
scum of Kent,
Mark'd for the gallows, lay your weapons down;
Home to your cottages, forsake this groom:
The King is merciful, if you revolt.

WILLIAM STAFFORD: But angry, wrathful, and inclin'd to
blood,
If you go forward: therefore yield, or die.

CADE: As for these silken-coated slaves I pass not:
It is to you, good people, that I speak,
Over whom, in time to come, I hope to reign;
For I am rightful heir unto the crown,
Being descended from Lord Mortimer.

WILLIAM STAFFORD: Jack Cade, the Duke of York hath taught
you this.

CADE: He lies, for I invented it myself. Go to, sirrah, tell the
King from me, that for his father's sake, Henry the Fifth, I
am content he shall reign; but I'll be Protector over him.

SIR HUMPHREY STAFFORD: O gross and miserable ignorance!

CADE: Ah, thou serge, nay, thou buckram lord! now art thou
within point-blank of our jurisdiction regal. What canst
thou answer to my Majesty for giving up of Normandy
unto the Dauphin of France? Be it known unto thee by
these presence, even the presence of Lord Mortimer, that I
am the besom that must sweep the court clean of such filth
as thou art. Thou hast most traitorously corrupted the
youth of the realm in erecting a grammar school. Thou hast

appointed justices of peace, to call poor men before them
about matters they were not able to answer. Moreover,
thou hast put them in prison; and because they could not
read, thou hast hang'd them.

SIR HUMPHREY STAFFORD: Herald, away; and throughout
every town
Proclaim them traitors that are up with Cade;
That those which fly before the battle ends
May, even in their wives' and children's sight,
Be hang'd up for example at their doors.
And you that be the King's friends, follow me.
(*Exeunt the two Staffords, and soldiers.*)

CADE: And you that love the commons, follow me.
Now show yourselves men; 'tis for liberty.
We will not leave one lord, one gentleman:
Spare none but such as go in clouted shoon.
Let the bodies be dragg'd at my horse heels till I do come
to London, where we will have the mayor's sword borne
before us.

BUTCHER: If we mean to thrive and do good, break open the
gaols and let out the prisoners.

CADE: Fear not that, I warrant thee. Come; let's march towards
London.
(*Exeunt omnes.*)

SCENE 2

London. The palace.
Enter KING HENRY *and* QUEEN MARGARET, *the* DUKE OF
EXETER *and* OLD CLIFFORD.

EXETER: What answer makes your Grace to the rebels'
supplication?

KING HENRY: I'll send some holy bishop to entreat;
For God forbid so many simple souls
Should perish by the sword! And I myself,
Rather than bloody war shall cut them short,
Will parley with Jack Cade their general.

But stay, I'll read it over once again.
Lord Clifford, Jack Cade hath sworn to have thy head.

OLD CLIFFORD: Ay, but I hope your Highness shall have his.
(*Enter* YOUNG CLIFFORD.)

KING HENRY: How now? Young Clifford? Why com'st thou in
such haste?

YOUNG CLIFFORD: The rebels are in Southwark; fly my lord!
Jack Cade proclaims himself Lord Mortimer,
And vows to crown himself in Westminster.
His army is a ragged multitude
Of hinds and peasants, rude and merciless:
All scholars, lawyers, courtiers, gentlemen,
They call false caterpillars, and intend their death.

KING HENRY: O graceless men! they know not what they do.

EXETER: My gracious lord, retire to Killingworth,
Until a power be rais'd to put them down.
(*Enter* SOMERSET.)

SOMERSET: Jack Cade hath almost gotten London Bridge.
The citizens fly and forsake their houses.

QUEEN MARGARET: Ah, were the Duke of Suffolk now alive,
These Kentish rebels would be soon appeas'd!

KING HENRY: How, madam? Still lamenting Suffolk's death?
If fear me, love, if that I had been dead,
Thou would'st not have mourn'd so much for me.

QUEEN MARGARET: My love; I should not mourn, but die for
thee.

EXETER: Then linger not, my lord; away! take horse.

KING HENRY: Come, Margaret: God, our hope, will succour
us.
Farewell, my lord; trust not the Kentish rebels.

QUEEN MARGARET: My hope is gone, now Suffolk is deceas'd.

EXETER: The trust I have is in mine innocence,
And therefore am I bold and resolute.
(*Exeunt omnes.*)

SCENE 3

London. Cannon Street.
Enter JACK CADE *and his followers.*

CADE: Now is Mortimer lord of this city. I charge and
command that, of the city's cost, the pissing-conduit run
nothing but claret wine this first year of our reign. And
now henceforward it shall be treason for any that calls me
other than Lord Mortimer.
(*Enter a* SOLDIER, *running.*)

SOLDIER: Jack Cade! Jack Cade!

CADE: Knock him down there.
(*They kill him.*)

WEAVER: If this fellow be wise, he'll never call ye Jack Cade
more: I think he hath a very fair warning.

BUTCHER: My lord, there's an army gathered together in
Smithfield.

CADE: Come then, let's go fight with them. But first, go and set
London Bridge afire, and, if you can, burn down the
Tower too. Away! burn all the records of the realm; my
mouth shall be the parliament of England. And
henceforward all things shall be in common. The proudest
peer in the realm shall not wear a head on his shoulders,
unless he pay me tribute; there shall not a maid be married,
but she shall pay to me her maidenhead, ere they have it.
Up Fish Street! down Saint Magnus' Corner! Kill and
knock down! throw them into Thames!
(*A parley.*)
What noise is this I hear? Dare any be so bold to sound
retreat or parley, when I command them kill?
(*Enter* EXETER, OLD CLIFFORD *and* YOUNG CLIFFORD.)

EXETER: Ay, here they be that dare and will disturb thee:
Know, Cade, we come ambassadors from the King
Unto the commons, whom thou hast misled;
And here pronounce free pardon to them all
That will forsake thee and go home in peace.

OLD CLIFFORD: What say ye, countrymen? Will ye relent
And yield to mercy, whilst 'tis offer'd you,
Or let a rebel lead you to your deaths?
Who loves the King, and will embrace his pardon,
Fling up his cap, and say, 'God save his Majesty!'
Who hateth him, and honours not his father,
Henry the Fifth, that made all France to quake,

Shake he his weapon at us, and pass by.

ALL: God save the King! God save the King!

CADE: What! Exeter and Clifford, are ye so brave? And you,
base peasants, do ye believe him? Will you needs be hang'd
with your pardons about your necks? I though ye would
never have given out these arms till you had recover'd your
ancient freedom; but you are all recreants and dastards,
and delight to live in slavery to the nobility. Let them
break your backs with burdens, take your houses over your
heads, ravish your wives and daughters before your faces.
For me, I will make shift for one, and so God's curse light
upon you all!

ALL: We'll follow Cade, we'll follow Cade!

OLD CLIFFORD: Is Cade the son of Henry the Fifth,
That thus you do exclaim you'll go with him?
Will he conduct you through the heart of France,
And make the meanest of you earls and dukes?
Alas! he hath no home, no place to fly to;
Nor knows he how to live but by the spoil,
Unless by robbing of your friends and us.
Were't not a shame, that whilst you live at jar,
The fearful French, whom you late vanquished,
Should make a start o'er seas and vanquish you?
Methinks already in this civil broil
I see them lording it in London streets,
Crying, 'Villiago!' unto all they meet.
Better ten thousands base-born Cades miscarry
Than you should stoop unto a Frenchman's mercy.
To France, to France! and get what you have lost;
Spare England, for it is your native coast.
Henry hath money, you are strong and manly;
God on our side, doubt not of victory.

ALL: A Clifford! a Clifford! we'll follow the King and Clifford.

CADE: Was ever feather so lightly blown to and fro as this
multitude? The name of Henry the Fifth hales them to an
hundred mischiefs, and makes them leave me desolate. My
sword make way for me, for here is no staying. In despite
of the devils and hell, have through the very midst of you!
and heavens and honour be witness, that no want of

resolution in me, but only my followers' base and
ignominious treasons, makes me betake me to my heels.
(*Exit.*)

EXETER: What, is he fled? Go some, and follow him;
And he that brings his head unto the King
Shall have a thousand crowns for his reward.
(*Exeunt some of them.*)
Follow me, soldiers; we'll devise a mean
To reconcile you all unto the King.
(*Exeunt omnes.*)

SCENE 4

Kenilworth Castle.
Trumpets. Enter KING HENRY, QUEEN MARGARET, *and*
SOMERSET, *on the terrace.*

KING HENRY: Was ever king that joy'd an earthly throne
And could command no more content than I?
No sooner was I crept out of my cradle
But I was made a king at nine months old;
Was never subject long'd to be a king
As I do long and wish to be a subject.
(*Enter* EXETER *and* OLD CLIFFORD.)
EXETER: Health and glad tidings to your Majesty!
KING HENRY: Why, Exeter, is the traitor Cade surpris'd?
OLD CLIFFORD: He is fled, my lord, and all his powers do
yield.
KING HENRY: Then, heaven, set ope thy everlasting gates,
To entertain my vows of thanks and praise!
(*Enter* SOMERSET.)
SOMERSET: Please it, your Grace,
The Duke of York is newly come from Ireland,
And with a puissant and a mighty power
Is marching hitherward in proud array.
KING HENRY: Thus stands my state, 'twixt Cade and York
distress'd;
Like to a ship that, having scap'd a tempest,

Is straightway calm'd, and boarded with a pirate.
But now is Cade driven back, his men dispers'd,
And now is York in arms to second him.
I pray thee, Exeter, go and meet him,
And ask him what's the reason for these arms.
But mark ye be not too rough in terms,
For he is fierce and cannot brook hard language.
EXETER: I will, my lord; and doubt not so to deal
As all things shall redound unto your good.
KING HENRY: Come, wife, let's in, and learn to govern better;
For yet may England curse my wretched reign.
(*Flourish. Exeunt.*)

SCENE 5

Fields between Dartford and Blackheath.
Enter YORK *and his army of Irish, with drum and colours.*

YORK: From Ireland thus comes York to claim his right,
And pluck the crown from feeble Henry's head.
Edward the Third, my lord, had seven sons:
The third was Lionel Duke of Clarence, fourth
Was John of Gaunt, the Duke of Lancaster.
Henry doth claim the crown from John of Gaunt,
The fourth son; York claims it from the third.
Till Lionel's issue fails, his should not reign:
It fails not yet, but flourishes in me,
And in my sons, fair slips of such a stock.
Ring, bells, aloud; burn, bonfires, clear and bright,
To entertain great England's lawful King.
Ah! sancta majestas, who'd not buy thee dear?
I cannot give due action to my words,
Except a sword or sceptre balance it.
A sceptre shall it have, have I a sword,
On which I'll toss the flower-de-luce of France.

Kent. Iden's garden.

CADE: Fie on ambitions! fie on myself, that have a sword, and
yet am ready to famish! These five days have I hid me in
these woods and durst not peep out, for all the country is
laid for me; but now am I so hungry, that if I might have a
lease of my life for a thousand years, I could stay no longer.
Wherefore, on a brick wall have I climb'd into this garden,
to see if I can eat grass, or pick a sallet.
(*Enter* IDEN.)

IDEN: Lord! who would live turmoiled in the court,
And may enjoy such quiet walks as these?
This small inheritance my father left me
Contenteth me, and worth a monarchy.
Sufficeth, that I have maintains my state,
And sends the poor well pleased from my gate.

CADE: Here's the lord of the soil come to seize me for a stray.
Ah, villain, thou wilt betray me, and get a thousand crowns
of the King by carrying my head to him; but I'll make thee
eat iron like an ostrich, and swallow my sword like a great
pin, ere thou and I part.

IDEN: Why, rude companion, whatsoe'er thou be,
I know thee not; why then should I betray thee?
Is't not enough to break into my garden,
And like a thief to come to rob my grounds,
But thou wilt brave me with these saucy terms?

CADE: I have eat no meat these five days; yet, come thou and
thy five men, and if I do not leave you all as dead as a door-
nail, I pray God I may never eat grass more.

IDEN: Nay, it shall ne'er be said, while England stands,
That Alexander Iden, esquire of Kent,
Took odds to combat a poor famish'd man.
Oppose thy steadfast-gazing eyes to mine,
See if thou canst outface me with thy looks:
And if mine arm be heaved in the air,
Thy grave is digg'd already in the earth.

CADE: By my valour, the most complete champion that ever I
heard!
(*They fight.*)
O, I am slain! Famine and no other hath slain me; let ten
thousand devils come against me, and give me but the ten
meals I have lost, and I'd defy them all. Wither, garden;
and be henceforth a burying-place to all that do dwell in
this house, because the unconquered soul of Cade is fled.
IDEN: Is't Cade that I have slain, that monstrous traitor?
Sword, I will hallow thee for this thy deed,
And hang thee o'er my tomb when I am dead.
CADE: Iden, farewell; and be proud of thy victory. Tell Kent
from me, she hath lost her best man, and exhort all the
world to be cowards; for I, that never fear'd any, am
vanquish'd by famine, not by valour.
(*Dies.*)
IDEN: Die, damned wretch, the curse of her that bare thee!
And as I thrust thy body in with my sword,
So wish I I might thrust thy soul to hell.
Hence will I drag thee headlong by the heels
Unto a dunghill, which shall be thy grave,
And there cut off thy most ungracious head;
Which I will bear in triumph to the King,
Leaving thy trunk for crows to feed upon.
(*Exit.*)

SCENE 7

London. The Parliament House.
Enter YORK, EDWARD, RICHARD, GEORGE, RUTLAND,
WARWICK, NORFOLK, *and others with white roses.*

WARWICK: This is the palace of the fearful King,
And this the regal seat; possess it, York;
For this is thine and not King Henry's heirs'.
YORK: Assist me then, sweet Warwick, and I will;
For hither we have broken in by force.
WARWICK: And when the King comes, offer him no violence,
Unless he seek to thrust you out perforce.

YORK: By words or blows here let us win our right.

RICHARD: Arm'd as we are, let's stay within this house.

WARWICK: The bloody parliament shall this be call'd
Unless Plantagenet, Duke of York, be king.

YORK: Then leave me not; my sons, be resolute;
I mean to take possession of my right.

WARWICK: Neither the King, nor he that loves him best,
The proudest he that holds up Lancaster,
Dares stir a wing if Warwick shake his bells.
I'll plant Plantagenet, root him up who dares.
Resolve thee, Richard; claim the English crown.
(*Flourish. Enter* KING HENRY, OLD CLIFFORD, YOUNG
CLIFFORD, SOMERSET, EXETER, OXFORD, *and soldiers
with red roses in their hats.*)

KING HENRY: My lords, look where the sturdy rebel sits,
Even, in the chair of state! Belike he means,
Back'd by the power of Warwick, that false peer,
To aspire unto the crown and reign as king.

OLD CLIFFORD: Why, what a brood of traitors have we here!

YORK: Look in a glass, and call thy image so.
I am thy King and thou a false-heart traitor.

OLD CLIFFORD: This is my King, York; I do not mistake;
But thou mistakes me much to think I do.
To Bedlam with him! Is the man grown mad!

KING HENRY: Ay, Clifford; a bedlam and ambitious humour
Makes him oppose himself against his King.

OLD CLIFFORD: He is a traitor; let him to the Tower,
And chop away that factious pate of his.

OXFORD: What! shall we suffer this? Let's pluck him down:
My heart for anger burns: I cannot brook it.

KING HENRY: Be thou patient, gentle Earl of Oxford.

OLD CLIFFORD: Patience is for poltroons, such as he;
He durst not sit there had your father liv'd.

YOUNG CLIFFORD: My gracious lord, here in the parliament
Let us assail the family of York.

SOMERSET: O monstrous traitor! I arrest thee, York,
Of capital treason 'gainst the King and crown.
Obey, audacious traitor; kneel for grace.

KING HENRY: Far be the thought of this from Henry's heart,

To make a shambles of the Parliament House!
Cousin of Somerset, frowns, words and threats,
Shall be the war that Henry means to use.
Thou factious Duke of York, descend my throne,
And kneel for grace and mercy at my feet;
I am thy sovereign.

YORK: I am thine.

EXETER: For shame, come down; he made thee Duke of York.

YORK: 'Twas my inheritance, as the earldom was.

EXETER: Thy father was a traitor to the crown.

WARWICK: Exeter, thou art a traitor to the crown
    In following this usurping Henry.

YORK: Will you we show our title to the crown?
    If not, our swords shall plead it in the field.

KING HENRY: What title hast thou, traitor, to the crown?
    Thy father was, as thou art, Duke of York.
    Thy grandfather, Roger Mortimer, Earl of March.
    I am the son of Henry the Fifth,
    Who made the Dauphin and the French to stoop,
    And seiz'd upon their towns and provinces.

WARWICK: Talk not of France, sith thou hast lost it all.

KING HENRY: The Lord Protector lost it, and not I:
    When I was crown'd I was but nine months old.

RICHARD: You are old enough now, and yet, methinks, you
                                   lose.
    Father, tear the crown from the usurper's head.

EDWARD: Sweet father, do so; set it on your head.

GEORGE: Good father, as thou lov'st and honourest arms,
    Let's fight it out and not stand cavilling thus.

RICHARD: Sound drums and trumpets, and the King will fly.

YOUNG CLIFFORD: Hence, heap of wrath, foul indigested
                                lump,
    As crooked in thy manners as thy shape!

RICHARD: Nay we shall heat you thoroughly anon.

YOUNG CLIFFORD: Take heed lest by your heat you burn
    yourself.

YORK: Sons, peace!

KING HENRY: Peace, thou! And give King Henry leave to
    speak.

WARWICK: Plantagenet shall speak first: hear him, lords;
    And be you silent and attentive too,
    For he that interrupts him shall not live.
YORK: Now, York, unloose thy long-imprison'd thoughts
    And let thy tongue be equal with thy heart.
    King art thou called; thou art not King.
    That head of thine doth not become a crown;
    Thy hand is made to grasp a palmer's staff,
    And not to grace an awful princely sceptre.
    That gold must round engirt these brows of mine.
    Here is a hand to hold a sceptre up,
    And with the same to act controlling laws.
    Give place; by heaven, thou shalt rule no more
    O'er him whom heaven created for thy ruler.
KING HENRY: Plantagenet, why seek'st thou to depose me?
    Are we not both Plantagenets by birth,
    And from two brothers lineally descent?
    Suppose by right and equity thou be King,
    Thinkest thou that I will leave my kingly throne,
    Wherein my grandsire and my father sat?
    No: first shall war unpeople this my realm;
    Ay, and their colours, often borne in France,
    And now in England to our heart's great sorrow,
    Shall be my winding-sheet. Why faint you, lords?
    My title's good, and better far than his.
WARWICK: Prove it, Henry, and thou shalt be King.
KING HENRY: Henry the Fourth by conquest got the crown.
YORK: 'Twas by rebellion against his King.
KING HENRY: (*Aside*) I know not what to say; my title's weak.
    Tell me, may not a king adopt an heir?
YORK: What then?
KING HENRY: An if he may, then am I lawful king;
    For Richard, in the view of many lords,
    Resign'd the crown to Henry the Fourth.
YORK: He rose against him, being his sovereign,
    And made him to resign his crown perforce.
WARWICK: Suppose, my lords, he did it unconstrain'd,
    Think you 'twere prejudicial to his crown?
EXETER: No; Richard could not so resign his crown

But that the next heir should succeed and reign.

KING HENRY: Art thou against us, Duke of Exeter?

EXETER: My lord, I have consider'd with myself
    The title of this most renowned Duke;
    And in my conscience do repute his Grace
    The rightful heir to England's royal seat.

KING HENRY: Hast thou not sworn allegiance unto me?

EXETER: I have.

KING HENRY: (*Aside*) All will revolt from me and turn to him.

OLD CLIFFORD: King Henry, be thy title right or wrong,
    Lord Clifford vows to fight in thy defence.

KING HENRY: O Clifford, how thy words revive my heart!

YORK: Henry of Lancaster, resign thy crown.

WARWICK: Do right unto this princely Duke of York,
    Or I will fill the house with armed men,
    And o'er the chair of state, where now he sits,
    Write up his title with usurping blood.
    (*He stamps with his foot, and the soldiers show themselves.*)

KING HENRY: My Lord of Warwick, hear me but one word;
    Let me for this my lifetime reign as King.

YORK: Confirm the crown to me and to mine heirs,
    And thou shalt reign in quiet whilst thou liv'st.

KING HENRY: Convey the soliders hence, and then I will.
    I am content; Richard Plantagenet,
    Enjoy the kingdom after my decease.

YOUNG CLIFFORD: What wrong is this unto the Prince your
    son!

WARWICK: What good is this to England and himself!

OLD CLIFFORD: How hast thou injur'd both thyself and us!
    I cannot stay to hear these articles.

YOUNG CLIFFORD: Nor I.

OLD CLIFFORD: Come, my son, let us tell the Queen these
    news.

OXFORD: Farewell, faint-hearted and degenerate King,
    In whose cold blood no spark of honour bides.

SOMERSET: Be thou a prey unto the house of York,
    And die in bands for this unmanly deed!
    (*Exit.*)

WARWICK: Turn this way, Henry, and regard them not.

EXETER: They seek revenge and therefore will not yield.

KING HENRY: Ah, Exeter!

WARWICK: Why should you sigh, my lord?

KING HENRY: Not for myself, Lord Warwick, but my son,
Whom I unnaturally shall disinherit.
But be it as it may.
(*To* YORK:)
                    I here entail.
The crown to thee and to thine heirs for ever;
Conditionally that here thou take an oath
To cease this civil war and, whilst I live,
To honour me as thy King and sovereign;
And neither by treason nor hostility
To seek to put me down and reign thyself.

YORK: This oath I willingly take and will perform.

WARWICK: Long live King Henry! Plantagenet, embrace him.

KING HENRY: And long live thou and these thy forward sons!

YORK: Now York and Lancaster are reconcil'd.

EXETER: Accurs'd be he that seeks to make them foes!

YORK: Farewell, my gracious lord; I'll to my castle.
(*Exeunt* YORK *and his sons.*)

WARWICK: And I'll keep London with my soldiers.
(*Exit.*)

KING HENRY: And I with grief and sorrow to the court.
(*Enter* QUEEN MARGARET *and the* PRINCE OF WALES.)

EXETER: Here comes the Queen.

QUEEN MARGARET: Ah! wretched man, would I had died a
                                        maid,
And never seen thee, never borne thee son,
Seeing thou has proved so unnatural a father.
Hadst thou but lov'd him half so well as I,
Or felt that pain which I did for him once,
Thou wouldst have left thy dearest heart-blood there,
Rather than made that savage Duke thine heir,
And disinherited thine only son.

PRINCE OF WALES: Father, you cannot disinherit me;
If you be King, why should not I succeed?

KING HENRY: Pardon me, Margaret; pardon me, sweet son;
The Earl of Warwick and the Duke enforc'd me.

QUEEN MARGARET: Enforc'd thee! Art thou King, and wilt
                      be forc'd?
    I shame to hear thee speak. Ah! timorous wretch,
    Thou hast undone thyself, thy son and me;
    And given unto the house of York such head
    As thou shalt reign but by their sufferance.
    To entail him and his heirs unto the crown,
    What is it but to make thy sepulchre,
    And creep into it far before thy time?
    Had I been there, which am a silly woman,
    The soldiers should have toss'd me on their pikes
    Before I would have granted to that act;
    But thou prefer'st thy life before thine honour;
    And seeing thou dost, I here divorce myself
    Both from thy table, Henry, and thy bed,
    Until that act of parliament be repeal'd
    Whereby my son is disinherited.
    The northern lords, that have forsworn thy colours,
    Will follow mine, if once they see them spread;
    And spread they shall be, to thy foul disgrace,
    And utter ruin of the house of York.
    Thus do I leave thee. Come, son, let's away.

KING HENRY: Stay, gentle Margaret, and hear me speak.

QUEEN MARGARET: Thou has spoke too much already: get thee
    gone.

KING HENRY: Gentle son Edward, thou wilt stay with me?

PRINCE OF WALES: When I return with victory from the field
    I'll see your Grace: till then I'll follow her.

QUEEN MARGARET: Our army is ready; come, we'll after them.
    (*Exeunt* QUEEN MARGARET *and* PRINCE OF WALES.)

SCENE 8

Sandal Castle, Yorkshire.
Enter RICHARD *and* EDWARD.

RICHARD: Brother, though I be youngest, give me leave.

EDWARD: No, I can better play the orator.

GEORGE: But I have reasons strong and forcible.

(*Enter the* DUKE *and* DUCHESS OF YORK.)

YORK: Why, how now, my sons! at a strife?
    What is your quarrel? How began it first?
EDWARD: No quarrel, but a slight contention.
YORK: About what?
RICHARD: About that which concerns your Grace and us –
    The crown of England, father, which is yours.
YORK: Mine, boy? Not till King Henry be dead.
RICHARD: Your right depends not on his life or death.
EDWARD: Now you are heir; therefore enjoy it now:
    By giving the house of Lancaster leave to breathe,
    It will outrun you, father, in the end.
GEORGE: But think
    How sweet it is to wear a crown,
    Within whose circuit is Elysium
    And all that poets feign of bliss and joy.
YORK: I took an oath that he should quietly reign.
EDWARD: But for a kingdom any oath may be broken;
    I would break a thousand oaths to reign one year.
RICHARD: No; God forbid your Grace should be forsworn.
DUCHESS OF YORK: He shall be, if he claim by open war.
RICHARD: I'll prove the contrary, father, if you'll hear me speak.
YORK: Thou canst not, son; it is impossible.
RICHARD: An oath is of no moment, being not took
    Before a true and lawful magistrate
    That hath authority over him that swears.
    Henry had none, but did usurp the place;
    Then, seeing 'twas he that made you to depose,
    Your oath, my lord, is vain and frivolous.
    Therefore, to arms!
    Why do we linger thus? I cannot rest
    Until the white rose that I wear be dy'd
    Even in the lukewarm blood of Henry's heart.
YORK: Richard, enough! I will be king, or die.
    (*Enter a* MESSENGER.)
    But stay; what news?
MESSENGER: The Queen and Somerset with all the northern
                              earls
    Intend here to besiege you in your castle.

She is hard by with twenty thousand men;
And therefore fortify your hold, my lord.

YORK: Ay, with my sword. What! Thinkest thou that we
fear them?
Prepare, my sons, we'll meet her in the field.

GEORGE: What, with five thousand men!

RICHARD: Ay, with five hundred for a need.
A woman's general; what should we fear?

EDWARD: I hear their drums: let's set our men in order,
And issue forth and bid them battle straight.

YORK: Five men to twenty! Though the odds be great,
I doubt not, Rutland, of our victory.
Many a battle have I won in France,
When as the enemy hath been ten to one;
Why should I not now have the like success?
(*Exeunt omnes.*)

SCENE 9

Field of battle between Sandal Castle and Wakefield.
Enter YORK *to* OLD CLIFFORD.

YORK: Clifford of Cumberland, 'tis York that calls:
Now, when the angry trumpet sounds alarum,
And dead men's cries do fill the empty air,
Clifford, I say, come forth and fight with me!
(*They fight.*)

OLD CLIFFORD: What seest thou in me, York? Why dost thou
pause?

YORK: With thy brave bearing should I be in love,
But that thou art so fast mine enemy.

OLD CLIFFORD: Nor should thy prowess want praise and
esteem,
But that 'tis shown ignobly and in treason.

YORK: So let it help me now against thy sword
As I in justice and true right express it.

OLD CLIFFORD: My soul and body on the action both!
(*They fight.* YORK *kills* OLD CLIFFORD.)

YORK: Thus war hath given thee peace, for thou art still.

Peace with his soul, heaven, if it be thy will!
(*Exit. Enter* YOUNG CLIFFORD.)
YOUNG CLIFFORD: Shame and confusion! all is on the rout:
    Fear frames disorder, and disorder wounds
    Where it should guard. O war, thou son of hell,
    Whom angry heavens do make their minister,
    Throw in the frozen bosoms of our part
    Hot coals of vengeance! Let no soldier fly.
    He that is truly dedicate to war
    Hath no self-love; nor he that loves himself
    Hath not essentially, but by circumstance,
    The name of valour.
(*He sees his dead father.*)
                O, let the vile world end,
    Now let the general trumpet blow his blast,
    Particularities and petty sounds
    To cease! Even at this sight
    My heart is turn'd to stone; and while 'tis mine
    It shall be stony. York not our old men spares;
    No more will I their babes: tears virginal
    Shall be to me even as the dew to fire;
    Henceforth I will not have to do with pity:
    Meet I an infant of the house of York,
    Into as many gobbets will I cut it
    As wild Medea young Absyrtus did;
    In cruelty will I seek out my fame.
(*Exit with his father on his back. Enter* EDWARD, GEORGE
and RUTLAND.)
RUTLAND: Ah, whither shall I fly to scape their hands?
GEORGE: York!
EDWARD: Fly Rutland, fly!
    (*Exeunt* EDWARD, GEORGE *and* RUTLAND. *Enter* RICHARD
    and SOMERSET.)
RICHARD: How now, my Lord of Somerset.
SOMERSET: Foul monstrous traitor, overweening cur,
    Take up your weapon and lay down your life.
RICHARD: Fie! charity for shame! speak not in spite,
    For you shall sup with Jesu Christ tonight.
SOMERSET: Foul stigmatic, that's more than thou canst tell.

RICHARD: If not in heaven, you'll surely sup in hell.
    (*They fight.* SOMERSET *is killed.*)
    So, lie thou there;
    Sword, hold thy temper; heart, be wrathful still;
    Priests pray for enemies, but princes kill.
    (*Exit. Enter* RUTLAND. *Enter* YOUNG CLIFFORD *and
    soldiers.*)
RUTLAND: Ah, gentle Clifford, kill me with thy sword,
    And not with such a cruel threatening look.
    Sweet Clifford, hear me speak before I die:
    I am too mean a subject for thy wrath;
    Be thou reveng'd on men, and let me live.
YOUNG CLIFFORD: In vain thou speak'st, poor boy; my father's
                                   blood
    Hath stopp'd the passage where thy words should enter.
RUTLAND: Then let my father's blood open it again;
    He is a man, and, Clifford, cope with him.
YOUNG CLIFFORD: The sight of any of the house of York
    Is as a Fury to torment my soul;
    And till I root out their accursed line
    And leave not one alive, I live in hell.
    Therefore –
    (*He lifts his sword.*)
RUTLAND: O, let me pray before I take my death!
    To thee I pray; sweet Clifford, pity me.
    I never did thee harm; why wilt thou slay me?
YOUNG CLIFFORD: Thy father slew my father; therefore die.
    (*He stabs* RUTLAND, *who dies.*)
    Plantagenet, I come, Plantagenet!
    And this thy son's blood cleaving to my blade
    Shall rust upon my weapon, till thy blood,
    Congeal'd with this, do make me wipe off both.
    (*Exit. Enter* YORK.)
YORK: The army of the Queen hath got the field:
    And all my followers to the eager foe
    Turn back and fly, like ships before the wind.
    My sons, God knows what hath bechanced them;
    Three times did Richard make a lane to me,
    And thrice cried, 'Courage, father! fight it out!'

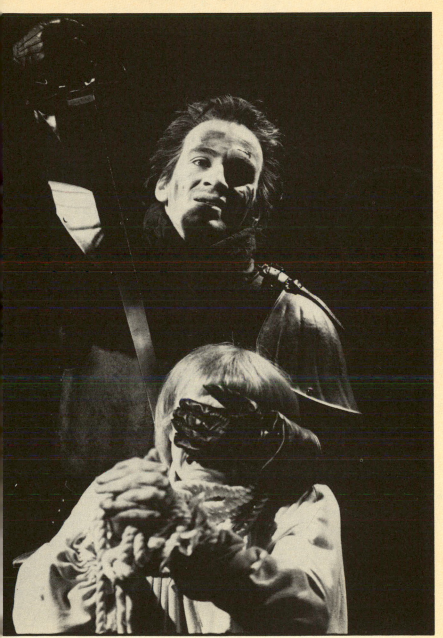

And full as oft came Edward to my side
And cried, 'A crown, or else a glorious tomb!
A sceptre or an earthly sepulchre!'
With this we charg'd again; but out alas!
We budg'd again; as I have seen a swan
With bootless labour swim against the tide
And spend her strength with overmatching waves.
(*A short alarum within.*)
Ah, hark! the fatal followers do pursue,
And I am faint and cannot fly their fury;
The sands are number'd that makes up my life;
Here must I stay, and here my life must end.
(*Enter* QUEEN MARGARET, YOUNG CLIFFORD, EXETER,
the young PRINCE OF WALES *and soldiers.*)
Come, bloody Clifford, and thou proud Queen,
I am your butt, and I abide your shot.

EXETER: Yield to our mercy, proud Plantagenet.

YOUNG CLIFFORD: Ay, to such mercy as his ruthless arm
With downright payment show'd unto my father.

YORK: My ashes, as the phoenix, may bring forth
A bird that will revenge upon you all;
And in that hope I throw mine eyes to heaven,
Scorning whate'er you can afflict me with.

YOUNG CLIFFORD: I will not bandy with thee word for word,
But buckler with thee blows twice two for one.
(*He draws his sword.*)

QUEEN MARGARET: Hold, valiant Clifford; for a thousand
causes
I would prolong awhile the traitor's life.
Come make him stand upon this molehill here,
That raught at mountains with outstretched arms,
Yet parted but the shadow with his hand.
What, was it you that would be England's king?
Was't you that revell'd in our parliament
And made a preachment of your high descent?
Where are your mess of sons to back you now –
The wanton Edward and the lusty George?
And where's that valiant crook-back prodigy,
Dicky your boy, that with his grumbling voice

Was wont to cheer his dad in mutinies?
Or, with the rest, where is your darling Rutland?
Look, York: I stain'd this napkin with the blood
That valiant Clifford with his rapier's point
Made issue from the bosom of the boy;
And if thine eyes can water for his death,
I give thee this to dry thy cheeks withal.
Alas, poor York! but that I hate thee deadly,
I should lament thy miserable state.
I prithee grieve, to make me merry, York.
What! Hath thy fiery heart so parch'd thine entrails
That not a tear can fall for Rutland's death?
Why art thou patient, man? thou shouldst be mad;
And I to make thee mad do mock thee thus.
Stamp, rave, and fret, that I may sing and dance.
Thou would'st be fee'd, I see, to make me sport;
York cannot speak unless he wear a crown.
A crown for York! and, lords, bow low to him:
Hold you his hands whilst I do set it on.
(*She puts a paper crown on* YORK's *head*.)
Ay, marry, sir, now looks he like a king!
Ay, this is he that took King Henry's chair,
And this is he was his adopted heir.
But how is it that great Plantagenet
Is crown'd so soon and broke his solemn oath?
As I bethink me, you should not be king
Till our King Henry had shook hands with Death.
O, 'tis a fault too, too unpardonable!
Off with the crown, and, with the crown, his head;
And, whilst we breathe, take time to do him dead.
YORK: She-wolf of France, but worse than wolves of France,
   Whose tongue more poisons than the adder's tooth!
   How ill-beseeming is it in thy sex
   To triumph like an Amazonian trull
   Upon their woes whom fortune captivates!
   But that thy face is vizard-like, unchanging,
   Made impudent with use of evil deeds,
   I would assay, proud Queen, to make thee blush.
   'Tis beauty that doth oft make women proud;

But God he knows thy share thereof is small.
'Tis virtue that doth make them most admir'd;
The contrary doth make thee wondered at.
'Tis government that makes them seem divine;
The want thereof makes thee abominable.
O tiger's heart wrapped in a woman's hide!
How could'st thou drain the life blood of the child,
To bid the father wipe his eyes withal,
And yet be seen to bear a woman's face?
Women are soft, mild, pitiful, and flexible;
Thou, stern, obdurate, flinty, rough, remorseless.
Bid'st thou me rage? Why, now thou hast thy wish.
Would'st have me weep? Why, now thou hast thy will.
For raging wind blows up incessant showers,
And when the rage allays, the rain begins.
These tears are my sweet Rutland's obsequies,
And every drop cries vengeance for his death
'Gainst thee, fell Clifford, and thee, false Frenchwoman.
EXETER: Beshrew me, but his passion moves me so
    That hardly can I check my eyes from tears.
YORK: That face of his the hungry cannibals
    Would not have touch'd, would not have stain'd with blood;
    But you are more inhuman, more inexorable –
    O, ten times more – than tigers of Hyrcania.
    See, ruthless Queen, a hapless father's tears.
    This cloth thou dipp'dst in blood of my sweet boy,
    And I with tears do wash the blood away.
    Keep thou the napkin, and go boast of this.
    There, take the crown, and with the crown my curse;
    And in thy need such comfort come to thee
    As now I reap at thy too cruel hand!
EXETER: Had he been slaughterman to all my kin
    I should not for my life but weep with him.
QUEEN MARGARET: What, weeping-ripe, my Lord of Exeter?
    Think but upon the wrong he did us all,
    And that will quickly dry thy melting tears.
YOUNG CLIFFORD: Here's for my oath, here's for my father's
    death.
    (*He stabs* YORK.)

QUEEN MARGARET: And here's to right our gentle-hearted King.
  (*She stabs* YORK.)
YORK: Open thy gate of mercy, gracious God!
  My souls flies through these wounds to seek out thee.
  (*He dies.*)
QUEEN MARGARET: Off with his head, and set it on York
                                                    gates;
  So York may overlook the town of York.
  (*Exeunt omnes.*)

SCENE 10

A plain near Mortimer's Cross in Herefordshire.
Enter EDWARD, RICHARD *and* GEORGE.

GEORGE: I wonder how our princely father scap'd,
  Or whether he be scap'd away or no.
EDWARD: Had he been ta'en, we should have heard the news;
  Had he been slain, we should have heard the news;
  Or had he scap'd, methinks we should have heard
  The happy tidings of his good escape.
RICHARD: Methought he bore him in the thickest troop
  As doth a lion in a herd of neat;
  So far'd our father with his enemies;
  Methinks 'tis prize enough to be his son.
  See how the morning opes her golden gates,
  And takes her farewell of the glorious sun;
  How well resembles it the prime of youth,
  Trimm'd like a younker prancing to his love!
EDWARD: Dazzle mine eyes, or do I see three suns?
RICHARD: Three glorious suns, each one a perfect sun;
  Not separated with the racking clouds,
  But sever'd in a pale clear-shining sky.
  See, see! they join, embrace, and seem to kiss,
  As if they vow'd some league inviolable:
  Now are they but one lamp, one light, one sun.
  In this the heaven figures some event.
EDWARD: 'Tis wondrous strange, the like yet never heard of.
  I think it cites us, brother, to the field,

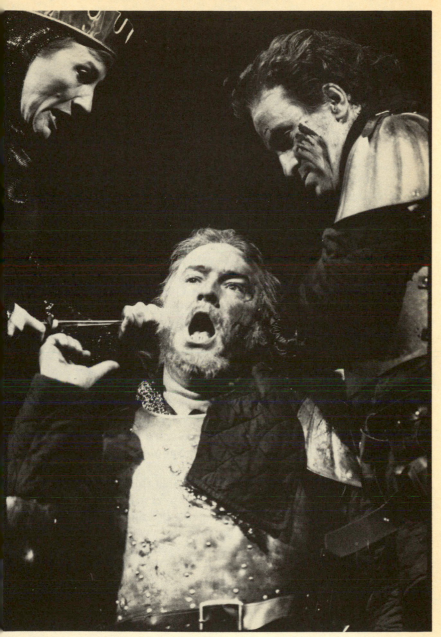

That we, the sons of brave Plantagenet,
Each one already blazing by our meeds,
Should notwithstanding join our lights together,
And over-shine the earth, as this the world.
Whate'er it bodes, henceforward will I bear
Upon my target three fair-shining suns.

RICHARD: Nay, bear three daughters: by your leave I speak it,
You love the breeder better than the male.
But what art thou, those heavy looks foretell
Some dreadful story hanging on thy tongue?
(*Enter a* MESSENGER.)

MESSENGER: Ah, one that was a woeful looker-on
When as the noble Duke of York was slain.

EDWARD: O, speak no more, for I have heard too much.

RICHARD: Say how he died, for I will hear it all.

MESSENGER: Environed he was with many foes,
But only slaughter'd by the ireful arm
Of unrelenting Clifford, and the Queen,
Who crown'd the gracious Duke in high despite,
Laugh'd in his face; and after many scorns,
They took his head, and on the gates of York
They set the same; and there it doth remain.

EDWARD: Sweet Duke of York, our prop to lean upon,
Now thou art gone, we have no staff, no stay.

GEORGE: O Clifford, boisterous Clifford! thou hast slain
The flower of Europe for his chivalry;
And treacherously hast thou vanquish'd him,
For hand to hand he would have vanquish'd thee.

EDWARD: Now my soul's palace is become a prison;
Ah, would she break from hence, that this my body
Might in the ground be closed up in rest!

RICHARD: I cannot weep, for all my body's moisture
Scarce serves to quench my furnace-burning heart;
Tears then for babes; blows and revenge for me!
Richard, I bear thy name; I'll venge thy death,
Or die renowned by attempting it.
(*Enter* WARWICK.)

WARWICK: How now, fair lords! What fare? What news
abroad?

EDWARD: O valiant lord, the Duke of York is slain!
WARWICK: Ten days ago I drown'd these news in tears.
    Tidings as swiftly as the posts could run
    Were brought me of your loss and his depart.
    I, then in London, gather'd flocks of friends
    And straightway marched to intercept the Queen.
    Short tale to make, our battles fiercely join'd.
    But whether 'twas the coldness of the King,
    Who look'd full gently on his warlike Queen,
    Or whether 'twas report of her success;
    Or more than common fear of Clifford's rigour,
    I cannot judge: but, to conclude with truth,
    Our soldiers had no heart to win the fight,
    So that we fled, here to join with you.
RICHARD: 'Twas odds, belike, when valiant Warwick fled:
    Oft have I heard his praises in pursuit,
    But ne'er till now his scandal of retire.
WARWICK: Nor now my scandal, Richard, dost thou hear;
    For thou shalt know this strong right hand of mine
    Can pluck the diadem from faint Henry's head,
    Were he as famous and as bold in war
    As he is fam'd for mildness, peace, and prayer.
RICHARD: But in this troublous time what's to be done?
    Shall we go throw away our coats of steel,
    And wrap our bodies in black mourning gowns?
    Or shall we on the helmets of our foes
    Tell our devotion with revengeful arms?
    If for the last, say ay, and to it, lords.
WARWICK: Why, therefore Warwick came to seek you out.
    Attend me, lords. The proud insulting Queen
    Hath wrought the easy-melting King like wax.
    He sware consent to your succession,
    His oath enrolled in the parliament;
    And now to London all the crew are gone,
    To frustrate both his oath and what beside
    May make against the house of Lancaster.
    Why, Via! to London will we march amain,
    And once again bestride our foaming steeds,
    And once again cry, 'Charge upon our foes!'

But never once again turn back and fly.

EDWARD: Lord Warwick, on thy shoulder will I lean;
And when thou fall'st – as God forbid the hour! –
Must Edward fall, which peril heaven forfend!

WARWICK: Then King of England shalt thou be proclaim'd
In every borough as we pass along;
And he that throws not up his cap for joy
Shall for the fault make forfeit of his head.

RICHARD: Then, Clifford, were thy heart as hard as steel,
As thou hast shown it flinty by thy deeds,
I come to pierce it, or to give thee mine.

EDWARD: Then strike up, drums! God and Saint George for us!

(*Exeunt omnes.*)

SCENE II

Before York
Enter KING HENRY, QUEEN MARGARET, YOUNG CLIFFORD,
NORTHUMBERLAND *and the* PRINCE OF WALES.

QUEEN MARGARET: Welcome, my lord, to this brave town of
York.
Yonder's the head of that arch-enemy
That sought to be encompass'd with your crown:
Doth not the object cheer your heart, my lord?

KING HENRY: Ay, as the rocks cheer them that fear their wrack:
To see this sight, it irks my very soul.
Withhold revenge, dear God! 'tis not my fault,
Nor wittingly have I infring'd my vow.

YOUNG CLIFFORD: My gracious liege, this too much lenity
And harmful pity must be laid aside.
Ambitious York did level at thy crown.
Thou, being a King, bless'd with a goodly son,
Didst yield consent to disinherit him,
Which argued thee a most unloving father.
Were it not pity that this goodly boy
Should lose his birthright by his father's fault,
And long hereafter say unto his child,
'What my great-grandfather and grandsire got

My careless father fondly gave away'?
KING HENRY: But, Clifford, tell me, didst thou never hear
That things evil got had ever bad success?
And happy always was it for that son
Whose father for his hoarding went to hell?
I'll leave my son my virtuous deeds behind;
And would my father had left me no more!
QUEEN MARGARET: My lord, cheer up your spirits; our foes are
nigh,
And this soft courage makes your followers faint.
You promis'd knighthood to our forward son;
Unsheathe your sword, and dub him presently.
Edward, kneel down.
KING HENRY: Edward Plantagenet, arise a knight;
And learn this lesson: Draw thy sword in right.
PRINCE OF WALES: My gracious father, by your kingly leave,
I'll draw it as apparent to the crown,
And in that quarrel use it to the death.
YOUNG CLIFFORD: Why, that is spoken like a toward prince.
(*Enter* BASSET.)
BASSET: Royal commanders, be in readiness;
For with a band of thirty thousand men
Comes Warwick, backing of the Duke of York;
And in the towns, as they do march along,
Proclaims him king, and many fly to him.
YOUNG CLIFFORD: I would your highness would depart the
field;
The Queen hath best success when you are absent.
QUEEN MARGARET: Ay, good my lord, and leave us to our
fortune.
KING HENRY: Why, that's my fortune too; therefore I'll stay.
YOUNG CLIFFORD: Be it with resolution then to fight.
(*March. Enter* EDWARD, GEORGE, RICHARD, WARWICK,
NORFOLK *and soldiers.*)
EDWARD: Now, perjur'd Henry, wilt thou kneel for grace,
And set thy diadem upon my head;
Or bide the mortal fortune of the field?
QUEEN MARGARET: Go rate thy minions, proud insulting boy!
Becomes it thee to be thus bold in terms

Before thy sovereign and thy lawful King?

EDWARD: I am his King, and he should bow his knee:
I was adopted heir by his consent:
Since when his oath is broke.

YOUNG CLIFFORD: And reason too:
Who should succeed the father but the son?

RICHARD: Are you there, butcher? O, I cannot speak!

YOUNG CLIFFORD: Ay, Crook-back, here I stand to answer
thee.

RICHARD: 'Twas you that kill'd young Rutland, was it not?

YOUNG CLIFFORD: Ay, and old York, and yet not satisfied.

RICHARD: For God's sake, lords, give signal to the fight.

WARWICK: What say'st thou, Henry, wilt thou yield the crown?

QUEEN MARGARET: Why, how now, long-tongu'd Warwick!
dare you speak?
When you and I met at St Albans last,
Your legs did better service than your hands.

RICHARD: Break off the parley; for scarce I can refrain
The execution of my big-swoln heart
Upon that Clifford, that cruel child-killer.

KING HENRY: Have done with words, my lords, and hear me
speak.

QUEEN MARGARET: Defy them then, or else hold close thy lips.

KING HENRY: I prithee give no limits to my tongue:
I am a King, and privileg'd to speak.

YOUNG CLIFFORD: My liege, the wound that bred this meeting
here
Cannot be cur'd by words; therefore be still.

RICHARD: Then, executioner, unsheathe thy sword.

PRINCE OF WALES: My royal father, cheer these noble lords
Unsheathe your sword, good father: cry, 'Saint George!'

RICHARD: Whoever got thee, there thy mother stands;
For well I wot thou hast thy mother's tongue.

QUEEN MARGARET: But thou art neither like thy sire nor dam,
But like a foul misshapen stigmatic.

RICHARD: Iron of Naples, hid with English gilt,
Sham'st thou not, knowing whence thou art extraught,
To let thy tongue detect thy base-born heart?

EDWARD: A wisp of straw were worth a thousand crowns

To make this shameless callet know herself.
For what hath broach'd this tumult but thy pride?
Hadst thou been meek, our title still had slept;
And in our resolution we defy thee;
Not willing any longer conference,
Since thou deniest the gentle King to speak.

QUEEN MARGARET: Stay, Edward.

EDWARD: No wrangling woman, we'll no longer stay:
These words will cost ten thousand lives this day.
(*Exeunt omnes.*)

SCENE 12

A field of battle between Towton and Saxton, in Yorkshire.
Alarum. Excursions. Enter WARWICK.

WARWICK: Forspent with toil, as runners with a race,
I lay me down a little while to breathe.
(*Enter* EDWARD, *running.*)

EDWARD: Smile, gentle heaven, or strike, ungentle death;
For this world frowns, and Edward's sun is clouded.

WARWICK: How now, my lord! What hap? What hope of good?
(*Enter* GEORGE.)

GEORGE: Our ranks are broke, and ruin follows us.
What counsel give you? Wither shall we fly?

EDWARD: Bootless is flight, they follow us with wings.
(*Enter* RICHARD.)

RICHARD: Ah, Warwick, why has thou withdrawn thyself?
Thy brother's blood the thirsty earth hath drunk,
Broach'd with the steely point of Clifford's lance.

WARWICK: Here on my knee I vow to God above
I'll never pause again, never stand still,
Till either death hath clos'd these eyes of mine,
Or fortune given me measure of revenge.

EDWARD: O Warwick, I do bend my knee with thine;
And in this vow do chain my soul to thine!
And ere my knee rise from the earth's cold face,
I throw my hands, mine eyes, my heart to thee,
Thou setter up and plucker down of kings.

RICHARD: Brother, give me thy hand; and, gentle Warwick,
Let me embrace thee in my weary arms.

GEORGE: And let us all together to our troops,
And give them leave to fly that will not stay,
And call them pillars that will stand to us.

WARWICK: Away, away! Once more, sweet lords, farewell.
(*Exeunt omnes. Excursions. Enter* RICHARD *and* YOUNG
CLIFFORD.)

RICHARD: Now, Clifford, I have singled thee alone.
Suppose this arm is for the Duke of York,
And this for Rutland; both bound to revenge,
Wert thou environ'd with a brazen wall.

YOUNG CLIFFORD: Now, Richard, I am with thee here alone.
This is the hand that stabb'd thy father York,
And this the hand that slew thy brother Rutland;
And here's the heart that triumphs in their death
And cheers these hands, that slew thy sire and brother,
To execute the like upon thyself;
And so, have at thee!

(*They fight.* WARWICK *comes;* YOUNG CLIFFORD *flies.*)

RICHARD: Nay, Warwick, single out some other chase;
For I myself will hunt this wolf to death.

(*Exeunt* RICHARD *and* WARWICK. *Alarum. Enter* KING
HENRY *alone.*)

KING HENRY: This battle fares like to the morning's war,
When dying clouds contend with growing light,
What time the shepherd, blowing of his nails,
Can neither call it perfect day nor night.
Now sways it this way, like a mighty sea
Forc'd by the tide to combat with the wind;
Now sways it that way, like the selfsame sea
Forc'd to retire by fury of the wind.
Sometime the flood prevails, and then the wind;
Now one the better, then another best;
Both tugging to be victors, breast to breast;
Yet neither conquerors nor conquered.
So is the equal poise of this fell war.
Here on this molehill will I sit me down.
To whom God will, there be the victory!

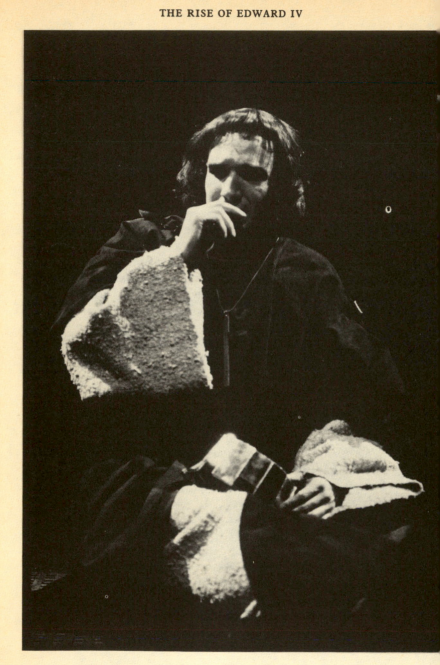

For Margaret my Queen, and Clifford too
Have chid me from the battle, swearing both
They prosper best of all when I am thence.
Would I were dead, if God's good will were so!
For what is in this world but grief and woe?
O God! methinks it were a happy life
To be no better than a homely swain;
To sit upon a hill, as I do now,
To carve out dials quaintly, point by point,
Thereby to see the minutes how they run –
How many makes the hour full complete,
How many hours brings about the day,
How many days will finish up the year,
How many years a mortal man may live.
When this is known, then to divide the times –
So many hours must I tend my flock;
So many hours must I take my rest;
So many hours must I contemplate;
So many hours must I sport myself;
So many days my ewes have been with young;
So many weeks ere the poor fools will ean;
So many years ere I shall shear the fleece;
So minutes, hours, days, weeks, months and years,
Pass'd over to the end they were created,
Would bring white hairs unto a quiet grave.
Ah, what a life were this! how sweet! how lovely!
Gives not the hawthorn bush a sweeter shade
To shepherds looking on their silly sheep,
Than doth a rich embroider'd canopy
To kings that fear their subjects' treachery?
O yes, it doth; a thousandfold it doth.
And to conclude, the shepherd's homely curds,
His cold thin drink out of his leather bottle,
His wonted sleep under a fresh tree's shade,
All which secure and sweetly he enjoys,
Is far beyond a prince's delicates –
His viands sparkling in a golden cup,
His body couched in a curious bed,
When Care, Mistrust, and Treason waits on him.

(*Alarum. Enter a* SON *that hath killed his father, with the body in his arms.*)

SON: Ill blows the wind that profits nobody.
This man whom hand to hand I slew in fight
May be possessed with some store of crowns;
And I, that haply take them from him now,
May yet ere night yield both my life and them
To some man else, as this dead man doth me.
Who's this? O God! it is my father's face.
O heavy times, begetting such events!
From London by the King was I press'd forth;
My father, being the Earl of Warwick's man,
Came on the part of York, press'd by his master;
And I, who at his hands receiv'd my life,
Have by my hands of life bereaved him.
Pardon me, God, I knew not what I did:
And pardon, father, for I knew not thee.

KING HENRY: O piteous spectacle! O bloody times!
Whilst lions war and battle for their dens,
Poor harmless lambs abide their enmity.
Weep, wretched man; I'll aid thee tear for tear;
And let our hearts and eyes, like civil war,
Be blind with tears, and break o'ercharg'd with grief.

(*Enter a* FATHER *that hath killed his son, with the body in his arms.*)

FATHER: Thou that so stoutly hast resisted me,
Give me thy gold, if thou hast any gold,
For I have bought it with an hundred blows.
But let me see: is this our foeman's face?
Ah, no, no, no; it is mine only son!
Ah, boy, if any life be left in thee,
Throw up thine eye! see, see, what showers arise,
Blown with the windy tempest of my heart
Upon thy wounds, that kills mine eye and heart!
O, pity, God, this miserable age!
What stratagems, how fell, how butcherly,
Erroneous, mutinous, and unnatural,
This deadly quarrel daily doth beget!

KING HENRY: Woe above woe! grief more than common grief!

O that my death would stay these ruthful deeds!
O pity, pity, gentle heaven, pity!
SON: How will my mother for a father's death
    Take on with me and ne'er be satisfied!
FATHER: How will my wife for slaughter of my son
    Shed seas of tears and ne'er be satisfied!
KING HENRY: How will the country for these woeful chances
    Misthink the King and not be satisfied!
SON: Was ever son so rued a father's death?
FATHER: Was ever father so bemoan'd his son?
KING HENRY: Was ever king so griev'd for subjects' woe?
    Much is your sorrow; mine, ten times so much.
SON: I'll bear thee hence, where I may weep my fill.
    (*Exit with body.*)
FATHER: These arms of mine shall be thy winding-sheet;
    I'll bear thee hence; and let them fight that will,
    For I have murder'd where I should not kill.
    (*Exit with the body.*)
KING HENRY: Sad-hearted men, much overgone with care,
    Here sits a King more woeful than you are.
    (*Alarums. Excursions. Enter* QUEEN MARGARET, *the*
    PRINCE OF WALES, OXFORD *and* EXETER.)
PRINCE OF WALES: Fly, father, fly! for all your friends are fled.
    Away! for death doth hold us in pursuit.
QUEEN MARGARET: Mount you, my lord; towards Berwick
                          post amain.
    Edward and Richard, like a brace of greyhounds
    Having the fearful-flying hare in sight,
    Are at our backs; and therefore hence amain.
OXFORD: Away! for vengeance comes along with them!
EXETER: Away! make speed,
    Or else come after, I'll away before.
KING HENRY: Nay, take me with thee, good sweet Exeter:
    Not that I fear to stay, but love to go
    Whither the Queen intends. Forward; away!
OXFORD: Away! or henceforth fly no more.
    (*Exeunt omnes. A loud alarum. Enter* YOUNG CLIFFORD
    wounded, with an arrow in his neck.)
YOUNG CLIFFORD: Here burns my candle out; ay, here it dies,

Which, whiles it lasted, gave King Henry light.
Oh, Lancaster, I fear thy overthrow
More than my body's parting with my soul.
The foe is merciless and will not pity;
For at their hands I have deserv'd no pity.
Come, York and Richard, Warwick and the rest;
I stabb'd your fathers' bosoms: split my breast.
(*He faints. Alarum and retreat. Enter* EDWARD, GEORGE,
RICHARD, MONTAGUE, WARWICK, *and soldiers.*)

EDWARD: Now breathe we, lords: good fortune bids us pause
And smooth the frowns of war with peaceful looks.
Some troops pursue the bloody-minded Queen,
That led calm Henry, though he were a King,
But think you, lords, that Clifford fled with them?

WARWICK: No, 'tis impossible he should escape;
For, though before his face I speak the words,
Your brother Richard mark'd him for the grave;
And, wheresoe'er he be, he's surely dead.
(YOUNG CLIFFORD *groans and dies.*)

RICHARD: Whose soul is that which takes her heavy leave?

GEORGE: A deadly groan, like life and death's departing.

RICHARD: See who it is.

EDWARD: And now the battle's ended,
If friend or foe, let him be gently us'd.

RICHARD: Revoke that doom of mercy, for 'tis Clifford.

WARWICK: Speak, Clifford, dost thou know who speaks to
thee?
Dark cloudy death o'ershades his beams of life,
And he nor sees, nor hears us, what we say.

RICHARD: O, would he did! and so, perhaps, he doth:
'Tis but his policy to counterfeit.

GEORGE: If so thou think'st, vex him with eager words.

RICHARD: Clifford, ask mercy, and obtain no grace.

EDWARD: Clifford, repent in bootless penitence.

WARWICK: Clifford, devise excuses for thy faults.

GEORGE: While we devise fell tortures for thy faults.

RICHARD: Thou didst love York, and I am son to York.

EDWARD: Thou pitiedst Rutland, I will pity thee.

GEORGE: Where's Captain Margaret, to fence you now?

WARWICK: They mock thee, Clifford; swear as thou wast wont.
RICHARD: What, not an oath? Nay, then the world goes hard
    When Clifford cannot spare his friends an oath.
    I know by that he's dead.
WARWICK: Off with the traitor's head,
    And rear it in the place your father's stands.
    Measure for measure must be answered.
    And now to London with triumphant march,
    There to be crowned England's royal King;
    From whence shall Warwick cut the sea to France,
    And ask the Lady Bona for thy Queen.
    So shalt thou sinew both these lands together;
    And, having France thy friend, thou shalt not dread
    The scatter'd foe that hopes to rise again.
EDWARD: Even as thou wilt, sweet Warwick, let it be;
    For in thy shoulder do I build my seat,
    And never will I undertake the thing
    Wherein thy counsel and consent is wanting.
    Richard, I will create thee Duke of Gloucester;
    And George, of Clarence; Warwick, as ourself,
    Shall do and undo as him pleaseth best.
RICHARD: Let me be Duke of Clarence, George of Gloucester,
    For Gloucester's dukedom is too ominous.
WARWICK: Tut, that's a foolish observation:
    Richard, be Duke of Gloucester. Now to London,
    To see these honours in possession.
    (*Exeunt omnes.*)

ACT TWO

SCENE I

London. The palace.
Enter KING EDWARD; RICHARD, *now* DUKE OF GLOUCESTER;
GEORGE, *now* DUKE OF CLARENCE, *and* LADY ELIZABETH GREY.

KING EDWARD: Brother of Gloucester, at St Albans field
    This lady's husband, Sir John Grey, was slain,
    His lands then seiz'd on by the conqueror.
    Her suit is now to repossess those lands.
GLOUCESTER: It were dishonour to deny it her.
KING EDWARD: It were no less; but yet I'll make a pause.
GLOUCESTER: (*Aside to* CLARENCE) Yea, is it so?
    I see the lady hath a thing to grant,
    Before the King will grant her humble suit.
CLARENCE: (*Aside to* GLOUCESTER) He knows the game: how
    true he keeps the wind!
GLOUCESTER: (*Aside to* CLARENCE) Silence!
KING EDWARD: Widow, we will consider of your suit;
    And come some other time to know our mind.
LADY GREY: Right gracious lord, I cannot brook delay:
    May it please your Highness to resolve me now;
    And what your pleasure is shall satisfy me.
GLOUCESTER: (*Aside to* CLARENCE) Ay, widow? then I'll
                warrant you all your lands,
    And if what pleases him shall pleasure you.
    Fight closer or, good faith, you'll catch a clap.
KING EDWARD: Lords, give us leave.
    (GLOUCESTER *and* CLARENCE *retire.*)
EDWARD: Now tell me, madam, do you love your children?
LADY GREY: Ay, full as dearly as I love myself.
KING EDWARD: And would you not do much to do them good?
LADY GREY: To do them good, I would sustain some harm.
KING EDWARD: Then get your husband's lands, to do them
                      good.
LADY GREY: Therefore I came unto your Majesty.
KING EDWARD: I'll tell you how these lands are to be got.

LADY GREY: So shall you bind me to your Highness' service.

KING EDWARD: What service wilt thou do me if I give them?

LADY GREY: What you command that rests in me to do.

KING EDWARD: But you will take exceptions to my boon.

LADY GREY: No, gracious lord, except I cannot do it.

KING EDWARD: Ay, but thou canst do what I mean to ask.

LADY GREY: Why, then I will do what your Grace commands.

GLOUCESTER: (*Aside to* CLARENCE) He plies her hard; and much rain wears the marble.

CLARENCE: (*Aside to* GLOUCESTER) As red as fire! Nay, then, her wax must melt.

LADY GREY: Why stops my lord? Shall I not hear my task?

KING EDWARD: An easy task; 'tis but to love a king.

LADY GREY: That's soon perform'd, because I am a subject.

KING EDWARD: Why, then, thy husband's lands I freely give thee.

LADY GREY: I take my leave with many thousand thanks.

GLOUCESTER: (*Aside to* CLARENCE) The match is made; she seals it with a curtsy.

KING EDWARD: But stay thee – 'tis the fruits of love I mean.

LADY GREY: The fruits of love I mean, my loving liege.

KING EDWARD: Ay, but, I fear me, in another sense.

LADY GREY: Why, then, you mean not as I thought you did.

KING EDWARD: But now you partly may perceive my mind.

LADY GREY: My mind will never grant what I perceive
Your Highness aims at, if I aim aright.

KING EDWARD: To tell thee plain, I aim to lie with thee.

LADY GREY: To tell thee pain, I had rather lie in prison.

KING EDWARD: Why, then thou shalt not have thy husband's lands.

LADY GREY: Why then mine honesty shall be my dower;
Almighty lord, this merry inclination
Accords not with the sadness of my suit:
Please you dismiss me, either with ay or no.

KING EDWARD: Ay, if thou wilt say ay to my request;
No, if thou dost say no to my demand.

LADY GREY: Then, no, my lord. My suit is at an end.

GLOUCESTER: (*Aside to* CLARENCE) The widow likes him not, she knits her brows.

CLARENCE: (*Aside to* GLOUCESTER) He is the bluntest wooer in
Christendom.

KING EDWARD: Say that King Edward take thee for his queen?

LADY GREY: 'Tis better said than done, my gracious lord:
I am a subject, fit to jest withal,
But far unfit to be a sovereign.

KING EDWARD: Sweet widow, by my state I swear to thee
I speak no more than what my soul intends;
And that is to enjoy thee for my love.

LADY GREY: And that is more than I will yield unto.
I know I am too mean to be your queen,
And yet too good to be your concubine.

KING EDWARD: You cavil, widow, I did mean my queen.

LADY GREY: 'Twill grieve your Grace my sons should call you
father.

KING EDWARD: No more than when my daughters call thee
mother.
Thou art a widow, and thou hast some children;
And by God's mother, I, being but a bachelor,
Have other some. Why, 'tis a happy thing
To be the father unto many sons.
Answer no more, for thou shalt be my queen.

GLOUCESTER: (*Aside to* CLARENCE) The ghostly father now
hath done his shrift.

CLARENCE: (*Aside to* GLOUCESTER) When he was made a
shriver, 'twas for shift.

KING EDWARD: Brothers, you muse what chat we two have
had.

GLOUCESTER: The widow likes it not, for she looks vex'd.

KING EDWARD: You'd think it strange if I should marry her.

CLARENCE: To whom, my lord?

KING EDWARD: Why, Clarence, to myself.
Well, jest on, brothers: I can tell you both
Her suit is granted for her husband's lands.
Widow, go you along. Lords, use her honourably.
(*Exeunt all but* GLOUCESTER.)

GLOUCESTER: Ay, Edward will use women honourably.
Would he were wasted, marrow, bones, and all,
That from his loins no hopeful branch may spring,

To cross me from the golden time I look for!
And yet, between my soul's desire and me –
The lustful Edward's title buried –
Is Clarence, Henry, and his son young Edward,
And all the unlook'd for issue of their bodies,
To take their rooms ere I can plant myself –
A cold premeditation for my purpose!
Why then I do but dream on sovereignty;
Like one that stands upon a promontory
And spies a far-off shore where he would tread,
Wishing his foot were equal with his eye;
And chides the sea, that sunders him from thence.
My eye's too quick, my heart o'erweens too much,
Unless my hand and strength could equal them.
Well, say there is no kingdom then for Richard;
What other pleasure can the world afford?
I'll make heaven in a lady's lap,
And deck my body in gay ornaments,
And 'witch sweet ladies with my words and looks.
O miserable thought! and more unlikely,
Than to accomplish twenty golden crowns.
Why, Love foreswore me in my mother's womb:
And, for I should not deal in her soft laws,
She did corrupt frail Nature with some bribe,
To shrink mine arm up like a wither'd shrub;
To make an envious mountain on my back,
Where sits Deformity to mock my body;
To shape my legs of an unequal size;
To disproportion me in every part,
Like to a chaos, or unlick'd bear-whelp
That carries no impression like the dam.
And am I then a man to be belov'd?
O monstrous fault to harbour such a thought!
Then, since this earth affords no joy to me
But to command, to check, to o'erbear such
As are of better person than myself,
I'll make my heaven to dream upon the crown;
And, whiles I live, t'account this world but hell,
Until my misshap'd trunk that bears this head

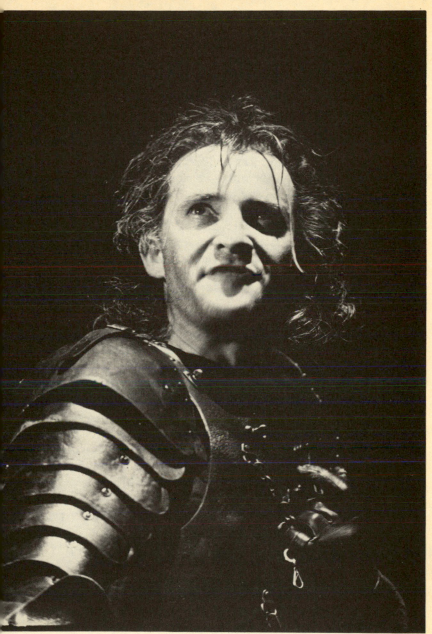

Be round impaled with a glorious crown.
And yet I know not how to get the crown,
For many lives stand between me and home:
And I – like one lost in a thorny wood,
That rents the thorns and is rent with the thorns,
Seeking a way, and straying from the way;
Not knowing how to find the open air,
But toiling desperately to find it out –
Torment myself to catch the English crown:
And from that torment I will free myself,
Or hew my way out with a bloody axe.
Why, I can smile, and murder whiles I smile,
And cry 'Content!' to that that grieves my heart,
And wet my cheeks with artificial tears,
And frame my face to all occasions.
Can I do this, and cannot get a crown?
Tut! were it further off, I'll pluck it down.
(*Exit.*)

SCENE 2

A chase in the north of England.
Enter two KEEPERS, *with crossbows in their hands.*

FIRST KEEPER: Under this thick-grown brake we'll shroud
                                        ourselves,
  For through this laund anon the deer will come.
SECOND KEEPER: I'll stay above the hill, so both may shoot.
FIRST KEEPER: That cannot be; the noise of thy crossbow
  Will scare the herd, and so my shot is lost.
  Here stand we both, and aim we at the best.
SECOND KEEPER: Here comes a man; let's stay till he be past.
  (*Enter* KING HENRY, *disguised, with a prayer book.*)
KING HENRY: From Scotland am I stol'n, even of pure love,
  To greet mine own land with my wishful sight.
  No, Harry, Harry, 'tis no land of thine;
  Thy place is fill'd, thy sceptre wrung from thee,
  Thy balm wash'd off wherewith thou wast anointed:
  No bending knee will call thee Caesar now,

No humble suitors press to speak for right:
For how can I help them and not myself?

FIRST KEEPER: Ay, here's a deer whose skin's a keeper's fee:
This is the quondam King; let's seize upon him.

SECOND KEEPER: Forbear awhile; we'll hear a little more.

KING HENRY: My queen and son are gone to France for aid;
And, as I hear, the great commanding Warwick
Is thither gone, to crave the French King's sister
To wife for Edward. If this news be true,
Poor Queen and son, your labour is but lost;
For Warwick is a subtle orator
And Lewis a prince soon won with moving words.

SECOND KEEPER: Say, what art thou that talk'st of kings and
queens?

KING HENRY: More than I seem, and less than I was born to:
A man at least, for less I should not be;
And men may talk of kings, and why not I?

SECOND KEEPER: Ay, but thou talk'st as if thou wert a king.

KING HENRY: Why, so I am, in mind; and that's enough.

SECOND KEEPER: But if thou be a king, where is thy crown?

KING HENRY: My crown is in my heart, not on my head;
Not deck'd with diamonds and Indian stones,
Nor to be seen: my crown is call'd content;
A crown it is that seldom kings enjoy.

SECOND KEEPER: Well, if you be a king crown'd with content,
Your crown content, and you, must be contented
To go along with us; for, as we think,
You are the king King Edward hath depos'd;
And we his subjects, sworn in all allegiance,
Will apprehend you as his enemy.

KING HENRY: But did you never swear, and break an oath?

SECOND KEEPER: No, never such an oath; nor will not now.

KING HENRY: Where did you dwell when I was King of
England?

SECOND KEEPER: Here in this country, where we now remain.

KING HENRY: I was anointed King at nine months old;
My father and my grandfather were kings,
And you were sworn true subjects unto me:
And tell me then, have you not broke your oaths?

FIRST KEEPER: No, we were subjects but while you were King.

KING HENRY: Why, am I dead? do I not breathe a man?
Ah, simple men, you know not what you sware.
Look, as I blow this feather from my face,
And as the air blows it to me again,
Obeying with my wind when I do blow,
And yielding to another when it blows,
Commanded always by the greater gust,
Such is the lightness of you common men.
But do not break your oaths; for of that sin
My mild entreaty shall not make you guilty.

FIRST KEEPER: We are true subjects to the King, King
Edward.

KING HENRY: So would you be again to Henry,
If he were seated as King Edward is.

FIRST KEEPER: Therefore we charge you, in God's name, and
the King's,
To go with us unto the officers.

KING HENRY: In God's name, lead; your King's name be
obey'd:
And what God will, that let your King perform;
And what he will, I humbly yield unto.
(*Exeunt omnes.*)

SCENE 3

France. The King's palace.
Flourish. Enter LEWIS, *the French King, his sister,* BONA;
PRINCE EDWARD (*formerly the* PRINCE OF WALES), QUEEN
MARGARET *and* OXFORD. LEWIS *sits, and rises up again.*

KING LEWIS: Fair Queen of England, worthy Margaret,
Sit down with us: it ill befits thy state
And birth that thou should'st stand while Lewis doth sit.

QUEEN MARGARET: No, mighty King of France: now Margaret
Must strike her sail, and learn awhile to serve
Where kings command. I was, I must confess,
Great Albion's Queen in former golden days;
But now mischance hath trod my title down

And with dishonour laid me on the ground,
Where I must take like seat unto my fortune.
KING LEWIS: Be plain, Queen Margaret, and tell thy grief;
   It shall be eas'd, if France can yield relief.
QUEEN MARGARET: Those gracious words revive my drooping
                                          thoughts.
   Now, therefore, be it known to noble Lewis
   That Henry, sole possessor of my love,
   Is, of a King, become a banish'd man;
   While proud ambitious Edward, Duke of York,
   Usurps the title and the regal seat.
   This is the cause that I, poor Margaret,
   Am come to crave thy just and lawful aid;
   And if thou fail us, all our hope is done.
KING LEWIS: Renowned Queen, with patience calm the storm,
   While we bethink a means to break it off.
QUEEN MARGARET: The more we stay, the stronger grows our
   foe.
KING LEWIS: The more I stay, the more I'll succour thee.
QUEEN MARGARET: But see where comes the breeder of my
   sorrow.
   (*Enter* WARWICK.)
KING LEWIS: Welcome, brave Warwick! What brings thee to
   France?
   (*He descends. She arises.*)
QUEEN MARGARET: Ay, now begins a second storm to rise;
   For this is he that moves both wind and tide.
WARWICK: From worthy Edward, King of Albion,
   I come, in kindness and unfeigned love,
   First, to do greetings to thy royal person,
   And then to crave a league of amity,
   With nuptial knot, if thou vouchsafe to grant
   That virtuous Lady Bona, thy fair sister.
QUEEN MARGARET: (*Aside*) If that go forward, Henry's hope is
   done.
WARWICK: (*To* BONA) And, gracious madam, in our King's
                                          behalf,
   I am commanded, with your leave and favour,
   Humbly to kiss your hand, and with my tongue

To tell the passion of my sovereign's heart;
Where Fame, late entering at his heedful ears,
Hath plac'd thy beauty's image and thy virtue.

QUEEN MARGARET: King Lewis and Lady Bona, hear me
speak.

His demand springs not from Edward's honest love,
But from Deceit, bred by Necessity;
But how can tyrants safely govern home
Unless abroad they purchase great alliance?

WARWICK: Injurious Margaret!

PRINCE EDWARD: And why not Queen?

WARWICK: Because thy father Henry did usurp;
And thou no more art prince that she is Queen.

OXFORD: Why, Warwick, canst thou speak against thy liege,
Whom thou obey'dst thirty and six years,
And not bewray thy treason with a blush?

WARWICK: Can Oxford, that did ever fence the right,
Now buckler falsehood with a pedigree?
For shame! leave Henry, and call Edward King.

OXFORD: Call him my King by whose injurious doom
My elder brother, the Lord Aubrey Vere,
Was done to death? and more than so, my father,
Even in the downfall of his mellow'd years,
When Nature brought him to the door of Death?
No, Warwick, no; while life upholds this arm,
This arm upholds the House of Lancaster.

WARWICK: And I the House of York.

QUEEN MARGARET: Peace, impudent and shameless Warwick,
peace,

Proud setter up and puller down of kings!

KING LEWIS: Queen Margaret, Prince Edward and Oxford,
Vouchsafe at our request to stand aside,
While I use further conference with Warwick.
(*They stand aloof.*)

QUEEN MARGARET: Heavens grant that Warwick's words
bewitch him not!

KING LEWIS: Now, Warwick, tell me, even upon thy
conscience,
Is Edward your true King? for I were loath

To link with him that were not lawful chosen.

WARWICK: Thereon I pawn my credit and mine honour.

KING LEWIS: But is he gracious in the people's eye?

WARWICK: The more that Henry was unfortunate.

KING LEWIS: Then further: all dissembling set aside,
Tell me the measure of his love for Bona.

WARWICK: Such as beseems a monarch like himself.

KING LEWIS: Now, sister, let us hear your firm resolve.

BONA: (*To* WARWICK) I must confess that often ere this day,
When I have heard your King's desert recounted,
Mine ear hath temper'd judgement to desire.

KING LEWIS: Then, Warwick, thus: our sister shall be
Edward's.
Draw near, Queen Margaret, and be a witness
That Bona shall be wife to the English King.

QUEEN MARGARET: Deceitful Warwick, it was thy device
By this alliance to make void my suit:
Before thy coming Lewis was Henry's friend.

KING LEWIS: And still is friend to him and Margaret:
But if your title to the crown be weak,
Then 'tis but reason that I be releas'd
From giving aid which late I promised.
Yet shall you have all kindness at my hand
That your estate requires and mine can yield.
(*A* POST *blowing a horn within.*)
Warwick, this is some post to us or thee.
(*Enter the* POST.)

POST: (*To* WARWICK) My lord ambassador, these are for you.
(*To* KING LEWIS) These from our King unto your Majesty.
(*To* QUEEN MARGARET) And, madam, these for you; from
whom I know not.
(*They all read their letters.*)

OXFORD: I like it well that our fair Queen and mistress
Smiles at her news, while Warwick frowns at his.

PRINCE EDWARD: Nay, mark how Lewis stamps as he were
nettled:
I hope all's for the best.

KING LEWIS: What? has your King married the Lady Grey?
And now, to soothe your forgery and his,

Sends me a paper to persuade me patience?
Is this th'alliance that he seeks with France?
Dare he presume to scorn us in this manner?
QUEEN MARGARET: I told your Majesty as much before:
This proveth Edward's love and Warwick's honesty.
WARWICK: King Lewis, I here protest in sight of heaven,
And by the hope I have of heavenly bliss,
That I am clear from this misdeed of Edward's —
No more my King, for he dishonours me,
And to repair my honour lost for him
I here renounce him and return to Henry.
My noble Queen, let former grudges pass,
And henceforth I am thy true servitor.
I will revenge his wrongs to Lady Bona,
And replant Henry in his former state.
QUEEN MARGARET: Warwick, these words have turn'd my hate
to love;
And I forgive and quite forget old faults,
And joy that thou becom'st King Henry's friend.
WARWICK: So much his friend, ay, his unfeigned friend,
That if King Lewis vouchsafe to furnish us
With some few bands of chosen soldiers,
I'll force the tyrant from his seat by war.
BONA: Dear brother, how shall Bona be reveng'd
But by thy help to this distressed Queen?
My quarrel and this English Queen's are one.
KING LEWIS: Then, England's messenger, return in post
And tell false Edward, thy supposed King,
That Lewis of France is sending over maskers
To revel it with him and his new bride.
BONA: Tell him, in hope he'll prove a widower shortly,
I'll wear the willow garland for his sake.
QUEEN MARGARET: Tell him my mourning weeds are laid
aside,
And I am ready to put armour on.
WARWICK: Tell him from me that he hath done me wrong,
And therefore I'll uncrown him ere't be long.
There's thy reward; be gone.
(*Exit* POST.)

KING LEWIS: But, Warwick,
　　Thou and Oxford, with five thousand men,
　　Shall cross the seas and bid false Edward battle;
　　And, as occasion serves, this noble Queen
　　And Prince shall follow with a fresh supply.
　　I long till Edward fall by war's mischance
　　For mocking marriage with a dame of France.
　　(*Exeunt all but* WARWICK.)
WARWICK: Had he none else to make a stale but me?
　　Then none but I shall turn his jest to sorrow.
　　I was the chief that rais'd him to the crown,
　　And I'll be chief to bring him down again:
　　Not that I pity Henry's misery,
　　But seek revenge on Edward's mockery.
　　(*Exit.*)

SCENE 4

London. The palace.
Enter GLOUCESTER, CLARENCE *and* RIVERS.

GLOUCESTER: Now tell me, brother Clarence, what think you
　　Of this new marriage with the Lady Grey?
　　Hath not our brother made a worthy choice?
CLARENCE: Alas, you know 'tis far from hence to France!
　　Could he not stay till Warwick made return?
　　Here comes the King.
GLOUCESTER: And his well-chosen bride.
　　(*Flourish. Enter* KING EDWARD, *attended;* QUEEN
　　ELIZABETH (*formerly* LADY GREY); HASTINGS, *and others.*)
CLARENCE: I mind to tell him plainly what I think.
KING EDWARD: Now, brother of Clarence, how like you our
　　　　　　　　　　　　　　　　　　choice,
　　That you stand pensive, as half malcontent?
CLARENCE: As well as Lewis of France or the Earl of Warwick,
　　Which are so weak of courage and in judgement
　　That they'll take no offence at our abuse.
KING EDWARD: Suppose they take offence without a cause;
　　They are but Lewis and Warwick: I am Edward,

Your King and Warwick's, and must have my will.
Say, brother Richard, are you offended too?

GLOUCESTER: No, God forfend that I should wish them sever'd
Whom God hath join'd: ay, and 'twere pity
To sunder them that yoke so well together.

KING EDWARD: Setting your scorns and your mislike aside,
Tell me some reason why the Lady Grey
Should not become my wife and England's Queen.

CLARENCE: Then this is my opinion: that King Lewis
Becomes your enemy for mocking him
About the marriage of the Lady Bona.

GLOUCESTER: And Warwick, doing what you gave in charge,
Is now dishonour'd by this marriage.

KING EDWARD: What if both Lewis and Warwick be appeas'd
By such invention as I can devise?

CLARENCE: Yet to have join'd with France in such alliance
Would more have strengthen'd this our commonwealth
'Gainst foreign storms than any home-bred marriage.

HASTINGS: Why, knows not Clarence that of itself
England is safe, if true within itself?

CLARENCE: The safer, Hastings, when 'tis back'd with France.

HASTINGS: 'Tis better using France than trusting France.
Let us be back'd with God and with the seas
Which he hath given for fence impregnable.

CLARENCE: For this one speech Lord Hastings well deserves
To have the heirdom of Lord Hungerford.

KING EDWARD: Ay, what of that? it was my will and grant;
And for this once my will shall stand for law.

GLOUCESTER: And yet, methinks, your Grace hath not done
well
To give the heir and daughter of Lord Scales
Unto the brother of your loving bride,
My Lord Rivers here.
She better would have fitted me, or Clarence:
But in your bride you bury brotherhood.

KING EDWARD: Alas, poor Clarence! is it for a wife
That thou art malcontent? I will provide thee.

CLARENCE: In choosing for yourself you show'd your
judgement,

Which being shallow, you shall give me leave
To play the broker in mine own behalf;
And to that end I shortly mind to leave you.

KING EDWARD: Leave me, or tarry, Edward will be King,
And not be tied unto his brother's will.

QUEEN ELIZABETH: My lords, before it pleas'd his Majesty
To raise my state to title of a queen,
Do me but right, and you must all confess
That I was not ignoble of descent;
And meaner than myself have had like fortune.
But as this title honours me and mine,
So your dislikes, to whom I would be pleasing,
Doth cloud my joys with danger and with sorrow.

KING EDWARD: My love, forbear to fawn upon their frowns:
What danger or what sorrow can befall thee
So long as Edward is thy constant friend?

GLOUCESTER: (*Aside*) I hear, yet say not much, but think the
more.
(*Enter a* POST.)

KING EDWARD: Now, messenger, what letters or what news
from France?
What answer makes King Lewis to our suit?

POST: At my depart, these were his very words:
'Go tell false Edward, thy supposed King,
That Lewis of France is sending over maskers
To revel it with him and his new bride.'

KING EDWARD: But what said Warwick to our news?

POST: He more incens'd against your Majesty
Than all the rest, discharg'd me with these words:
'Tell him from me that he hath done me wrong,
And therefore I'll uncrown him ere't be long.'

KING EDWARD: Ha! durst the traitor breathe out so proud
words?
Well, I will arm me, being thus forewarn'd:
They shall have wars and pay for their presumption.

CLARENCE: But say, is Warwick friends with Margaret?

POST: Ay, good my lord, they are so link'd in friendship
That young Prince Edward marries Warwick's daughter,
The Lady Anne.

CLARENCE: Now, brother king, farewell, and sit you fast,
    For I will hence to Warwick's other daughter;
    That, though I want a kingdom, yet in marriage
    I may not prove inferior to yourself.
    You that love me and Warwick, follow me.
    (*Exit* CLARENCE.)
KING EDWARD: My brother Clarence gone to Warwick!
    Well, haste is needful in this desperate case.
    Go levy men and make prepare for war;
    Myself in person will straight follow you.
    Now, brother Richard, will you stand by us?
GLOUCESTER: Ay, in despite of all that shall withstand you.
HASTINGS: And Hastings as he favours Edward's cause!
NOBLEMAN: My gracious lord, Henry, your foe, is taken,
    And brought your prisoner to your palace gate.
KING EDWARD: Why, so! then am I sure of victory.
    See that he be conveyed unto the tower.
    Now, therefore, let us hence, and lose no hour
    Till we meet Warwick with his foreign power.
    (*Exeunt omnes.*)

SCENE 5

A plain in Warwickshire.
Enter WARWICK *and* OXFORD, *with French soldiers.*

WARWICK: Trust me, my lord, all hitherto goes well;
    The common people by numbers swarm to us.
    (*Enter* CLARENCE.)
    But see where Edward's brother comes.
    Speak suddenly, Clarence: are we all friends?
CLARENCE: Fear not that, my lord.
WARWICK: Then, gentle duke, welcome unto Warwick;
    I hold it cowardice
    To rest mistrustful where a noble heart
    Hath pawn'd an open hand in sign of love;
    And so, sweet Clarence; my daughter shall be thine.
    And now what rests but, in night's coverture,
    Thy brother being carelessly encamp'd,

We may surprise and take him at our pleasure?
Our scouts have found the adventure very easy:
So we, well cover'd with the night's black mantle,
At unawares may beat down Edward's guard,
And seize himself –

King Edward's camp near Warwick.
Enter three WATCHMEN *to guard the King's tent.*
FIRST WATCHMAN: Come on, my masters, each man take his
                                                stand:
    The King by this is set him down to sleep.
SECOND WATCHMAN: What, will he not to bed?
FIRST WATCHMAN: Why, no; for he hath made a solemn vow
    Never to lie and take his natural rest
    Till Warwick or himself be quite suppress'd.
SECOND WATCHMAN: Tomorrow then belike shall be the day,
    If Warwick be so near as men report.
THIRD WATCHMAN: But say, I pray, what nobleman is that
    That with the King here resteth in his tent?
FIRST WATCHMAN: 'Tis the Lord Hastings, the King's chiefest
    friend.
    (WARWICK, OXFORD *and the French soldiers silently*
    approach.)
WARWICK: This is his tent; and see where stand his guard.
FIRST WATCHMAN: Who goes there?
SECOND WATCHMAN: Stay, or thou diest.
    (WARWICK *and the rest cry all,* 'Warwick! Warwick!' *and set*
    upon the guard, who fly, crying, 'Arm! Arm!', WARWICK *and*
    the rest following them.)

The drum playing and the trumpet sounding, enter WARWICK *and*
the rest bringing KING EDWARD *out in his gown,* GLOUCESTER
and HASTINGS *fly over the stage.*
OXFORD: What are they that fly there?
WARWICK: Richard and Hastings; let them go;
    Here is the Duke.
KING EDWARD: Why, Warwick, when we parted,
    Thou call'dst me King.
WARWICK: Ay, but the case is alter'd.

When you disgrac'd me in my embassade,
Then I degraded you from being King,
And come now to create you Duke of York.
Alas, how should you govern any kingdom
That know not how to use ambassadors,
Nor how to be contented with one wife,
Nor how to use your brothers brotherly,
Nor how to study for the people's welfare,
Nor how to shroud yourself from enemies?

KING EDWARD: Yea, brother of Clarence, art thou here too?
Nay, then I see that Edward needs must down.
Yet, Warwick, in despite of all mischance,
Of thee thyself and all thy complices,
Edward will always bear himself a king.
Though Fortune's malice overthrow my state,
My mind exceeds the compass of her wheel.

WARWICK: Then, for his mind, be Edward England's King;
(*Takes off his crown.*)
But Henry now shall wear the English crown
And be true King indeed; thou but the shadow.
(*They lead him out forcibly.*)

OXFORD: What now remains, my lords, for us to do
But march to London with our soldiers?

WARWICK: Ay, that's the first thing that we have to do,
To free King Henry from imprisonment
And see him seated in the regal throne.
(*Exeunt omnes.*)

SCENE 6

London. The palace.
Enter QUEEN ELIZABETH *and* RIVERS.

RIVERS: Madam, what makes in you this sudden change?
QUEEN ELIZABETH: Why, brother Rivers, are you yet to learn
What late misfortune is befall'n King Edward?
RIVERS: What, loss of some pitch'd battle against Warwick?
QUEEN ELIZABETH: No, but the loss of his own royal person.
RIVERS: Then is my sovereign slain?

QUEEN ELIZABETH: Ay, almost slain, for he is taken prisoner.
RIVERS: These news, I must confess, are full of grief.
QUEEN ELIZABETH: Yet I the rather wean me from despair
    For love of Edward's offspring in my womb:
    This is it that makes me bridle passion
    And bear with mildness my misfortune's cross,
    Lest with my signs or tears I blast or drown
    King Edward's fruit, true heir to th' English crown.
RIVERS: But, madam, where is Warwick then become?
QUEEN ELIZABETH: I am inform'd that he comes towards
                        London
    To set the crown once more on Henry's head.
    I'll hence forthwith unto the sanctuary.
    There shall I rest secure from force and fraud.
    Come, therefore, let us fly while we may fly:
    If Warwick take us, we are sure to die.
    (*Exeunt both.*)

SCENE 7

London. The Tower.
Flourish. Enter KING HENRY, CLARENCE, WARWICK, EXETER,
young RICHMOND, OXFORD *and the* LIEUTENANT OF THE
TOWER.

KING HENRY: Master Lieutenant, now that God and friends
    Have shaken Edward from the regal seat
    And turn'd my captive state to liberty,
    Be thou sure, I'll well requite thy kindness,
    For that it made my prisonment a pleasure.
    Good Warwick, after God, thou set'st me free,
    And chiefly therefore I thank God and thee;
    He was the author, thou the instrument.
    Therefore, that I may conquer Fortune's spite
    By living low where Fortune cannot hurt me,
    Warwick, although my head still wear the crown,
    I here resign my government to thee;
    I make you Lord Protector of this land,

While I myself will lead a private life
And in devotion spend my latter days
To sin's rebuke and my Creator's praise.

WARWICK: Why then, though loath, yet must I be content.
And now, my lord, it is more than needful
Forthwith that Edward be pronounc'd a traitor
And all his lands and goods be confiscate.

CLARENCE: What else? And that succession be determin'd.

WARWICK: Ay, therein Clarence shall not want his part.

KING HENRY: But with the first of all your chief affairs
Let me entreat – for I command no more –
That Margaret your Queen and my son Edward
Be sent for to return from France with speed;
For till I see them here, by doubtful fear
My joy of liberty is half eclips'd.

CLARENCE: It shall be done, my sovereign, with all speed.

KING HENRY: My Lord of Exeter, what youth is that,
Of whom you seem to have so tender care?

EXETER: My liege, it is young Henry, Earl of Richmond.

KING HENRY: Come hither, England's hope.
(*Lays his hand on his head.*)
                                                            If secret powers
Suggest but truth to my divining thoughts,
This pretty lad will prove our country's bliss.
His looks are full of peaceful majesty;
His head by nature fram'd to wear a crown,
His hand to wield a sceptre; and himself
Likely in time to bless a regal throne.
Make much of him, my lords, for this is he
Must help you more than you are hurt by me.
(*Enter* OXFORD.)

WARWICK: What news, my friend?

OXFORD: That Edward is escaped from your brother
And fled, as he hears since, to Burgundy.

WARWICK: Unsavoury news! But how made he escape?

OXFORD: He was convey'd by Richard, Duke of Gloucester,
And the Lord Hastings, who attended him,
And now is he returned with hasty Germans
And blunt Hollanders

And is pass'd in safety through the narrow seas,
And with his troops doth march amain in London;
And many giddy people flock to him.
KING HENRY: Let's levy men and beat him back again.
CLARENCE: A little fire is quickly trodden out,
Which, being suffer'd, rivers cannot quench.
WARWICK: In Warwickshire I have true-hearted friends,
Those will I muster up, and thou, son Clarence,
Shalt stir in Suffolk, Norfolk, and in Kent,
The knights and gentlemen to come with thee.
OXFORD: In Oxfordshire, I'll muster up my friends.
WARWICK: My sovereign, with the loving citizens,
Shall rest in London till we come to him.
CLARENCE: In sign of truth, I kiss your Highness' hand.
KING HENRY: Well-minded Clarence, be thou fortunate;
Fair lords, take leave and stand not to reply.
WARWICK: Farewell, sweet lords; let's meet at Coventry.
(*Exeunt all but* KING HENRY *and* EXETER.)
KING HENRY: Here at the Tower will I rest a while.
Cousin of Exeter, what thinks your lordship?
Methinks the power that Edward hath in field
Should not be able to encounter mine.
EXETER: The doubt is that he will seduce the rest.
KING HENRY: That's not my fear; my meed hath got me fame:
I have not stopp'd mine ears to their demands;
My pity hath been balm to heal their wounds,
My mildness hath allay'd their swelling griefs,
My mercy dried their water-flowing tears;
I have not been desirous of their wealth,
Nor forward of revenge, though they much err'd.
Then why should they love Edward more than me?
No, Exeter, these graces challenge grace;
And, when the lion fawns upon the lamb,
The lamb will never cease to follow him.
(*Exit.*)
EXETER: As Henry's late presaging prophecy
Did glad my heart with hope of this young Richmond,
So doth my heart misgive me, in these conflicts,
What may befall him to his harm and ours.

Therefore, I'll send him hence to Brittany,
Till storms be past of civil enmity.
Ay, for if Edward repossess the crown,
'Tis like that Richmond with the rest shall down.

SCENE 8

Before Coventry.
Flourish. Enter KING EDWARD, GLOUCESTER, HASTINGS *and*
soldiers.

KING EDWARD: Now, brother Richard, Hastings, and the rest,
Yet thus far Fortune maketh us amends,
And says that once more I shall interchange
My waned state for Henry's regal crown.
(*March. Enter* BUCKINGHAM *with drum and soldiers.*)
GLOUCESTER: Brother, this is the Duke of Buckingham,
Our trusty friend, unless I be deceiv'd.
KING EDWARD: Welcome, great Duke! But why come you in
arms?
BUCKINGHAM: To help King Edward in his time of storm,
As every loyal subject ought to do.
KING EDWARD: Thanks, Buckingham; but now do we forget
Our title to the crown, and only claim
Our dukedom till God please to send the rest.
BUCKINGHAM: Then fare you well, for I will hence again:
I came to serve a king and not a duke.
(*The drum begins to march.*)
KING EDWARD: Nay, stay, a while; and we'll debate
By what safe means the crown may be recover'd.
BUCKINGHAM: What talk you of debating? In few words:
If you'll not here proclaim yourself our King,
I'll leave you to your fortune and be gone.
Why shall we fight, if you pretend no title?
KING EDWARD: When we grow stronger, then we'll make our
claim:
Till then 'tis wisdom to conceal our meaning.
HASTINGS: Away with scrupulous wit! Now arms must rule.
GLOUCESTER: And fearless minds climb soonest unto crowns.

Brother, we will proclaim you out of hand.

KING EDWARD: Then be it as you will; for 'tis my right,
And Henry but usurps the diadem.

BUCKINGHAM: Ay, now my sovereign speaketh like himself,
And now will I be Edward's champion.

HASTINGS: Sound trumpet; Edward shall be here proclaim'd.
Before the gates of Coventry,
Where peremptory Warwick know remains.
(*Flourish.*)

BUCKINGHAM: Long live Edward the Fourth!

ALL: Long live Edward the Fourth!

KING EDWARD: Thanks, brave Buckingham, and thanks unto
you all.
(*March. Flourish.*)

GLOUCESTER: See how the surly Warwick mans the wall.

WARWICK: O unbid spite! Is sportful Edward come?

KING EDWARD: Now, Warwick, wilt thou ope the city gates,
Call Edward King, and at his hands beg mercy,
And he shall pardon thee these outrages?

WARWICK: Nay, rather, wilt thou draw thy forces hence,
Confess who set thee up and pluck'd thee down,
And thou shalt still remain – the Duke of York?

GLOUCESTER: I thought at least he would have said the King.

WARWICK: Nay, Henry is my King, Warwick his subject.

KING EDWARD: But Warwick's King is Edward's prisoner;
And, gallant Warwick, do but answer this:
What is the body when the head is off?

GLOUCESTER: Come, Warwick, take the time; kneel down,
kneel down.
Nay, when? Strike now, or else the iron cools.

WARWICK: I had rather chop this hand off at a blow
And with the other fling it at thy face,
Than bear so low a sail to strike to thee.

KING EDWARD: Sail how thou canst, have wind and tide thy
friend,
This hand, fast wound about thy silver hair,
Shall, whiles thy head is warm and new cut off,
Write in the dust this sentence with thy blood:
'Wind-changing Warwick now can change no more.'

(*Enter* CLARENCE *with drum and colours.*)

WARWICK: O cheerful colours! See where succour comes!
 Lo now, where George of Clarence sweeps along,
 Of force enough to bid his brother battle.

CLARENCE: Clarence, Clarence, for Lancaster!

KING EDWARD: Et tu, Brute! wilt thou stab Caesar too?
 Sound a parley, to George of Clarence.
 (*Sound of parley.* GLOUCESTER *and* CLARENCE *whisper.*)

WARWICK: Come, Clarence, come; thou wilt if Warwick call.
 (CLARENCE *takes the red rose from his hat and throws it at*
 WARWICK.)

CLARENCE: Father of Warwick, know you what this means?
 Look, here I throw my infamy at thee:
 I will not ruinate my father's house,
 And am so sorry for my trespass made,
 That, to deserve well at my brother's hands,
 I here proclaim myself thy mortal foe;
 With resolution, wheresoe'er I meet thee,
 To plague thee for thy foul misleading me.
 And so, proud-hearted Warwick, I defy thee,
 And to my brother turn my blushing cheeks,
 Pardon me, Edward, I will make amends:
 And, Richard, do not frown upon my faults,
 For I will henceforth be no more unconstant.

KING EDWARD: Now welcome more, and ten times more
 belov'd,
 Than if thou never hadst deserv'd our hate.

GLOUCESTER: Welcome, good Clarence; this is brother-like.

WARWICK: O passing traitor, perjur'd and unjust!

KING EDWARD: What, Warwick, wilt thou leave the town and
 fight?
 Or shall we beat the stones about thine ears?

WARWICK: Alas, I am not coop'd here for defence!
 I will away towards Barnet presently
 And bid thee battle, Edward, if thou dar'st.

KING EDWARD: Yes, Warwick, Edward dares, and leads the
 way.
 Lords, to the field; Saint George and victory!
 (*Exeunt. March.* WARWICK *and his company follow.*)

A field of battle near Barnet.
Enter WARWICK.

WARWICK: Ah, who is nigh? Come to me, friend or foe,
　　　And tell me who is victor, York or Warwick?
　　　Why ask I that my mangled body shows? –
　　　My blood, my want of strength, my sick heart shows? –
　　　That I must yield my body to the earth,
　　　And, by my fall, the conquest to my foe.
　　　Thus yields the cedar to the axe's edge
　　　Whose arms gave shelter to the princely eagle,
　　　Under whose shade the rampling lion slept.
　　　These eyes, that now are dimm'd with death's black veil,
　　　Have been as piercing as the midday sun
　　　To search the secret treasons of the world;
　　　The wrinkles in my brows, now fill'd with blood,
　　　Were liken'd oft to kingly sepulchres;
　　　For who liv'd King but I could dig his grave?
　　　Lo now my glory smear'd in dust and blood!
　　　My parks, my walks, my manors that I had,
　　　Even now forsake me; and of all my lands
　　　Is nothing left me but my body's length.
　　　Why, what is pomp, rule, reign, but earth and dust?
　　　And live we how we can, yet die we must.
　　　(*Enter* KING EDWARD, GLOUCESTER, CLARENCE *and the
　　　rest.*)
KING EDWARD: So, lie thou there: die thou, and die our fear;
　　　For Warwick was a bug that fear'd us all.
　　　Thus far our fortune keeps an upward course,
　　　And we are grac'd with wreaths of victory:
　　　But in the midst of this bright-shining day
　　　I spy a black suspicious threatening cloud
　　　That will encounter with our glorious sun –
　　　I mean, my lord, those powers that the Queen
　　　Hath rais'd in Gallia have arriv'd our coast,
　　　And, as we hear, march on to fight with us.
CLARENCE: A little gale will soon disperse that cloud.

KING EDWARD: We are advertis'd by our loving friends
    That they do hold their course toward Tewkesbury.
    We, having now the best at Barnet field,
    Will thither straight, for willingness rids way.
    Strike up the drum, cry 'courage!' and away.
    (*Exeunt omnes.*)

SCENE 10

Plains near Tewkesbury.
Flourish. March. Enter QUEEN MARGARET, PRINCE EDWARD,
OXFORD *and soldiers.*

QUEEN MARGARET: Great lords, wise men ne'er sit and wail
                                their loss,
    But cheerly seek how to redress their harms.
    Say Warwick was our anchor; what of that?
    And Clifford our top-mast; what of him?
    Our slaughter'd friends the tackles; what of these?
    Why, is not Oxford here another anchor?
    We will not from the helm to sit and weep,
    But keep our course, though the rough wind say no,
    From shelves and rocks that threaten us with wrack.
    And what is Edward but a ruthless sea?
    What Clarence but a quicksand of deceit?
    And Richard but a ragged fatal rock?
    Say you can swim – alas, 'tis but a while!
    Tread on the sand – why, there you quickly sink:
    Bestride the rock – the tide will wash you off,
    Or else you famish; that's a threefold death.
    This speak I, lords, to let you understand,
    If case some one of you would fly from us,
    That there's no hop'd-for mercy with the brothers.
PRINCE EDWARD: Methinks a woman of this valiant spirit
    Should, if a coward heard her speak these words,
    Infuse his breast with magnanimity.
OXFORD: Women and children of so high a courage,
    And warriors faint! why, 'twere perpetual shame.
    He that will not fight for such a hope

Go home to bed and, like the owl by day,
If he arise, be mock'd and wonder'd at.
(*Enter a* MESSENGER.)
MESSENGER: Prepare you, lords, for Edward is at hand.
OXFORD: I thought no less: it is his policy
  To haste thus fast, to find us unprovided.
QUEEN MARGARET: But he's deceiv'd; we are in readiness.
  (*Flourish, and march. Enter* KING EDWARD, GLOUCESTER,
  CLARENCE *and soldiers.*)
KING EDWARD: Brave followers, yonder stands the thorny
                                                      wood
  Which by the heavens' assistance and your strength
  Must by the roots be hewn up yet ere night.
  I need not add more fuel to your fire,
  For well I wot ye blaze to burn them out.
  Give signal to the fight, and to it, lords!
QUEEN MARGARET: Lords, knights, and gentlemen, what I
                                                  should say
  My tears gainsway; for every word I speak
  Ye see I drink the water of my eye.
  Therefore no more but this: Henry, your sovereign,
  Is prisoner to the foe, his state usurp'd,
  His realm a slaughter-house, his subjects slain,
  His statutes cancell'd, and his treasure spent;
  And yonder stands the wolf that makes this spoil.
  You fight in justice: then, in God's name, lords,
  Be valiant, and give signal to the fight.
  (*Alarum. Retreat. Excursions. Exeunt omnes.*)

Flourish. Enter KING EDWARD, GLOUCESTER, CLARENCE *and
soldiers with* QUEEN MARGARET, OXFORD, BASSET *and
prisoners.*
KING EDWARD: Now here a period of tumultuous broils.
  Away with Oxford to Hames Castle straight:
  For Basset, off with his guilty head.
  Go, bear them hence; I will not hear him speak.
OXFORD: For my part, I'll not trouble thee with words.
BASSET: Nor I; but stoop with patience to my fortune.

(*Exeunt* OXFORD *and* BASSET, *guarded.*)

QUEEN MARGARET: So part we sadly in this troublous world,
To meet with joy in sweet Jerusalem.

KING EDWARD: Is proclamation made that who finds Edward
Shall have a high reward, and he his life?

GLOUCESTER: It is: and lo where youthful Edward comes.
(*Enter soldiers, with* PRINCE EDWARD.)

KING EDWARD: Bring forth the gallant: let us hear him speak.
Edward, what satisfaction canst thou make
For bearing arms, for stirring up my subjects?

PRINCE EDWARD: Speak like a subject, proud ambitious York.
Suppose that I am now my father's mouth;
Resign thy chair, and where I stand kneel thou.

QUEEN MARGARET: Ah, that thy father had been so resolv'd!

GLOUCESTER: For God's sake, take away this captive scold.

PRINCE EDWARD: Nay, take away this scolding crookback
rather.

KING EDWARD: Peace, wilful boy, or I will charm your tongue.

CLARENCE: Untutor'd lad, thou art too malapert.

PRINCE EDWARD: Lascivious Edward, and thou perjur'd
George,
And thou misshapen Dick, I tell ye all
I am your better, traitors as ye are.

KING EDWARD: Take that, the likeness of this railer here.
(*Stabs him.*)

GLOUCESTER: Sprawl'st thou? Take that to end thy agony.
(*Stabs him.*)

CLARENCE: And there's for twitting me with perjury.
(*Stabs him.*)

QUEEN MARGARET: O, kill me too!

GLOUCESTER: Marry, and shall.
(*Offers to kill her.*)

KING EDWARD: Hold, Richard, hold; for we have done too
much.

GLOUCESTER: Why should she live to fill the world with words?

KING EDWARD: What, doth she swoon? Use means for her
recovery.

GLOUCESTER: Clarence, excuse me to the King my brother:
I'll hence to London on a serious matter.

CLARENCE: What? what?

GLOUCESTER: The Tower! the Tower! I'll root them
    out.
    (*Exit.*)

QUEEN MARGARET: O Ned, sweet Ned, speak to thy mother,
                                    boy!

    Canst thou not speak? O traitors! murderers!
    Butchers and villains! bloody cannibals!
    How sweet a plant have you untimely cropp'd!
    You have no children, butchers; if you had,
    The thought of them would have stirr'd up remorse:
    But if you ever chance to have a child,
    Look in his youth to have him so cut off.

KING EDWARD: Away with her; go bear her hence perforce.

QUEEN MARGARET: Nay, never bear me hence; dispatch me
                                    here:
    Here sheath thy sword; I'll pardon thee my death.
    What, wilt thou not? Then, Clarence, do it thou.

CLARENCE: By heaven, I will not do thee so much ease.

QUEEN MARGARET: Good Clarence, do; sweet Clarence, do
    thou do it.

CLARENCE: Didst thou not hear me swear I would not do it?

QUEEN MARGARET: Ay, but thou usest to forswear thyself.
    'Twas sin before, but now 'tis charity.
    What! wilt thou not? Where is that devil's butcher?
    Richard, hard-favour'd Richard, where art thou,
    Thou art not here: murder is thy alms-deed;
    Petitioners for blood thou ne'er put'st back.

KING EDWARD: Away, I say; I charge ye bear her hence.

QUEEN MARGARET: So come to you and yours as to this prince!
    (*Exit, led out forcibly.*)

KING EDWARD: Where's Richard gone?

CLARENCE: To London all in post, and, as I guess,
    To make a bloody supper in the Tower.

KING EDWARD: He's sudden if a thing come in his head.
    Now march we hence: discharge the common sort
    With pay and thanks, and let's away to London
    And see our gentle Queen how well she fares:
    By this, I hope, she hath a son for me.

London. The Tower.
Enter KING HENRY *and* GLOUCESTER, *with the* LIEUTENANT,
on the walls.

GLOUCESTER: Good day, my lord. What, at your book so hard?
KING HENRY: Ay, my good lord – my lord, I should say rather.
GLOUCESTER: Sirrah, leave us to ourselves; we must confer.
   (*Exit* LIEUTENANT.)
KING HENRY: So flies the reckless shepherd from the wolf;
   So first the harmless sheep doth yield his fleece,
   And next his throat unto the butcher's knife.
   What scene of death hath Roscius now to act?
GLOUCESTER: Suspicion always haunts the guilty mind;
   The thief doth fear each bush an officer.
KING HENRY: The bird that hath been limed in a bush
   With trembling wings misdoubteth every bush;
   And I, the hapless male to one sweet bird,
   Have now the fatal object in my eye
   Where my poor young was lim'd, was caught, and kill'd.
   Ah, kill me with thy weapon, not with words!
   My breast can better brook thy dagger's point
   Than can my ears that tragic history.
   But wherefore dost thou come? Is't for my life?
GLOUCESTER: Think'st thou I am an executioner?
KING HENRY: A persecutor I am sure thou art:
   If murdering innocents be executing,
   Why then thou art an executioner.
GLOUCESTER: Thy son I kill'd for his presumption.
KING HENRY: Hadst thou been kill'd when first thou didst
                   presume,
   Thou hadst not liv'd to kill a son of mine.
   And thus I prophesy: that many a thousand
   Which now mistrust no parcel of my fear,
   And many an old man's sigh, and many a widow's,
   And many an orphan's water-standing eye –
   Men for their sons', wives for their husbands',
   Orphans for their parents' timeless death –

Shall rue the hour that ever thou wast born.
The owl shriek'd at thy birth – an evil sign;
The night crow cried, aboding luckless time;
Dogs howl'd and hideous tempests shook down trees;
The raven rook'd her on the chimney's top,
And chattering pies in dismal discords sung;
Thy mother felt more than mother's pain,
And yet brought forth less than a mother's hope,
To wit, an indigest deformed lump,
Not like the fruit of such a goodly tree.
Teeth hadst thou in thy head when thou wast born,
To signify thou cam'st to bite the world;
And if the rest be true which I have heard,
Thou cam'st –

GLOUCESTER: I'll hear no more: die, prophet, in thy speech.
(*Stabs him.*)
For this, amongst the rest, was I ordain'd.

KING HENRY: Ay, and for much more slaughter after this.
O God, forgive my sins and pardon thee!
(*Dies.*)

GLOUCESTER: What, will the aspiring blood of Lancaster
Sink in the ground? I thought it would have mounted.
See how my sword weeps for the poor King's death.
O, may such purple tears be alway shed
From those that wish the downfall of our house!
If any spark of life be yet remaining,
Down, down to hell; and say I sent thee thither –
(*Stabs him again.*)
I that have neither pity, love, nor fear.
Indeed 'tis true that Henry told me of:
For I have often heard my mother say
I came into the world with my legs forward.
Had I not reason, think ye, to make haste
And seek their ruin that usurp'd our right?
The midwife wonder'd, and the women cried,
'O Jesu bless us, he is born with teeth!'
And so I was, which plainly signified
That I should snarl, and bite, and play the dog.
Then, since the heavens have shap'd my body so,

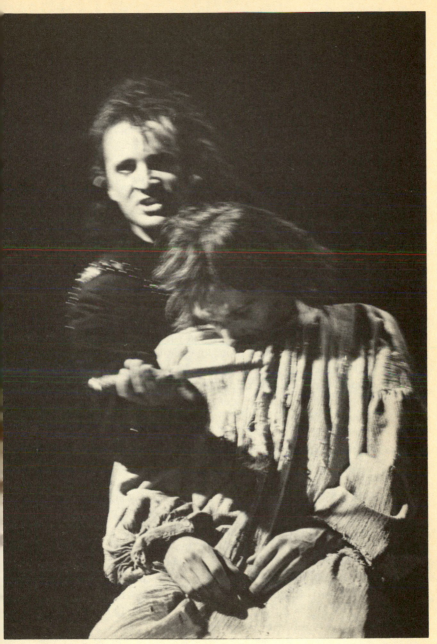

Let hell make crook'd my mind to answer it.
I have no brother, I am like no brother;
And this word 'love', which greybeards call divine,
Be resident in men like one another,
And not in me: I am myself alone.
Clarence, beware; thou keep'st me from the light,
King Henry and the Prince his son are gone;
Clarence, thy turn is next, and then the rest,
Counting myself but bad till I be best.
I'll throw thy body in another room,
And triumph, Henry, in thy day of doom.
(*Exit, with the body.*)

SCENE 12

London. The palace.
Flourish. Enter KING EDWARD, QUEEN ELIZABETH,
CLARENCE, GLOUCESTER, HASTINGS *and a* NURSE *with the*
young PRINCE *and attendants.*

KING EDWARD: Once more we sit in England's royal throne,
Repurchas'd with the blood of enemies.
What valiant foemen, like to autumn's corn,
Have we mow'd down in tops of all their pride!
Come hither, Bess, and let me kiss my boy.
Young Ned, for thee thine uncles and myself
Have in our armours watch'd the winter's night,
Went all afoot in summer's scalding heat,
That thou might'st repossess the crown in peace;
And of our labours thou shalt reap the gain.
GLOUCESTER: (*Aside*) I'll blast his harvest, if your head were
laid;
For yet I am not look'd on in the world.
This shoulder was ordain'd so thick to heave,
And heave it shall some weight, or break my back:
Work thou the way, and that shalt execute.
KING EDWARD: Clarence and Gloucester, love my lovely
Queen;
And kiss your princely nephew, brothers both.

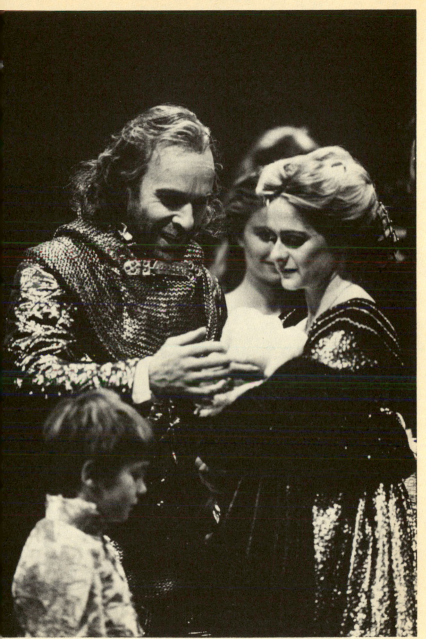

CLARENCE: The duty that I owe unto your Majesty
   I seal upon the lips of this sweet babe.
QUEEN ELIZABETH: Thanks, noble Clarence; worthy brother,
   thanks.
GLOUCESTER: And, that I love the tree from whence thou
                                        sprang'st,
   Witness the loving kiss I give the fruit.
KING EDWARD: Now am I seated as my soul delights,
   Having my country's peace and brothers' loves.
CLARENCE: What will your Grace have done with Margaret?
KING EDWARD: Away with her and waft her hence to France.
   And now what rests but that we spend the time
   With stately triumphs, mirthful comic shows,
   Such as befits the pleasure of the court?
   Sound drums and trumpets! Farewell, sour annoy!
   For here, I hope, begins our lasting joy.
GLOUCESTER: Now . . . !

RICHARD III,
HIS DEATH

Richard III, His Death was first performed at the Royal Shakespeare Theatre, Stratford-upon-Avon, on 13 October 1988, and subsequently transferred to the Barbican Theatre, London, on 27 March 1989.

The cast was as follows:

For York

EDWARD IV	Ken Bones
ELIZABETH	Joanne Pearce
GEORGE, DUKE OF CLARENCE	David Morrissey
RICHARD, DUKE OF GLOUCESTER, *later* RICHARD III	Anton Lesser
DUCHESS OF YORK	Marjorie Yates
PRINCE EDWARD	Lee Barton/Paul Curran
RICHARD, DUKE OF YORK	Lee Broom/Guy Newey
ANTHONY WOODVILLE, LORD RIVERS	Edward Harbour
LORD GREY	Kevin Doyle
MARQUESS OF DORSET	Jo James
WILLIAM, LORD HASTINGS	Edward Peel
DUKE OF BUCKINGHAM	Oliver Cotton
SIR WILLIAM CATESBY	Patrick Robinson
SIR RICHARD RATCLIFFE	Richard Bremmer
LORD STANLEY	Darryl Forbes-Dawson

For Lancaster

HENRY VI, *his ghost*	Ralph Fiennes
MARGARET	Penny Downie
PRINCE EDWARD, *his ghost*	Lyndon Davies
LADY ANNE	Geraldine Alexander
EARL OF RICHMOND, *later* HENRY VII	Simon Dormandy

Directed by Adrian Noble
Designed by Bob Crowley
Lighting by Chris Parry
Music by Edward Gregson
Fight Director Malcolm Ranson
Sound by Paul Slocombe
Company voice work by Cicely Berry and Andrew Wade
Music Director Michael Tubbs
Assistant Director Stephen Rayne
Stage Manager Michael Dembowicz
Photographs by Richard Mildenhall

CHARACTERS

KING EDWARD IV

RICHARD, DUKE OF GLOUCESTER, his brother, *later*
  KING RICHARD III

GEORGE, DUKE OF CLARENCE, his brother (*later* GHOST)

DUKE OF BUCKINGHAM

STANLEY, EARL OF DERBY

LORD HASTINGS (*later* GHOST)

QUEEN MARGARET, widow to Henry VI

DUCHESS OF YORK, mother to Edward IV, Clarence and
  Richard III

QUEEN ELIZABETH, wife to Edward IV

EDWARD, PRINCE OF WALES, her son (*later* GHOST)

RICHARD, DUKE OF YORK, her son (*later* GHOST)

LORD RIVERS, her brother (*later* GHOST)

LORD GREY, her son (*later* GHOST)

MARQUESS OF DORSET, her son (*later* GHOST)

LADY ANNE, widow to the Prince of Wales, *later* Queen to
  Richard III (*later* GHOST)

SIR ROBERT BRAKENBURY, Lieutenant of the Tower

SIR WILLIAM CATESBY

SIR RICHARD RATCLIFFE

LORD LOVELL

SIR JAMES TYRELL

EARL OF RICHMOND, *later* Henry VII

SIR JAMES BLUNT

BISHOP OF ELY

LORD MAYOR OF LONDON

GHOST OF EDWARD, PRINCE OF WALES

GHOST OF HENRY VI

Gentlemen, Murderers, Keepers, Citizens, Messengers,
  Guards, Pallbearers, Attendants, Soldiers, Aldermen,
  Bishops

ACT ONE

SCENE I

London.
Enter RICHARD, DUKE OF GLOUCESTER, *alone.*

GLOUCESTER: Now is the winter of our discontent
    Made glorious summer by this sun of York;
    And all the clouds that lour'd upon our house
    In the deep bosom of the ocean buried.
    Now are our brows bound with victorious wreaths,
    Our bruised arms hung up, for monuments,
    Our stern alarums chang'd to merry meetings,
    Our dreadful marches to delightful measures.
    Grim-visaged war hath smooth'd his wrinkled front;
    And now, instead of mounting barbed steeds
    To fright the souls of fearful adversaries,
    He capers nimbly in a lady's chamber,
    To the lascivious pleasing of a lute.
    But I, that am not shap'd for sportive tricks,
    Nor made to court an amorous looking-glass;
    I, that am rudely stamp'd, and want love's majesty
    To strut before a wanton ambling nymph;
    I, that am curtail'd of this fair proportion,
    Cheated of feature by dissembling Nature,
    Deform'd, unfinish'd, sent before my time
    Into this breathing world, scarce half made up –
    And that so lamely and unfashionable
    That dogs bark at me, as I halt by them –
    Why, I, in this weak piping time of peace,
    Have no delight to pass away the time,
    Unless to spy my shadow in the sun,
    And descant on mine own deformity.
    And therefore, since I cannot prove a lover
    To entertain these fair well-spoken days,
    I am determined to prove a villain,
    And hate the idle pleasures of these days.
    Plots have I laid, inductions dangerous,

By drunken prophecies, libels, and dreams,
To set my brother Clarence and the King
In deadly hate, the one against the other;
And if King Edward be as true and just
As I am subtle, false, and treacherous,
This day should Clarence closely be mew'd up
About a prophecy, which says that 'G'
Of Edward's heirs the murderer shall be –
Dive, thoughts, down to my soul: here Clarence comes.
(*Enter* CLARENCE, *guarded, and* BRAKENBURY, *Lieutenant of the Tower.*)

GLOUCESTER: Brother, good day; what means this armed guard
That waits upon your Grace?

CLARENCE: His Majesty,
Tendering my person's safety, hath appointed
This conduct to convey me to the Tower.

GLOUCESTER: Upon what cause?

CLARENCE: Because my name is George.

GLOUCESTER: Alack, my lord, that fault is none of yours;
He should for that commit your godfathers.
O, belike his Majesty hath some intent
That you should be new-christen'd in the Tower.
But what's the matter, Clarence, may I know?

CLARENCE: Yea, Richard, when I know: for I protest
As yet I do not. But, as I can learn,
He hearkens after prophecies and dreams,
And says a wizard told him that by 'G'
His issue disinherited should be.
And for my name of George begins with G,
It follows in his thought that I am he.

GLOUCESTER: Why, this it is, when men are ruled by women:
'Tis not the King that sends you to the Tower;
My Lady Grey, his wife, Clarence, 'tis she
That tempers him to this extremity.
Was it not she, and that good man of worship,
Anthony Rivers, her brother there,
That made him send Lord Hastings to the Tower,
From whence this present day he is deliver'd?
We are not safe, Clarence, we are not safe!

CLARENCE: By heaven, I think there is no man secure,
 But the Queen's kindred.
BRAKENBURY: I beseech your graces both to pardon me:
 His Majesty hath straitly given in charge
 That no man shall have private conference –
 Of what degree soever – with his brother.
GLOUCESTER: Even so; And please your worship, Brakenbury,
 You may partake of anything we say.
 We speak no treason, man: we say the King
 Is wise and virtuous, and his noble Queen
 Well struck in years, fair, and not jealous
 And that the Queen's kindred are made gentlefolks.
BRAKENBURY: I do beseech your Grace to pardon me, and
                                               withal
 Forbear your conference with the noble Duke.
CLARENCE: We know thy charge, Brakenbury, and will obey.
GLOUCESTER: We are the Queen's abjects, and must obey.
 Brother, farewell. I will unto the King,
 And whatsoe'er you will employ me in,
 I will perform it to enfranchise you.
 Meantime, this deep disgrace in brotherhood
 Touches me deeper than you can imagine.
CLARENCE: I know it pleaseth neither of us well.
GLOUCESTER: Well, your imprisonment shall not be long:
 Meantime, have patience.
CLARENCE: I must perforce. Farewell.
 (*Exit* CLARENCE *with* BRAKENBURY *and guard*.)
GLOUCESTER: Simple, plain Clarence, I do love thee so
 That I will shortly send thy soul to heaven –
 If heaven will take the present at our hands.
 But who comes here? The new-deliver'd Hastings?
 (*Enter* LORD HASTINGS.)
HASTINGS: Good time of day unto my gracious lord.
GLOUCESTER: As much unto my good Lord Chamberlain:
 Well are you welcome to the open air.
 How hath your lordship brook'd imprisonment?
HASTINGS: With patience, noble lord, as prisoners must;
 But I shall live, my lord, to give them thanks
 That were the cause of my imprisonment.

GLOUCESTER: No doubt, no doubt; and so shall Clarence too:
  For they that were your enemies are his,
  And have prevail'd as much on him, as you.
HASTINGS: More pity that the eagles should be mew'd,
  Whiles kites and buzzards prey at liberty.
GLOUCESTER: What news abroad?
HASTINGS: No news so bad abroad as this at home:
  The King is sickly, weak and melancholy,
  And his physicians fear him mightily.
GLOUCESTER: Now by Saint John, that news is bad indeed.
  O, he hath kept an evil diet long,
  And over-much consum'd his royal person:
  'Tis very grievous to be thought upon.
  Where is he, in his bed?
HASTINGS: He is.
GLOUCESTER: Go you before, and I will follow you.
  (*Exit* HASTINGS.)
  He cannot live, I hope, and must not die
  Till George be pack'd with post-horse up to heaven.
  I'll in to urge his hatred more to Clarence;
  Which done, God take King Edward to His mercy,
  And leave the world for me to bustle in.
  For then I'll marry Warwick's eldest daughter –
  What though I kill'd her husband and her father?
  The readiest way to make the wench amends
  Is to become her husband, and her father;
  The which will I, not all so much for love
  As for another secret close intent,
  By marrying her which I must reach unto.
  But yet I run before my horse to market:
  Clarence still breathes, Edward still lives and reigns;
  When they are gone, then must I count my gains.
  (*Exit.*)

SCENE 2

Street.
Enter the corpse of HENRY VI *with halberds to guard it;* LADY
ANNE *being the mourner, attended.*

ANNE: Set down, set down your honourable load
    (If honour may be shrouded in a hearse)
    Whilst I awhile obsequiously lament
    Th'untimely fall of virtuous Lancaster.
    (*The bearers set down the hearse.*)
    Poor key-cold figure of a holy king,
    Pale ashes of the house of Lancaster,
    Thou bloodless remnant of that royal blood:
    Be it lawful that I invocate thy ghost
    To hear the lamentations of poor Anne,
    Wife to thy Edward, to thy slaughter'd son,
    Stabbed by the selfsame hand that made these wounds.
    O, cursed be the hand that made these holes;
    Cursed the heart that had the heart to do it;
    Cursed the blood that let this blood from hence.
    If ever he have child, abortive be it;
    If ever he have wife, let her be made
    More miserable by the life of him
    Than I am made by my young lord, and thee.
    Come now towards Chertsey with your holy load.
    (*The bearers take up the hearse. Enter* GLOUCESTER.)
GLOUCESTER: Stay, you that bear the corse, and set it down.
ANNE: What black magician conjures up this fiend
    To stop devoted charitable deeds?
GLOUCESTER: Villains! set down the corse or by Saint Paul
    I'll make a corse of him that disobeys!
    (*The bearers set down the hearse.*)
ANNE: What, do you tremble? Are you all afraid?
    Alas, I blame you not, for you are mortal,
    And mortal eyes cannot endure the devil.
GLOUCESTER: Sweet saint, for charity, be not so curst.
ANNE: Foul devil, for God's sake hence, and trouble us not;
    For thou hast made the happy earth thy hell.
    If thou delight to view they heinous deeds,
    Behold this pattern of thy butcheries.
    O gentlemen! See, see dead Henry's wounds
    Open their congeal'd mouths and bleed afresh.
    Blush, blush, thou lump of foul deformity:
    Thy deed inhuman and unnatural

Provokes this deluge most unnatural.
O God! which this blood mad'st, revenge his death;
Either heav'n with lightning strike the murderer dead,
Or earth gape open wide and eat him quick.

GLOUCESTER: Lady, you know no rules of charity.

ANNE: Villain, thou know'st no law of God nor man.
No beast so fierce but knows some touch of pity.

GLOUCESTER: But I know none, and therefore am no beast.

ANNE: O wonderful, when devils tell the truth!

GLOUCESTER: More wonderful. When angels are so angry.
Vouchsafe, divine perfection of a woman,
To give me leave but to acquit myself.

ANNE: Vouchsafe, diffus'd infection of a man,
But to give me leave to accuse thy cursed self.
Did'st thou not kill this King?

GLOUCESTER: I grant ye, yea.

ANNE: Dost grant me, hedgehog! Then God grant me too
Thou mayst be damnèd for that wicked deed.
O he was gentle, mild, and virtuous.

GLOUCESTER: The better for the King of Heaven that hath
him.

ANNE: He is in heaven, where thou shalt never come.

GLOUCESTER: Let him thank me that holp send him thither,
For he was fitter for that place than earth.

ANNE: And thou unfit for any place but hell.

GLOUCESTER: Yes, one place else, if you will hear me name it.

ANNE: Some dungeon.

GLOUCESTER: Your bedchamber.

ANNE: Ill rest betide the chamber where thou liest.

GLOUCESTER: So will it, madam, till I lie with you.

ANNE: I hope so!

GLOUCESTER: I know so. But, gentle Lady Anne,
Is not the causer of the timeless deaths
Of these Plantagenets, Henry and Edward,
As blameful as the executioner?

ANNE: Thou wast the cause and most accurs'd effect.

GLOUCESTER: Your beauty was the cause of that effect:
Your beauty, that did haunt me in my sleep
To undertake the death of all the world,

So I might live one hour in your sweet bosom.

ANNE: If I thought that, I tell thee, homicide,
These nails should rend that beauty from my cheeks.

GLOUCESTER: These eyes could not endure that beauty's wrack.

ANNE: Black night o'ershade thy day, and death thy life.

GLOUCESTER: Curse not thyself, fair creature; thou art both.

ANNE: I would I were, to be reveng'd on thee.

GLOUCESTER: It is a quarrel most unnatural,
To be reveng'd on him that loveth thee.

ANNE: It is a quarrel just and reasonable,
To be reveng'd on him that kill'd my husband.

GLOUCESTER: He that bereft thee, lady, of thy husband,
Did it to help thee to a better husband.

ANNE: Where is he?

GLOUCESTER: Here.
(*She spits at him.*)
                              Why dost thou spit at me?

ANNE: Would it were mortal poison, for thy sake.

GLOUCESTER: Never came poison from so sweet a place.

ANNE: Never hung poison on a fouler toad.
Out of my sight! Thou dost infect mine eyes.

GLOUCESTER: Thine eyes, sweet lady, have infected mine.

ANNE: Would they were basilisks, to strike thee dead.

GLOUCESTER: Those eyes of thine from mine have drawn salt
                                                    tears;
These eyes, which never shed remorseful tear,
No, when thy warlike father, like a child,
Told the sad story of my father's death,
And twenty times made pause to sob and weep,
My manly eyes did scorn an humble tear;
And what these sorrows could not thence exhale,
Thy beauty hath, and made them blind with weeping.
If thy revengeful heart cannot forgive,
Lo here I lend thee this sharp-pointed sword,
Which if thou please to hide in this true breast,
I lay it naked to the deadly stroke,
And humbly beg the death upon my knee.
(*He lays his breast open. She offers at it with his sword.*)
Nay, do not pause, for I did kill King Henry –

But 'twas thy beauty that provoked me.
Nay, now dispatch: 'twas I that stabb'd young Edward –
But 'twas thy heavenly face that set me on.
(*She lets fall the sword.*)
Take up the sword again, or take up me.
ANNE: Arise, dissembler; though I wish thy death,
    I will not be thy executioner.
GLOUCESTER: Then bid me kill myself, and I will do it.
ANNE: I have already.
GLOUCESTER: That was in thy rage:
    Speak it again, and even with the word,
    This hand, which for thy love did kill thy love,
    Shall for thy love kill a far truer love;
    To both their deaths shalt thou be accessary.
ANNE: I would I knew thy heart.
GLOUCESTER: 'Tis figured in my tongue.
ANNE: I fear me both are false.
GLOUCESTER: Then never was man true.
ANNE: Well, well, put up your sword.
GLOUCESTER: Say then my peace is made.
ANNE: That shalt thou know hereafter.
GLOUCESTER: But shall I live in hope?
ANNE: All men, I hope, live so.
GLOUCESTER: Vouchsafe to wear this ring.
ANNE: To take is not to give.
    (*She puts on the ring.*)
GLOUCESTER: Look how my ring encompasseth thy finger;
    Even so thy breast encloseth my poor heart;
    Wear both of them, for both of them are thine.
    And if thy poor devoted servant may
    But beg one favour at thy gracious hand,
    Thou dost confirm his happiness for ever.
ANNE: What is it?
GLOUCESTER: That it may please you leave these sad designs
    To him that hath more cause to be a mourner,
    And after I have solemnly interr'd
    At Chertsey Monastery this noble King,
    And wet his grave with my repentant tears,
    I will with all expedient duty see you.

Grant me this boon.

ANNE: With all my heart, and much it joys me too,
To see you are become so penitent.

GLOUCESTER: Bid me farewell.

ANNE: 'Tis more than you deserve;
But since you teach me how to flatter you,
Imagine I have said farewell already.
(*Exit* ANNE.)

GLOUCESTER: Sirs, take up the corse.

GENTLEMAN: Towards Chertsey, noble lord?

GLOUCESTER: No, to Whitefriars; there attend my coming.
(*Exeunt bearers and guard with corse.*)
Was ever woman in this humour woo'd?
Was ever woman in this humour won?
I'll have her, but I will not keep her long.
What? I that kill'd her husband and his father:
To take her in her heart's extremest hate,
And yet to win her, all the world to nothing!
Ha!
Hath she forgot already that brave prince,
Edward, her lord, whom I, some three months since,
Stabb'd in my angry mood at Tewkesbury?
And will she yet abase her eyes on me,
On me, that halts and am misshapen thus?
I do mistake my person all this while!
Upon my life, she finds – although I cannot –
Myself to be a marvellous proper man.
I'll be at charges for a looking-glass,
And entertain a score or two of tailors
To study fashions to adorn my body:
Since I am crept in favour with myself,
I will maintain it with some little cost.
But first I'll turn yon fellow in his grave,
And then return, lamenting, to my love.
Shine out, fair sun, till I have bought a glass,
That I may see my shadow as I pass.
(*Exit.*)

SCENE 3

The Court.
Enter QUEEN ELIZABETH, LORD RIVERS.

RIVERS: Have patience, madam; there's no doubt his Majesty
Will soon recover his accustomed health.
QUEEN ELIZABETH: If he were dead, what would betide on
me?
RIVERS: No other harm but loss of such a lord.
The heavens have bless'd you with a goodly son
To be your comforter when he is gone.
QUEEN ELIZABETH: Ah, he is young, and his minority
Is put unto the trust of Richard Gloucester,
A man that loves not me, nor none of you.
RIVERS: Is it concluded he shall be Protector?
QUEEN ELIZABETH: It is determin'd, not concluded yet;
But so it must be, if the King miscarry.
(*Enter* BUCKINGHAM *and* STANLEY, EARL OF DERBY.)
RIVERS: Here come the lords of Buckingham and Stanley.
BUCKINGHAM: Good time of day unto your royal Grace!
DERBY: God make your Majesty joyful, as you have been.
QUEEN ELIZABETH: Saw you the King today, my Lord
Stanley?
DERBY: But now the Duke of Buckingham and I
Are come from visiting his Majesty.
QUEEN ELIZABETH: What likelihood of his amendment, lords?
BUCKINGHAM: Madam, good hope; his Grace speaks
cheerfully.
QUEEN ELIZABETH: God grant him health. Did you confer
with him?
BUCKINGHAM: Ay, madam; he desires to make atonement
Between the Duke of Gloucester and your brothers,
And between them and my good Lord Hastings.
(*Enter* GLOUCESTER *and* HASTINGS.)
GLOUCESTER: They do me wrong, and I will not endure it!
Who is it that complains unto the King
That I, forsooth, am stern, and love them not?
By holy Paul, they love his Grace but lightly

189

That fill his ears with such dissentious rumours.
RIVERS: To whom in all this presence speaks your Grace?
GLOUCESTER: To thee, that hast nor honesty nor grace.
A plague upon you all! His royal Grace
Cannot be quiet scarce a breathing while
But you must trouble him with lewd complaints.
QUEEN ELIZABETH: Brother of Gloucester, you mistake the
matter:
The King, of his own royal disposition,
Aiming, belike, at your interior hatred,
That in your outward action shows itself
Against my children, brothers, and myself,
Makes him to send, that he may learn the ground.
GLOUCESTER: I cannot tell; the world is grown so bad
That wrens make prey where eagles dare not perch.
Since every Jack became a gentleman
There's many a gentle person made a Jack.
QUEEN ELIZABETH: Come, come: we know your meaning,
brother Gloucester.
You envy my advancement and my friends'.
God grant we never may have need of you.
GLOUCESTER: Meantime, God grants that I have need of you:
Our brother is imprisoned by your means.
QUEEN ELIZABETH: By Him that rais'd me to this careful
height
I never did incense his Majesty
Against the Duke of Clarence, but have been
An earnest advocate to plead for him.
GLOUCESTER: You may deny that you were not the mean
Of my Lord Hastings' late imprisonment.
RIVERS: She may, my lord, for –
GLOUCESTER: She may do more, sir, than denying that.
What may she not? She may – ay, marry may she –
RIVERS: What, marry may she?
GLOUCESTER: What, marry may she? Marry with a king;
A bachelor and a handsome stripling too.
QUEEN ELIZABETH: My Lord of Gloucester, I have too long
borne
Your blunt upbraidings and your bitter scoffs;

By heaven, I will acquaint his Majesty
Of those gross taunts that oft I have endur'd.
I had rather be a country servant maid
Than a great queen, with this condition,
To be so baited, scorn'd, and stormed at.
(*Enter old* QUEEN MARGARET, *behind.*)
Small joy have I in being England's Queen.

QUEEN MARGARET: (*Aside*) And lessen'd be that small, God I
beseech Him:

Thy honour, state, and seat is due to me.

GLOUCESTER: What, threat you me with telling of the King?
Tell him, and spare not: look what I have said
I will avouch't in presence of the King:
'Tis time to speak: my pains are quite forgot.

QUEEN MARGARET: (*Aside*) Out, devil! I do remember them
too well:

Thou kill'dst my husband Henry in the Tower,
And Edward, my poor son, at Tewkesbury.

GLOUCESTER: Ere you were Queen, yea, or your husband
King,

I was a packhorse in his great affairs;
A weeder-out of his proud adversaries:
To royalize his blood, I spent mine own.

QUEEN MARGARET: (*Aside*) Ay, and much better blood than
his, or thine.

GLOUCESTER: Let me put in your minds, if you forget,
What you have been ere this, and what you are;
Withal, what I have been, and what I am.

QUEEN MARGARET: (*Aside*) A murd'rous villain, and so still
thou art.

GLOUCESTER: Poor Clarence did forsake his father, Warwick,
Ay, and forswore himself – which Jesu pardon –

QUEEN MARGARET: (*Aside*) Which God revenge.

GLOUCESTER: To fight on Edward's party for the crown:
And for his meed, poor lord, he is mewed up.

RIVERS: My lord of Gloucester, in those busy days
We follow'd then our lord, our sovereign King:
So should we you, if you should be our King.

GLOUCESTER: If I should be? I had rather be a pedlar!

Far be it from my heart, the thought thereof.
(QUEEN MARGARET *comes forward.*)

QUEEN MARGARET: Hear me, you wrangling pirates, that fall
out
In sharing that which you have pill'd from me:
Which of you trembles not, that looks on me?
If not that I am Queen, you bow like subjects,
Yet that by you depos'd you quake like rebels.
Ah, gentle villain! do not turn away.

GLOUCESTER: Foul wrinkled witch, what mak'st thou in my
sight?

QUEEN MARGARET: But repetition of what thou hast marr'd;
That will I make, before I let thee go.

GLOUCESTER: Wert thou not banished on pain of death?

QUEEN MARGARET: I was, but I do find more pain in
banishment
Than death can yield me here by my abode.
A husband and a son thou ow'st to me;
And thou a kingdom; all of you, allegiance.
This sorrow that I have by rights is yours;
And all the pleasures you usurp are mine.

GLOUCESTER: The curse my noble father laid on thee
When thou didst crown his warlike brows with paper,
And with thy scorns drew'st rivers from his eyes,
And then to dry them, gav'st the Duke a clout
Steep'd in the faultless blood of pretty Rutland –
His curses then, from bitterness of soul
Denounc'd against thee, are all fall'n upon thee,
And God, not we, hath plagu'd thy bloody deed.

QUEEN ELIZABETH: So just is God, to right the innocent.

HASTINGS: O, 'twas the foulest deed to slay that babe,
And the most merciless, that e'er was heard of.

RIVERS: Tyrants themselves wept when it was reported.

DERBY: No man but prophesied revenge for it.

BUCKINGHAM: Old Exeter, then present, wept to see it.

QUEEN MARGARET: What? Were you snarling all before I
came,
Ready to catch each other by the throat,
And turn you all your hatred now on me?

Did York's dread curse prevail so much with heaven
That Henry's death, my lovely Edward's death,
Their kingdom's loss, my woeful banishment,
Should all but answer for that peevish brat?
Can curses pierce the clouds and enter heaven?
Why then, give way, dull clouds, to my quick curses:
Though not by war, by surfeit die your King,
As ours by murder, to make him a king!
Edward thy son, that now is Prince of Wales,
For Edward our son, that was Prince of Wales,
Die in his youth, by like untimely violence.
Thyself, a queen, for me that was a queen,
Outlive thy glory like my wretched self:
And die neither mother, wife nor England's Queen.
Rivers, methinks you were a stander-by,
And so wast thou, Lord Hastings, when my son
Was stabb'd with bloody daggers. God, I pray Him,
That none of you may live his natural age,
But by some unlook'd accident cut off.
GLOUCESTER: Have done thy charm, thou hateful wither'd hag!
QUEEN MARGARET: And leave out thee? Stay, dog, for thou
                                    shalt hear me.
If heaven have any grievous plague in store
Exceeding those that I can wish upon thee,
O, let them keep it till thy sins be ripe,
And then hurl down their indignation
On thee, the troubler of the poor world's peace.
The worm of conscience still begnaw thy soul;
Thy friends suspect for traitors while thou liv'st,
And take deep traitors for thy dearest friends;
Thou elvish-mark'd, abortive, rooting hog,
Thou that wast seal'd in thy nativity
The slave of Nature, and the son of hell;
Thou rag of honour, thou detested –
GLOUCESTER: Margaret!
QUEEN MARGARET: Richard!
GLOUCESTER: Ha?
QUEEN MARGARET: I call thee not.
GLOUCESTER: I cry thee mercy then, for I did think

That thou hadst call'd me all these bitter names.

QUEEN MARGARET: Why, so I did, but look'd for no reply.
O, let me make the period to my curse!

GLOUCESTER: 'Tis done by me, and ends in 'Margaret'.

QUEEN ELIZABETH: Thus have you breath'd your curse
against yourself.

QUEEN MARGARET: Poor painted Queen, vain flourish of my
fortune:
Why strew'st thou sugar on that bottled spider,
Whose deadly web ensnareth thee about?
Fool, fool; thou whet'st a knife to kill thyself.
The day will come that thou shalt wish for me
To help thee curse this poisonous bunch-back'd toad.

BUCKINGHAM: Have done, have done!

QUEEN MARGARET: O princely Buckingham, I'll kiss thy hand
In sign of league and amity with thee:
Now fair befall thee and thy noble house;
Thy garments are not spotted with our blood,
Nor thou within the compass of my curse.

BUCKINGHAM: Nor no one here; for curses never pass
The lips of those that breathe them in the air.

QUEEN MARGARET: I will not think but they ascend the sky,
And there awake God's gentle sleeping peace.
O Buckingham, take heed of yonder dog!
Look when he fawns he bites; and when he bites
His venom tooth will rankle to the death.
Have not to do with him; beware of him.

GLOUCESTER: What doth she say, my Lord of Buckingham?

BUCKINGHAM: Nothing that I respect, my gracious lord.

QUEEN MARGARET: What, dost thou scorn me for my gentle
counsel?
O, but remember this another day
When he shall split thy very heart with sorrow,
And say, poor Margaret was a prophetess.
Live, each of you, the subjects to his hate,
And he to yours, and all of you to God's.
(*Exit.*)

BUCKINGHAM: My hair doth stand on end to hear her curses.

RIVERS: And so doth mine; I muse why she's at liberty.

194

QUEEN ELIZABETH: I never did her harm, to my knowledge.
  (*Enter* CATESBY.)
CATESBY: Madam, his Majesty doth call for you,
  And for your Grace, and you, my gracious lords.
QUEEN ELIZABETH: Catesby, I come. Lords, will you go with
  me?
RIVERS: We wait upon your Grace.
  (*Exeunt all but* GLOUCESTER. *Enter two* MURDERERS.)
GLOUCESTER: How now, my hardy, stout, resolved mates;
  Are you now going to dispatch this thing?
FIRST MURDERER: We are, my lord, and come to have the
                                             warrant,
  That we may be admitted where he is.
GLOUCESTER: Well thought upon; I have it here about me.
  (*He gives the warrant.*)
  But, sirs, be sudden in the execution,
  Withal obdurate; do not hear him plead;
  For Clarence is well spoken, and perhaps
  May move your hearts to pity, if you mark him.
FIRST MURDERER: Tut, tut, my lord: we will not stand to
                                             prate.
  Talkers are no good doers; be assur'd
  We go to use our hands, and not our tongues.
GLOUCESTER: I like you, lads: about your business straight.
  Go, go, dispatch.
FIRST MURDERER: We will, my noble lord.
  (*Exeunt omnes.*)

SCENE 4

The Tower.
Enter CLARENCE *and* KEEPER.

KEEPER: Why looks your Grace so heavily today?
CLARENCE: O, I have pass'd a miserable night,
  So full of fearful dreams, of ugly sights,
  That, as I am a Christian faithful man,
  I would not spend another such a night
  Though 'twere to buy a world of happy days,

So full of dismal terror was the time.
KEEPER: What was your dream, my lord? I pray you tell me.
CLARENCE: Methoughts that I had broken from the Tower
 And was embarked to cross to Burgundy;
 And in my company my brother Gloucester,
 Who from my cabin tempted me to walk
 Upon the hatches; thence we look'd toward England,
 And cited up a thousand heavy times,
 During the wars of York and Lancaster,
 That had befall'n us. As we pac'd along
 Upon the giddy footing of the hatches,
 Methought that Gloucester stumbled, and in falling,
 Struck me (that thought to stay him) overboard,
 Into the tumbling billows of the main.
 O Lord! Methought what pain it was to drown:
 What dreadful noise of waters in mine ears;
 What sights of ugly death within mine eyes!
 Methoughts I saw a thousand fearful wrecks;
 Ten thousand men that fishes gnaw'd upon;
 Wedges of gold, great anchors, heaps of pearl,
 Inestimable stones, unvalu'd jewels,
 All scatter'd in the bottom of the sea.
 Some lay in dead men's skulls, and in the holes
 Where eyes did once inhabit, there were crept –
 As 'twere in scorn of eyes – reflecting gems,
 That woo'd the slimy bottom of the deep,
 And mock'd the dead bones that lay scatter'd by.
KEEPER: Had you such leisure in the time of death
 To gaze upon these secrets of the deep?
CLARENCE: Methought I had; and often did I strive
 To yield the ghost, but still the envious flood
 Stopp'd in my soul, and would not let it forth.
KEEPER: Awak'd you not in this sore agony?
CLARENCE: No, no; my dream was lengthen'd after life.
 O, then began the tempest to my soul;
 I pass'd, methought, the melancholy flood,
 With that sour ferryman which poets write of,
 Unto the kingdom of perpetual night.
 The first that there did greet my stranger-soul

Was my great father-in-law, renowned Warwick,
Who spake aloud, 'What scourge for perjury
Can this dark monarchy afford false, Clarence?'
And so he vanish'd. Then came wand'ring by
A shadow like an angel, with bright hair
Dabbled in blood; and he shriek'd out aloud,
'Clarence is come: false, fleeting, perjur'd Clarence,
That stabb'd me in the field by Tewkesbury!
Seize on him, Furies! Take him unto torment!'
With that, methoughts, a legion of foul fiends
Environ'd me, and howled in mine ears
Such hideous cries, that with the very noise
I trembling wak'd, and for a season after
Could not believe but that I was in hell,
Such terrible impression made my dream.

KEEPER: No marvel, lord, though it affrighted you;
I am afraid, methinks, to hear you tell it.

CLARENCE: Ah, keeper, keeper, I have done these things,
That now give evidence against my soul,
For Edward's sake: and see how he requites me.
O God, if my deep prayers cannot appease thee,
But Thou wilt be aveng'd on my misdeeds,
Yet execute Thy wrath in me alone;
O, spare my guiltless wife and my poor children.
Keeper, I prithee, sit by me awhile:
My soul is heavy, and I fain would sleep.

KEEPER: I will, my lord. God give your grace good rest!
(CLARENCE *sleeps. Enter* BRAKENBURY.)

BRAKENBURY: Sorrow breaks seasons and reposing hours,
Makes the night morning, and the noontide night.
Princes have but their titles for their glories,
And for unfelt imaginations
They often feel a world of restless cares.
(*Enter the two* MURDERERS.)

BRAKENBURY: What would'st thou, fellow? And how cam'st
thou hither?

SECOND MURDERER: I would speak with Clarence, and I came
hither on my legs.

197

FIRST MURDERER: Let him see our commission, and talk no more.

(BRAKENBURY *reads it.*)

BRAKENBURY: I am in this commanded to deliver
The noble Duke of Clarence to your hands.
I will not reason what is meant hereby,
Because I will be guiltless from the meaning.

(*Exit* BRAKENBURY *with* KEEPER.)

FIRST MURDERER: You may, sir; 'tis a point of wisdom. Fare you well.

SECOND MURDERER: What, shall I stab him as he sleeps?

FIRST MURDERER: No: he'll say 'twas done cowardly when he wakes.

SECOND MURDERER: Why, he shall never wake until Judgement Day.

FIRST MURDERER: Why, then he'll say we stabbed him sleeping.

SECOND MURDERER: The urging of that word, 'judgement', hath bred a kind of remorse in me.

FIRST MURDERER: What, art thou afraid?

SECOND MURDERER: Not to kill him – having a warrant – but to be damned for killing him, from the which no warrant can defend me.

FIRST MURDERER: I thought thou hadst been resolute.

SECOND MURDERER: So I am – to let him live.

FIRST MURDERER: I'll back to the Duke of Gloucester, and tell him so.

SECOND MURDERER: Nay, I prithee stay a little: I hope this passionate humour of mine will change. It was wont to hold me but while one tells twenty.

FIRST MURDERER: How dost thou feel thyself now?

SECOND MURDERER: Faith, some certain dregs of conscience are yet within me.

FIRST MURDERER: Remember our reward, when the deed's done.

SECOND MURDERER: Zounds, he dies! I had forgot the reward.

FIRST MURDERER: Where's thy conscience now?

SECOND MURDERER: O, in the Duke of Gloucester's purse. Come, shall we fall to work?

FIRST MURDERER: Take him on the costard with the hilts of thy sword, and then throw him into the malmsey-butt in the next room.

SECOND MURDERER: Oh excellent device! and make a sop of him.

FIRST MURDERER: Soft, he wakes.

SECOND MURDERER: Strike!

FIRST MURDERER: No, we'll reason with him.

CLARENCE: Where art thou, keeper? Give me a cup of wine.

SECOND MURDERER: You shall have wine enough, my lord, anon.

CLARENCE: In God's name, what art thou?

FIRST MURDERER: A man, as you are.

CLARENCE: But not as I am, royal.

SECOND MURDERER: Nor you as we are, loyal.

CLARENCE: Wherefore do you come?

SECOND MURDERER: To – to – to –

CLARENCE: To murder me?

MURDERERS: Ay, ay.

CLARENCE: You scarcely have the hearts to tell me so,
And therefore cannot have the hearts to do it.
Wherein, my friends, have I offended you?

FIRST MURDERER: Offended us you have not, but the King.

CLARENCE: I shall be reconcil'd to him again.
I charge you, as you hope to have redemption,
By Christ's dear blood, shed for our grievous sins,
That you depart and lay no hands on me:
The deed you undertake is damnable.

FIRST MURDERER: What we will do, we do upon command.

SECOND MURDERER: And he that hath commanded is our King.

CLARENCE: Erroneous vassals! The great King of kings
Hath in the table of His law commanded
That thou shalt do no murder. Will you then
Spurn at His edict, and fulfil a man's?
Take heed! For He holds vengeance in His hand
To hurl upon their heads that break His law.

SECOND MURDERER: And that same vengeance doth He hurl on thee,

For false forswearing, and for murder too.

FIRST MURDERER: How canst thou urge God's dreadful law to
us,
When thou hast broke it in such dear degree?

CLARENCE: Alas, for whose sake did I that ill deed?
For Edward, for my brother, for his sake.
He sends you not to murder me for this,
For in that sin he is as deep as I.
If you are hir'd for meed, go back again,
And I will send you to my brother Gloucester,
Who shall reward you better for my life
Than Edward will for tidings of my death.

SECOND MURDERER: You are deceiv'd: your brother
Gloucester hates you.

CLARENCE: O, do not slander him, for he is kind.

FIRST MURDERER: Right, as snow in harvest.
Come: you deceive yourself;
'Tis he that sends us to destroy you here.

CLARENCE: It cannot be: for he bewept my fortune,
And hugg'd me in his arms, and swore with sobs
That he would labour my delivery.

FIRST MURDERER: Why so he doth, when he delivers you
From his earth's thraldom to the joys of heaven.

SECOND MURDERER: Make peace with God, for you must die,
my lord.

CLARENCE: Have you that holy feeling in your souls
To counsel me to make my peace with God,
And are you yet to your own souls so blind
That you will war with God by murd'ring me?
O sirs, consider: they that set you on
To do this deed will hate you for the deed.

SECOND MURDERER: What shall we do?

CLARENCE: Relent, and save your souls.
(*To* SECOND MURDERER) My friend, I spy some pity in
thy looks:
O, if thine eye be not a flatterer,
Come thou on my side, and entreat for me.

SECOND MURDERER: Look behind you, my lord!
(FIRST MURDERER *stabs him*.)

FIRST MURDERER: If all this will not do, I'll drown you in the
malmsey-butt within.
(*Exit with the body.*)
SECOND MURDERER: A bloody deed, and desperately
dispatch'd.
How fain, like Pilate, would I wash my hands
Of this most grievous murder.
(*Enter* FIRST MURDERER.)
FIRST MURDERER: By heavens, the Duke shall know how
slack you have been.
SECOND MURDERER: I would he knew that I had sav'd his
brother.
Take thou the fee, and tell him what I say,
For I repent me that the Duke is slain.
(*Exit.*)
FIRST MURDERER: So do not I: go, coward as thou art.
Well, I'll go hide the body in some hole
Till that the Duke give order for his burial.
And when I have my meed, I will away:
For this will out, and then I must not stay.
(*Exit.*)

SCENE 5

The Court.
Flourish. Enter KING EDWARD, *sick,* QUEEN ELIZABETH,
DUCHESS OF YORK, RIVERS, HASTINGS, BUCKINGHAM, *and*
attendants.

KING EDWARD: Why, so: now have I done a good day's work:
You peers, continue this united league.
I every day expect an embassage
From my Redeemer, to redeem me hence;
And more in peace my soul shall part to heaven,
Since I have made my friends at peace on earth.
Hastings and Rivers, take each other's hand;
Dissemble not your hatred; swear your love.
Take heed you dally not before your King,

Lest He that is the supreme King of kings
Confound your hidden falsehood, and award
Either of you to be the other's end.

HASTINGS: So prosper I, as I swear perfect love.

RIVERS: And I, as I love Hastings with my heart.

KING EDWARD: Madam, yourself is not exempt from this.

QUEEN ELIZABETH: There, Hastings: I will never more
                                remember
Our former hatred, so thrive I and mine.

KING EDWARD: Now, princely Buckingham, seal thou this
                                   league
And make me happy in your unity.

BUCKINGHAM: (*To* QUEEN ELIZABETH) Whenever
                    Buckingham doth turn his hate
Upon your Grace, but with all duteous love
Doth cherish you and yours, God punish me
With hate in those where I expect most love.
(*They embrace.*)

KING EDWARD: A pleasing cordial, princely Buckingham,
Is this thy vow unto my sickly heart.
(*Enter* SIR RICHARD RATCLIFFE *and* GLOUCESTER.)

GLOUCESTER: Good morrow to my sovereign King and Queen;
And, princely peers, a happy time of day.

KING EDWARD: Happy indeed, as we have spent the day;
Gloucester, we have done deeds of charity,
Made peace of enmity, fair love of hate,
Between these swelling, wrong-incensed peers.

GLOUCESTER: A blessed labour, my most sovereign lord.
If I unwittingly, or in my rage,
Have aught committed that is hardly borne
By any in this presence, I desire
To reconcile me to his friendly peace:
'Tis death to me to be at enmity.
First, madam, I entreat true peace of you,
Of you, my noble cousin Buckingham,
If ever any grudge were lodg'd between us;
Of you, and you, Lord Rivers,
Dukes, earls, lords, gentlemen: indeed of all.
I do not know that Englishman alive

With whom my soul is any jot at odds,
More than the infant that is born tonight –
I thank my God for my humility.
QUEEN ELIZABETH: A holy day shall this be kept hereafter;
My sovereign lord, I do beseech your Highness
To take our brother Clarence to your grace.
GLOUCESTER: Why, madam, have I offer'd love for this,
To be so flouted in this royal presence?
Who knows not that the gentle Duke is dead?
(*They all start.*)
KING EDWARD: Who knows not he is dead! Who knows he is?
DUCHESS OF YORK: Oh! Clarence, my unhappy son.
QUEEN ELIZABETH: All-seeing heaven, what a world is this?
KING EDWARD: Is Clarence dead? The order was revers'd.
GLOUCESTER: But he, poor man, by your first order died,
And that a winged Mercury did bear;
Some tardy cripple bore the countermand,
That came too lag to see him buried.
(*Enter* DERBY.)
DERBY: A boon, my sovereign, for my service done!
KING EDWARD: I prithee peace; my soul is full of sorrow.
DERBY: I will not rise unless your Highness hear me.
KING EDWARD: Then say at once what is it thou requests.
DERBY: The forfeit, sovereign, of my servant's life
Who slew today a riotous gentleman
Lately attendant on the Duke of Norfolk.
KING EDWARD: Have I a tongue to doom my brother's death,
And shall that tongue give pardon to a slave?
Who sued to me for him? Who, in my wrath,
Kneel'd at my feet and bid me be advis'd?
Who spoke of brotherhood? Who spoke of love?
Who told me, in the field at Tewkesbury
When Oxford had me down, he rescued me
And said, 'Dear brother, live and be a king'?
Who told me, when we both lay in the field
Frozen almost to death, how he did lap me
Even in his garments, and did give himself,
All thin and naked, to the numb-cold night?
All this from my remembrance brutish wrath

Sinfully pluck'd, and not a man of you
Had so much grace to put it in my mind.
But when your carters or your waiting vassals
Have done a drunken slaughter, and defac'd
The precious image of our dear Redeemer,
You straight are on your knees for 'Pardon, pardon!'
And I, unjustly too, Must grant it you.
(DERBY *rises*.)
But for my brother not a man would speak,
Nor I, ungracious, speak unto myself
For him, poor soul. The proudest of you all
Have been beholden to him in his life,
Yet none of you would once beg for his life.
O God, I fear thy justice will take hold
On me, and you, and mine and yours for this.
Come, Hastings, help me to my closet.
Ah, poor Clarence!
(*Exeunt some with* KING EDWARD *and* QUEEN
ELIZABETH.)
GLOUCESTER: This is the fruits of rashness: mark'd you not
How that the guilty kindred of the Queen
Look'd pale when they did hear of Clarence' death?
O, they did urge it still unto the King:
God will revenge it. Come, lords, will you go
To comfort Edward with our company?
BUCKINGHAM: We wait upon your grace.
(*Enter* QUEEN ELIZABETH; RIVERS *after her*.)
GLOUCESTER: What noise is this?
QUEEN ELIZABETH: Ah! who shall hinder me to wail and weep,
To chide my fortune, and torment myself?
Edward, my lord, thy son, our King, is dead.
Why grow the branches, when the root is gone?
Why wither not the leaves that want their sap?
DUCHESS OF YORK: Ah, so much interest have I in thy sorrow
As I had title in thy noble husband.
I have bewept a worthy husband's death,
And liv'd with looking on his images:
But now two mirrors of his princely semblance
Are crack'd in pieces by malignant death:

Clarence and Edward. O, what cause have I,
Thine being but a moiety of my moan,
To overgo thy woes and drown thy cries.

QUEEN ELIZABETH: Give me no help in lamentation:
All springs reduce their currents to mine eyes,
That I, being govern'd by the watery moon,
May send forth plenteous tears to drown the world.

GLOUCESTER: Sister, have comfort: all of us have cause
To wail the dimming of our shining star,
But none can help our harms by wailing them.

QUEEN ELIZABETH: Ah, for my husband, for my dear lord
Edward!

DUCHESS OF YORK: Ah, for my children, Edward and
Clarence!

QUEEN ELIZABETH: What stay had I but Edward, and he is
gone.

DUCHESS OF YORK: What stays had I but they, and they are
gone.

QUEEN ELIZABETH: Was never widow had so dear a loss.

DUCHESS OF YORK: Was never mother had so dear a loss.
Alas, I am the mother of these griefs:
She for an Edward weeps, and so do I;
I for a Clarence weep, so doth not she;
Pour all your tears: I am your sorrow's nurse,
And I will pamper it with lamentation.

RIVERS: Madam, bethink you, like a careful mother,
Of the young prince your son: send straight for him;
Let him be crown'd; in him your comfort lives.
Drown desperate sorrow in dead Edward's grave,
And plant your joys in living Edward's throne.

BUCKINGHAM: Though we have spent our harvest of this King,
We are to reap the harvest of his son.
Meseemeth good that with some little train,
Forthwith from Ludlow the young Prince be fetch'd
Hither to London, to be crown'd our King.

RIVERS: Why with some little train, my Lord of Buckingham?

BUCKINGHAM: Marry, my lord, lest by a multitude
The new-heal'd wound of malice should break out.

GLOUCESTER: I hope the King made peace with all of us,

And the compact is firm and true in me.

RIVERS: And so in me, and so, I think, in all.
Therefore I say with noble Buckingham
That it is meet so few should fetch the Prince.

HASTINGS: And so say I.

GLOUCESTER: Then, be it so, and go we to determine
Who they shall be that straight shall post to Ludlow.
Madam, and you my sister, will you go
To give your censures in this business?

QUEEN ELIZABETH *and* DUCHESS OF YORK: With all our
hearts.

GLOUCESTER: Madam, my mother, I do cry you mercy:
Humbly on my knee I crave your blessing.

DUCHESS OF YORK: God bless thee, and put meekness in thy
breast;

Love, charity, obedience, and true duty.

GLOUCESTER: Amen! (*Aside*) And make me die a good old man!
(*Exuent all but* BUCKINGHAM *and* GLOUCESTER.)

BUCKINGHAM: My lord, whoever journeys to the Prince,
For God's sake let not us two stay at home;
For by the way I'll sort occasion,
As index to the story we late talk'd of,
To part the Queen's proud kindred from the Prince.

GLOUCESTER: My other self, my counsel's consistory,
My oracle, my prophet, my dear cousin:
I, as a child, will go by thy direction.
(*Exeunt.*)

SCENE 6

London street.
Enter two CITIZENS.

FIRST CITIZEN: Good morrow, neighbour: wither away so
fast?

SECOND CITIZEN: I promise you, I scarcely know myself.
Hear you the news abroad?

FIRST CITIZEN: Yes, that the King is dead.

SECOND CITIZEN: Ill news, by'r Lady; seldom comes the
  better.
  (*Enter two more* CITIZENS.)
THIRD CITIZEN: Neighbours, God speed.
FIRST CITIZEN: Give you good
  morrow, sir.
THIRD CITIZEN: Doth the news hold of good King Edward's
  death?
SECOND CITIZEN: Ay, sir, it is too true. God help the while.
THIRD CITIZEN: Then, friends, look to see a troublous world.
FIRST CITIZEN: No, no; by God's good grace, his son shall
  reign.
FOURTH CITIZEN: Woe to that land that's govern'd by a child!
FIRST CITIZEN: So stood the state when Henry the Sixth
  Was crown'd in Paris but at nine months old.
THIRD CITIZEN: Stood the state so? No, no, good friends.
  For then this land was famously enrich'd
  With politic grave counsel; then the King
  Had virtuous uncles to protect his Grace.
FIRST CITIZEN: Why, so hath this, both by his father and
  mother.
THIRD CITIZEN: O, full of danger is the Duke of Gloucester,
  And the Queen's sons and brothers, haught and proud;
  And were they to be rul'd, and not to rule,
  This sickly land might solace as before.
FIRST CITIZEN: Come, come: we fear the worst; all will be
  well.
FOURTH CITIZEN: When clouds are seen, wise men put on
                                 their cloaks;
  When great leaves fall, then winter is at hand;
  All may be well; but if God sort it so
  'Tis more than we deserve, or I expect.
FIRST CITIZEN: Well, leave we it to God. Whither away?
THIRD CITIZEN: Marry, we were sent for to the Mayor.
FIRST CITIZEN: And so was I: I'll bear you company.
SECOND CITIZEN: And so will I.
  (*Exeunt omnes.*)

SCENE 7

The Court.
Enter the young DUKE OF YORK, QUEEN ELIZABETH, *and the*
DUCHESS OF YORK.

QUEEN ELIZABETH: Last night, I hear, they lay at Stony
           Stratford,
 And at Northampton they do rest tonight;
 Tomorrow, or next day, they will be here.
DUCHESS OF YORK: I long with all my heart to see the Prince;
 I hope he is much grown since last I saw him.
QUEEN ELIZABETH: But I hear no: they say my son of York
 Has almost overta'en him in his growth.
YORK: Ay, mother, but I would not have it so.
DUCHESS OF YORK: Why, my young cousin? It is good to grow.
YORK: My uncle Gloucester says small herbs have grace,
 Great weeds do grow apace.
DUCHESS OF YORK: He was the wretched'st thing when he was
             young,
 So long a-growing, and so leisurely,
 That if his rule were true, he should be gracious.
YORK: Marry, they say my uncle grew so fast
 That he could gnaw a crust at two hours old.
DUCHESS OF YORK: I prithee, pretty York, who told thee this?
YORK: Grandam, his nurse.
DUCHESS OF YORK: His nurse? Why, she was dead ere thou
 wast born.
YORK: If 'twere not she, I cannot tell who told me.
QUEEN ELIZABETH: A parlous boy: go to, you are too shrewd.
DUCHESS OF YORK: Good madam, be not angry with the child.
QUEEN ELIZABETH: Pitchers have ears.
 (*Enter* DERBY.)
DUCHESS OF YORK: Here comes Lord Stanley. What news?
DERBY: Such news madam, as grieves me to report.
QUEEN ELIZABETH: How doth the Prince?
DERBY: Well, madam, and
 in health.

DUCHESS OF YORK: What is thy news?

DERBY: Lord Rivers and Lord Grey
  Are sent to Pomfret, prisoners.

DUCHESS OF YORK: Who hath committed them?

DERBY: The mighty
  Dukes, Gloucester and Buckingham.

QUEEN ELIZABETH: Ay me! I see the ruin of my house:
  The tiger now hath seiz'd the gentle hind;
  Insulting tyranny begins to jut
  Upon the innocent and aweless throne.
  Come, come my boy: we will to sanctuary.
  Madam, farewell.

DUCHESS OF YORK: Stay, I will go with you.

QUEEN ELIZABETH: You have no cause.

DERBY: (*To* QUEEN ELIZABETH) My gracious lady, go,
  And thither bear your treasure and your goods.
  Come; I'll conduct you to the sanctuary.
  (*Exeunt all but* DUCHESS OF YORK.)

DUCHESS OF YORK: Accursed and unquiet wrangling days,
  How many of you have mine eyes beheld!
  My husband lost his life to get the crown,
  And often up and down my sons were toss'd
  For me to joy and weep their gain and loss;
  And being seated, and domestic broils
  Clean overblown, themselves, the conquerors,
  Make war upon themselves, brother to brother,
  Blood to blood, self against self. O preposterous
  And frantic outrage, end thy damned spleen,
  Or let me die, to look on death no more.
  (*Exit.*)

SCENE 8

The trumpets sound. Enter the young EDWARD, PRINCE OF
WALES, GLOUCESTER *and* BUCKINGHAM, LORD MAYOR,
BISHOP OF ELY *and* CATESBY, *with others.*

BUCKINGHAM: Welcome, sweet Prince, to London, to your
    chamber.
GLOUCESTER: Welcome, dear cousin, my thoughts' sovereign.
    The weary way hath made you melancholy.
PRINCE EDWARD: Where is Uncle Rivers, where is Clarence?
    I want more uncles here to welcome me.
GLOUCESTER: Those uncles which you want were dangerous;
    God keep you from them, and from such false friends!
PRINCE EDWARD: God keep me from false friends – but they
    were none.
GLOUCESTER: My lord, the Mayor of London comes to greet
    you.
LORD MAYOR: God bless your Grace with health and happy
    days!
PRINCE EDWARD: I thank you, good my lord, and thank you
    all.
    (*The* LORD MAYOR *and his train stand aside.*)
    I thought my mother and my brother York
    Would long ere this have met us on the way.
    Fie, what a slug is Hastings, that he comes not
    To tell us whether they will come or no.
    (*Enter* HASTINGS.)
BUCKINGHAM: And in good time, here comes the sweating
    lord.
PRINCE EDWARD: Welcome, my lord. What, will our mother
    come?
HASTINGS: On what occasion God He knows, not I,
    The Queen your mother and your brother York
    Have taken sanctuary. The tender Prince
    Would fain have come with me to meet your Grace,
    But by his mother was perforce withheld.
BUCKINGHAM: Fie, what an indirect and peevish course
    Is this of hers! Lord Bishop, will your Grace
    Persuade the Queen to send the Duke of York
    Unto his princely brother presently?
ELY: God in heaven forbid we should infringe
    The holy privilege of blessed sanctuary.
BUCKINGHAM: Weigh it, but with the grossness of this age,
    You break not sanctuary in seizing him;

The benefit thereof is always granted
To those who have the wit to claim the place.
This prince hath neither claim'd it nor deserv'd it,
And therefore in mine opinion cannot have it.
Oft have I heard of sanctuary men,
But sanctuary children, never till now.

ELY: My lord, you shall o'errule my mind for once.
Come on, Lord Hastings, will you go with me?

HASTINGS: I go my lord.

PRINCE EDWARD: Good lords, make all the speedy haste you
may.
(*Exeunt* ELY *and* HASTINGS.)
Say, uncle Gloucester, if our brother come,
Where shall we sojourn till our coronation?

GLOUCESTER: Where it seems best unto your royal self.
If I may counsel you, some day or two
Your Highness shall repose you at the Tower.

PRINCE EDWARD: I do not like the Tower, of any place.
Did Julius Caesar build that place, my lord?

BUCKINGHAM: He did, my gracious lord, begin that place,
Which since, succeeding ages have re-edified.

PRINCE EDWARD: Is it upon record, or else reported
Successively from age to age, he built it?

BUCKINGHAM: Upon record, my gracious lord.

PRINCE EDWARD: But say, my lord, it were not register'd,
Methinks the truth should live from age to age,
As 'twere retail'd to all posterity,
Even to the general all-ending day.

GLOUCESTER: (*Aside*) So wise so young, they say, do never live
long.

PRINCE EDWARD: What say you, uncle?

GLOUCESTER: I say, without characters fame lives long.

PRINCE EDWARD: I'll tell you what, my cousin Buckingham.

BUCKINGHAM: What, my gracious lord?

PRINCE EDWARD: And if I live until I be a man,
I'll win our ancient right in France again,
Or die a soldier, as I liv'd a king.

GLOUCESTER: (*Aside*) Short summers lightly have a forward
spring.

(*Enter* YORK, HASTINGS *and* ELY.)

HASTINGS: Make way!

BUCKINGHAM: Now in good time here comes the Duke of
York.

PRINCE EDWARD: Richard of York; how fares our loving
brother?

YORK: Well, my dread lord – so, must I call you now.

PRINCE EDWARD: Ay, brother, to our grief, as it is yours.

GLOUCESTER: How fares our cousin, noble Lord of York?

YORK: I thank you, gentle uncle.
I pray you, uncle, give me this dagger.

GLOUCESTER: What, would you have my weapon, little lord?

YORK: I would, that I might thank you as you call me.

GLOUCESTER: How?

YORK: Little.

PRINCE EDWARD: My Lord of York will still be cross in talk;
Uncle, your Grace knows how to bear with him.

YORK: You mean to bear me, not to bear with me;
Uncle, my brother mocks both you and me;
Because that I am little like an ape,
He thinks that you should bear me on your shoulders!

GLOUCESTER: My lord, will't please you pass along?
Myself and my good cousin Buckingham
Will to your mother, to entreat of her
To meet you at the Tower and welcome you.

YORK: What, will you go unto the Tower, my lord?

PRINCE EDWARD: My Lord Protector needs will have it so.

YORK: I shall not sleep in quiet at the Tower.

GLOUCESTER: Why, what should you fear?

YORK: Marry, my uncle Clarence' angry ghost:
My grandam told me he was murdered there.

PRINCE EDWARD: I fear no uncles dead.

GLOUCESTER: Nor none that live, I hope?

PRINCE EDWARD: And if they live, I hope I need not fear.
But come, my lord; and with a heavy heart,
Thinking on them, go I unto the Tower.
(*A sennet. Exeunt* PRINCE EDWARD, YORK, HASTINGS,
ELY, *and others.* GLOUCESTER, BUCKINGHAM *and*
CATESBY *remain.*)

BUCKINGHAM: Well, let them rest. Come hither, Catesby:
    Thou art sworn as deeply to effect what we intend
    As closely to conceal what we impart.
    What think'st thou? Is it not an easy matter
    To make William Lord Hastings of our mind
    For the instalment of this noble Duke
    In the seat royal of this famous isle?

CATESBY: He for his father's sake so loves the Prince
    That he will not be won to aught against him.

BUCKINGHAM: What think'st thou then of Stanley? Will not
    he?

CATESBY: He will do all in all as Hastings doth.

BUCKINGHAM: Well, then, no more but this: go, gentle
                        Catesby,
    And as it were afar off, sound thou Lord Hastings
    How he doth stand affected to our purpose,
    And summon him tomorrow to the Tower
    To sit about the coronation.
    If he be leaden, icy, cold, unwilling,
    Be thou so too, and so break off the talk,
    And give us notice of his inclination.

GLOUCESTER: Tell him, Catesby, his ancient adversary, Lord
                        Rivers,
    Tomorrow is let blood at Pomfret Castle,

BUCKINGHAM: Good Catesby, go effect this business soundly.

CATESBY: My good lords both, with all the heed I can.
    (*Exit* CATESBY.)

BUCKINGHAM: Now, my lord, what shall we do if we perceive
    Lord Hastings will not yield to our complots?

GLOUCESTER: Chop off his head; something we will
                        determine,
    And look when I am King, claim thou of me
    The earldom of Hereford, and all the moveables
    Whereof the King my brother was possess'd.

BUCKINGHAM: I'll claim that promise at your Grace's hand.

GLOUCESTER: And look to have it yielded with all kindness.
    (*Exeunt.*)

SCENE 9

Hastings's house.
Enter a MESSENGER *to the door.*

MESSENGER: My lord, my lord!
HASTINGS: (*Within*) Who knocks?
MESSENGER: One from the Lord Stanley.
(*Enter* HASTINGS.)
HASTINGS: What is't a clock?
MESSENGER: Upon the stroke of four.
HASTINGS: Cannot my Lord Stanley sleep these tedious nights?
MESSENGER: So it appears by that I have to say.
   First, he commends him to your noble self.
HASTINGS: What then?
MESSENGER: And then he sends you word
   He dreamt the boar had razed off his helm.
   Therefore he sends to know your lordship's pleasure,
   If you will presently take horse with him
   And with all speed post with him toward the north,
   To shun the danger that his soul divines.
HASTINGS: Go, fellow, go; return unto thy lord;
   Tell him his fears are shallow, without instance;
   And for his dreams, I wonder he's so simple
   To trust the mockery of unquiet slumbers.
   To fly the boar before the boar pursues
   Were to incense the boar to follow us,
   Go, bid thy master rise, and come to me,
   And we will both together to the Tower,
   Where he shall see the boar will use us kindly.
MESSENGER: I'll go, my lord, and tell him what you say.
   (*Exit. Enter* CATESBY.)
CATESBY: Many good morrows to my noble lord!
HASTINGS: Good morrow, Catesby; you are early stirring,
   What news, what news in this our tott'ring state?
CATESBY: It is a reeling world indeed, my lord,
   And I believe will never stand upright
   Till Richard wear the garland of the realm.
HASTINGS: How, wear the garland? Dost thou mean the crown?

CATESBY: Ay, my good lord.

HASTINGS: I'll have this crown of mine cut from my shoulders
Before I'll see the crown so foul misplac'd.
But canst thou guess that he doth aim at it?

CATESBY: Ay, on my life, and hopes to find you forward
Upon his party for the gain thereof;
And thereupon he sends you this good news
That this same very day your enemies,
The kindred of the Queen, must die at Pomfret.

HASTINGS: Indeed, I am no mourner for that news,
Because they have been still my adversaries;
But that I'll give my voice on Richard's side
To bar my master's heirs in true descent,
God knows I will not do it, to the death.

CATESBY: God keep your lordship in that gracious mind.

HASTINGS: But I shall laugh at this twelve-month hence
That they which brought me in my master's hate,
I live to look upon their tragedy.

CATESBY: 'Tis a vile thing to die, my gracious lord,
When men are unprepar'd and look not for't.

HASTINGS: O monstrous, monstrous! And so falls it out
With Rivers, and Lord Grey: and so 'twill do
With some men else that think themselves as safe
As thou and I, who as thou know'st are dear
To princely Richard and to Buckingham.

CATESBY: The Princes both make high account of you –

HASTINGS: I know they do, and I have well deserv'd it.
(*Enter* DERBY.)
Come on, come on: Where is your boar-spear, man?
Fear you the boar, and go so unprovided?

DERBY: My lord, good morrow; good morrow, Catesby.
You may jest on, but by the holy Rood,
I do not like these several councils, I.

HASTINGS: My lord, I hold my life as dear as you do yours,
Think you, but that I know our state secure,
I would be so triumphant as I am?

DERBY: The lords at Pomfret, when they rode from London,
Were jocund, and suppos'd their states were sure,
But yet you see how soon the day o'ercast.

This sudden stab of rancour I misdoubt.
HASTINGS: Come, come: have with you. Wot you what, my
                                   lord?
Today the lords you talk'd of are beheaded.
DERBY: They, for their truth, might better wear their heads
Than some that have accus'd them wear their hats
But come, my lord, let us away.
HASTINGS: I'll wait upon your lordship.
(*Exeunt omnes.*)

SCENE 10

Pomfret Castle.
Enter RATCLIFFE, *leading* RIVERS *and* GREY *to death.*

RIVERS: Sir Richard Ratcliffe, let me tell thee this:
Today shalt thou behold a subject die
For truth, for duty, and for loyalty.
RATCLIFFE: Dispatch: the limit of your lives is out.
RIVERS: O Pomfret, Pomfret! O thou bloody prison,
Fatal and ominous to noble peers!
Within the guilty closure of thy walls
Richard the Second here was hack'd to death.
GREY: Now Margaret's curse is fall'n upon our heads,
For standing by when Richard stabb'd her son.
RIVERS: Then curs'd she Richard, then curs'd she Buckingham,
Then curs'd she Hastings. O remember, God,
To hear her prayer for them, as now for us.
RATCLIFFE: Make haste. The hour of death is expiate.
RIVERS: Come, Grey; let us embrace.
Farewell, until we meet again in heaven.
(*Exeunt omnes.*)

SCENE 11

The Council House.
Enter BUCKINGHAM, DERBY, HASTINGS, ELY, RATCLIFFE *and*
LOVELL *and with others.*

HASTINGS: Now, noble peers, the cause why we are met
  Is to determine of the coronation.
  In God's name, speak: when is the royal day?
BUCKINGHAM: Are all things ready for the royal time?
DERBY: They are, and wants but nomination.
ELY: Tomorrow, then, I judge a happy day.
BUCKINGHAM: Who knows the Lord Protector's mind herein?
  Who is most inward with the noble Duke?
ELY: Your Grace, we think, should soonest know his mind.
BUCKINGHAM: We know each other's faces; for our hearts
  He knows no more of mine than I of yours.
  Lord Hastings, you and he are near in love.
HASTINGS: I thank his Grace, I know he loves me well;
  But for his purpose in the coronation
  I have not sounded him, nor he deliver'd
  His gracious pleasure any way therein.
  But you, my honourable lords, my name the time,
  And in the Duke's behalf I'll give my voice,
  Which I presume he'll take in gentle part.
  (*Enter* GLOUCESTER.)
ELY: In happy time, here comes the Duke himself.
GLOUCESTER: My noble lords and cousins all, good morrow:
  I have been long a sleeper, but I trust
  My absence doth neglect no great design
  Which by my presence might have been concluded.
BUCKINGHAM: Had you not come upon your cue, my lord,
  William Lord Hastings had pronounc'd your part –
  I mean your voice for crowning of the King.
GLOUCESTER: Than my Lord Hastings no man might be
                                        bolder:
  His lordship knows me well, and loves me well.
  My Lord of Ely, when I was last in Holborn
  I saw good strawberries in your garden there;
  I do beseech you, send for some of them.
ELY: Marry, and will, my lord, with all my heart.
  (*Exit* ELY.)
GLOUCESTER: Cousin of Buckingham, a word with you.
  (*Takes him aside.*)
  Catesby hath sounded Hastings in our business,

And finds the testy gentleman so hot
That he will lose his head ere give consent.

BUCKINGHAM: Withdraw yourself awhile! I'll go with you.
(*Exeunt* GLOUCESTER *and* BUCKINGHAM.)

DERBY: We have not yet set down this day of triumph.
Tomorrow, in my judgement, is too sudden,
For I myself am not so well provided
As else I would be, were the day prolong'd.
(*Enter* ELY.)

ELY: Where is my Lord Protector?
I have sent for these strawberries.

HASTINGS: His Grace looks cheerfully and smooth this morning:
There's some conceit or other likes him well
When that he bids good morrow with such spirit.
I think there's never a man in Christendom
Can lesser hide his love or hate than he.

DERBY: What of his heart perceive you in his face
By any livelihood he show'd today?

HASTINGS: Marry, that with no man here he is offended,
For were he, he had shown it in his looks.
(*Enter* GLOUCESTER *and* BUCKINGHAM.)

GLOUCESTER: I pray you all, tell me what they deserve
That do conspire my death with devilish plots
Of damned witchcraft, and that have prevail'd
Upon my body with their hellish charms.

HASTINGS: The tender love I bear your Grace, my lord,
Makes me most forward in this princely presence,
To doom th'offenders, whatsoever they be:
I say, my lord, they have deserved death.

GLOUCESTER: Then be your eyes the witness of their evil.
See how I am bewitch'd! Behold, mine arm
Is like a blasted sapling wither'd up!
And this is Edward's wife, that monstrous witch,
That by her witchcraft thus has marked me.

HASTINGS: If she has done this deed, my noble lord —

GLOUCESTER: If? Thou protector of this damned strumpet,
Talk'st thou to me of ifs! Thou art a traitor:
Off with his head! Now by Saint Paul I swear
I will not dine until I see the same.

The rest that love me, rise and follow me.
(*Exeunt.* LOVELL *and* RATCLIFFE *remain with* HASTINGS.)
HASTINGS: Woe, woe for England; not a whit for me –
For I, too fond, might have prevented this.
Stanley did dream the boar did raze his helm,
And I did scorn it and disdain to fly;
O Margaret, Margaret, now thy heavy curse
Is lighted on poor Hastings' wretched head.
RATCLIFFE: Come, come, dispatch: the Duke would be at
                                    dinner;
Make a short shrift: he longs to see your head.
HASTINGS: O momentary grace of mortal men,
Which we more hunt for than the grace of God.
Who builds his hope in air of your good looks
Lives like a drunken sailor on a mast,
Ready with every nod to tumble down
Into the fatal bowels of the deep.
LOVELL: Come, come, dispatch: 'tis bootless to exclaim.
HASTINGS: O bloody Richard! Miserable England,
I prophesy the fearfull'st time to thee
That ever wretched age hath looked upon.
Come, lead me to the block; bear him my head.
They smile at me who shortly shall be dead.
(*Exeunt omnes.*)

SCENE 12

Enter GLOUCESTER *and* BUCKINGHAM *in rotten armour,*
marvellous ill-favoured.

GLOUCESTER: Come, cousin, canst thou quake and change thy
                                    colour,
As if thou wert distraught and mad with terror?
BUCKINGHAM: Tut, I can counterfeit the deep tragedian,
Tremble and start at wagging of a straw,
Intending deep suspicion. Ghastly looks
Are at my service, like enforced smiles,
And both are ready in their offices
At any time to grace my stratagems.

But what, is Catesby gone?

GLOUCESTER: He is, and see, he brings the Mayor along.

(*Enter the* LORD MAYOR *and* CATESBY.)

BUCKINGHAM: Lord Mayor, the reason we have sent –

GLOUCESTER: Look back! Defend thee, here are enemies!

BUCKINGHAM: Be patient, they are friends; Ratcliffe and
Lovell.

LOVELL: Here is the head of that ignoble traitor,
The dangerous and unsuspected Hastings.

GLOUCESTER: So dear I lov'd the man that I must weep.
I took him for the plainest harmless creature
That breath'd upon the earth a Christian.

BUCKINGHAM: This day he plotted in the Council House
To murder me and my good Lord of Gloucester.

LORD MAYOR: And do not doubt, right noble princes both,
But I'll acquaint our duteous citizens
With all your just proceedings in this cause.

GLOUCESTER: And to that end we wish'd your lordship here,
T'avoid the censures of the carping world.

BUCKINGHAM: And so, my good Lord Mayor, we bid farewell.

(*Exit* LORD MAYOR.)

GLOUCESTER: Go after, after, cousin Buckingham:
The Mayor towards Guildhall hies him in all post.
There, at your meet'st advantage of the time,
Infer the bastardy of Edward's children;
Moreover, urge his hateful luxury
And bestial appetite in change of lust,
Tell them, when that my mother went with child
Of that insatiate Edward, noble York
My princely father, then had wars in France,
And by true computation of the time
Found that the issue was not his begot;

BUCKINGHAM: Doubt not, my lord; I'll play the orator
As if the golden fee for which I plead
Were for myself; and so, my lord, adieu.

GLOUCESTER: And bring them, cousin, here to Baynard's Castle.

BUCKINGHAM: I go, and towards three or four o'clock
Look for the news that the Guildhall affords.

(*Exit* BUCKINGHAM.)

GLOUCESTER: Who is so gross
 That cannot see this palpable devise?
 Yet who's so bold but says he sees it not?

SCENE 13

Enter GLOUCESTER *and* BUCKINGHAM.

GLOUCESTER: How now, how now? What say the citizens?
BUCKINGHAM: The citizens are mum, say not a word.
GLOUCESTER: Touch'd you the bastardy of Edward's children?
BUCKINGHAM: I did, with his contract with Lady Lucy,
 Th'unsatiate greediness of his desire,
 His tyranny for trifles; his own bastardy,
 As being got, your father then in France,
 And his resemblance, being not like the Duke.
 Withal, I did infer your lineaments –
 Being the right idea of your father,
 Both in your form and nobleness of mind –
 Your discipline in war, wisdom in peace,
 Your bounty, virtue, fair humility;
 And when mine oratory drew toward end,
 I bid them that did love their country's good
 Cry, 'God save Richard, England's royal King!'
GLOUCESTER: And did they so?
BUCKINGHAM: No, so God help me: they spake not a word.
GLOUCESTER: What tongueless blocks were they? Would they
 not speak!
BUCKINGHAM: The Mayor is here at hand. Intend some fear;
 Be not you spoke with but by mighty suit.
 And look you get a prayer book in your hand,
 And stand between two churchmen, good my lord;
 For on that ground I'll make a holy descant.
 And be not easily won to our requests:
 Play the maid's part: say no, but take it.
GLOUCESTER: But take it.
 (*Exit* GLOUCESTER. *Enter* LORD MAYOR, *aldermen and
 citizens.*)
BUCKINGHAM: Welcome, my lord: I dance attendance here.

I think the Duke will not be spoke withal.
(*Enter* CATESBY.)
Now, Catesby, what says your lord to my request?

CATESBY: He doth entreat your Grace, my noble lord,
To visit him tomorrow, or next day:
He is within, with two right reverend fathers,
Divinely bent to meditation;
And in no worldly suits would he be mov'd
To draw him from his holy exercise.

BUCKINGHAM: Return, good Gatesby, to the gracious Duke;
Tell him myself, the Mayor and aldermen,
In deep designs, in matter of great moment,
No less importing than our general good,
Are come to have some conference with his Grace.

CATESBY: I'll signify so much unto him straight.
(*Exit.*)

BUCKINGHAM: Ah ha, my lord, this prince is not an Edward:
He is not lolling on a lewd love-bed,
But on his knees at meditation;
Not dallying with a brace of courtesans,
But meditating with two deep divines;
Happy were England, would this virtuous Prince
Take on his Grace the sovereignty thereof.
But sure I fear we shall not win him to it.

LORD MAYOR: Marry, God defend his Grace should say us nay!

BUCKINGHAM: I fear he will. Here Catesby comes again.
(*Enter* CATESBY.)
Now, Catesby, what says his Grace?

CATESBY: My Lord,
He wonders to what end you have assembled
Such troops of citizens to come to him,
He fears, my lord, you mean no good to him.

BUCKINGHAM: Sorry I am my noble cousin should
Suspect me that I mean no good to him.
By heaven, we come to him in perfect love;
And so once more return and tell his Grace.
(*Exit* CATESBY.)
When holy and devout religious men
Are at their beads, 'tis hard to draw them thence,

So sweet is zealous contemplation.
(*Enter* GLOUCESTER *aloft, between two bishops, and*
CATESBY.)
LORD MAYOR: See where his Grace sits, 'tween two clergymen!
BUCKINGHAM: Two props of virtue for a Christian Prince,
 To stay him from the fall of vanity;
 Famous Plantagenet, most gracious Prince,
 Lend favourable ear to our requests.
 And pardon us the interruption
 Of thy devotion and right Christian zeal.
GLOUCESTER: My lord, there needs no such apology;
 I do beseech your Grace to pardon me,
 Who – earnest in the service of my God –
 Neglect the visitation of my friends.
 But leaving this, what is your Grace's pleasure?
BUCKINGHAM: Even that, I hope, which pleaseth God above,
 And all good men of this ungovern'd isle.
GLOUCESTER: I do suspect I have done some offence
 That seems disgracious in the city's eye.
 And that you come to reprehend my ignorance.
BUCKINGHAM: You have, my lord: would it might please your
                Grace
 On our entreaties to amend that fault.
GLOUCESTER: Else wherefore breathe I in a Christian land?
BUCKINGHAM: Know then, it is your fault that you resign
 The sceptred office of your ancestors,
 To the corruption of a blemish'd stock;
 Which to recure, we heartily solicit
 Your gracious self to take on you the charge
 And kingly government of this your land;
 Not as Protector, steward, substitute,
 But as successively, from blood to blood,
 Your right of birth, your empery, your own.
 For this, consorted with the citizens –
 Your very worshipful and loving friends,
 And by their vehement instigation –
 In this just cause come I to move your Grace.
GLOUCESTER: I know not whether to depart in silence
 Or bitterly to speak in your reproof.

Your love deserves my thanks, but my desert
Unmeritable shuns your high request.
For so much is my poverty of spirit,
So mighty and so many my defects,
That I would rather hide me from my greatness –
But, God be thank'd, there is no need of me –
The royal tree hath left us royal fruit,
Which, mellowed by the stealing hours of time,
Will well become the seat of majesty,
And make, no doubt, us happy by his reign.

BUCKINGHAM: My lord, this argues conscience in your Grace;
But the respects thereof are nice and trivial.
You say Prince Edward is your brother's son:
So say we too – but not by Edward's wife.
For first was he contract to Lady Lucy
(Your mother lives a witness to his vow),
Then, good my lord, take to your royal self
This proffer'd benefit of dignity.

LORD MAYOR: Do, good my lord: your citizens entreat you.

BUCKINGHAM: Refuse not, mighty lord, this proffer'd love.

CATESBY: O, make them joyful; grant their lawful suit.

GLOUCESTER: Alas, why would you heap this care on me?
I am unfit for state and majesty.
I cannot, nor I will not, yield to you.

BUCKINGHAM: If you refuse it, as in love and zeal
Loath to depose the child, your brother's son –
Yet know, whe'er you accept our suit or no,
Your brother's son shall never reign our King,
And in this resolution here we leave you.
Come, citizens; zounds! I'll entreat no more.

GLOUCESTER: O, do not swear, my Lord of Buckingham!
(*Exeunt* BUCKINGHAM, *aldermen, and citizens.*)

CATESBY: Call them again, sweet Prince; accept their suit.

LORD MAYOR: Do, good my lord, lest all the land do rue it.

GLOUCESTER: Will you enforce me to a world of cares?
Call them again. I am not made of stones,
But penetrable to your kind entreaties,
Albeit against my conscience and my soul.
(*Enter* BUCKINGHAM *and the rest.*)

226

GLOUCESTER: Cousin of Buckingham, and sage grave men,
    Since you will buckle fortune on my back
    To bear her burden, whe'er I will or no,
    I must have patience to endure the load.
    For God doth know, and you may partly see,
    How far I am from the desire thereof.
LORD MAYOR: God bless your Grace: we see it, and will say it.
GLOUCESTER: In saying so, you shall but say the truth.
BUCKINGHAM: Then I salute you with this royal title:
    Long live Richard, England's worthy King!
LORD MAYOR: Amen.
ALL: Amen
BUCKINGHAM: Tomorrow may it please you to be crown'd?
GLOUCESTER: Even when you please, for you will have it so.
BUCKINGHAM: Tomorrow then we will attend your Grace;
    And so most joyfully we take our leave.
GLOUCESTER: (*To the* BISHOPS) Come, let us to our holy work
                          again.

    Farewell, my cousin, farewell, gentle friends.
    (*Exeunt omnes.*)

ACT TWO

SCENE I

The Tower.
Enter QUEEN ELIZABETH, *the* DUCHESS OF YORK,
BRAKENBURY, *the* MARQUESS OF DORSET *and* ANNE,
DUCHESS OF GLOUCESTER.

QUEEN ELIZABETH: Master Lieutenant, pray you by your leave:
How doth the Prince, and my young son of York?
BRAKENBURY: Well, madam, and in health. But by your leave
I may not suffer you to visit them:
The King hath strictly charg'd the contrary.
QUEEN ELIZABETH: The King! Who's that?
BRAKENBURY: I mean the Lord
Protector.
QUEEN ELIZABETH: The Lord protect him from that kingly title!
Hath he set bounds between their love and me?
I am their mother; who shall bar me from them?
DUCHESS OF YORK: I am their father's mother: I will see them.
BRAKENBURY: I do beseech your Graces all to pardon me.
I am bound by oath; and therefore pardon me.
(*Exit* BRAKENBURY. *Enter* DERBY.)
DERBY: Let me but meet you, ladies, one hour hence,
And I'll salute your Grace of York as mother
And reverend looker-on of two fair queens.
(*To* ANNE) Come, madam, you must straight to
Westminster,
There to be crowned Richard's royal Queen.
QUEEN ELIZABETH: Ah, cut my lace asunder,
That my pent heart may have some scope to beat,
Or else I swoon with this dead-killing news.
ANNE: Despiteful tidings! O unpleasing news!
DORSET: Madam have comfort: how fares your Grace?
QUEEN ELIZABETH: O Dorset, speak not to me; get thee gone.
Death and destruction dogs thee at thy heels;
If thou wilt outstrip death, go, cross the seas,
And live with Richmond, from the reach of hell.

228

Go: hie thee, hie thee from this slaughterhouse,
Lest thou increase the number of the dead.

DERBY: Full of wise care in this your counsel, madam.
　(*To* DORSET) Take all the swift advantage of the hours;
　You shall have letters from me to my son
　In your behalf, to meet you on the way.

DUCHESS OF YORK: O ill-dispersing wind of misery!
　O my accursed womb, the bed of death!
　A cockatrice hast thou hatch'd to the world,
　Whose unavoided eye is murderous.

DERBY: Come, madam, come: I in all haste was sent.

ANNE: And I with all unwillingness will go.
　O would to God that the inclusive verge
　Of golden metal that must round my brow
　Were red-hot steel, to sear me to the brains.

QUEEN ELIZABETH: Go, go, poor soul; I envy not thy glory.
　To feed my humour, wish thyself no harm.

ANNE: No? Why? When he that, is my husband now
　Came to me as I follow'd Henry's corse,
　This was my wish: 'Be thou', quoth I, 'accurs'd
　For making me, so young, so old a widow;
　And be thy wife – if any be so mad –
　More miserable by the life of thee
　Than thou hast made me by my dear lord's death.'
　Lo, ere I can repeat this curse again,
　Within so small a time, my woman's heart
　Grossly grew captive to his honey words,
　And prov'd the subject of mine own soul's curse,
　For never yet one hour in his bed
　Did I enjoy the golden dew of sleep,
　But with his timorous dreams was still awak'd.
　Besides, he hates me for my father Warwick,
　And will, no doubt, shortly be rid of me.

QUEEN ELIZABETH: Poor heart, adieu, I pity thy complaining.

ANNE: No more than with my soul I mourn for yours.

DORSET: Farewell, thou woeful welcomer of glory.

ANNE: Adieu, poor soul, that tak'st thy leave of it.

DUCHESS OF YORK: (*To* DORSET) Go thou to Richmond, and
　good fortune guide thee;

(*To* QUEEN ELIZABETH) Go thou to sanctuary, and good
thoughts possess thee;
(*To* ANNE) Go thou to Richard, and good angels tend thee;
I to my grave, where peace and rest lie with me!
QUEEN ELIZABETH: Stay, yet look back with me unto the
Tower.

Pity, you ancient stones, those tender babes
Whom envy hath immur'd within your walls –
Rough cradle for such little pretty ones,
Rude ragged nurse, old sullen playfellow
For tender princes, use my babies well.
So foolish sorrow bids your stones farewell.
(*Exeunt omnes.*)

SCENE 2

A Sennet. Enter RICHARD *as King, in pomp,* BUCKINGHAM,
CATESBY, RATCLIFFE, LOVELL, *a page, and attendants.*

KING RICHARD: Stand all apart. Cousin of Buckingham!
BUCKINGHAM: My gracious sovereign!
KING RICHARD: Give me thy hand. Thus far, by thy advice
And thy assistance, is King Richard seated.
But shall we wear these glories for a day,
Or shall they last, and we rejoice in them?
BUCKINGHAM: Still live they, and for ever let them last!
KING RICHARD: Ah, Buckingham, now do I play the touch
To try if thou be current gold indeed.
Young Edward lives – think now what I would speak.
BUCKINGHAM: Say on, my loving lord.
KING RICHARD: Why, Buckingham, I say I would be King.
BUCKINGHAM: Why so you are, my thrice-renowned lord.
KING RICHARD: Ha, am I King? 'Tis so – but Edward lives.
BUCKINGHAM: True, noble prince.
KING RICHARD: O bitter consequence
That Edward still should live – true noble prince!
Cousin, thou wast not wont to be so dull.
Shall I be plain? I wish the bastards dead,
And I would have it suddenly perform'd.

What say'st thou now? Speak suddenly, be brief.

BUCKINGHAM: Your Grace may do your pleasure.

KING RICHARD: Tut, tut, thou art all ice; thy kindness freezes.
Say, have I thy consent that they shall die?

BUCKINGHAM: Give me some little breath, some pause, dear
lord,
Before I positively speak in this;
I will resolve you herein presently.
(*Exit* BUCKINGHAM.)

CATESBY: (*Aside*) The King is angry: see, he gnaws his lip.

KING RICHARD: I will converse with iron-witted fools
And unrespective boys; none are for me
That look into me with considerate eyes.
High-reaching Buckingham grows circumspect. –
Ratcliffe!

RATCLIFFE: My lord?

KING RICHARD: Know'st thou not any whom corrupting gold
Will tempt unto a close exploit of death?

RATCLIFFE: I know a discontented gentleman.
Whose humble means match not his haughty spirit.

KING RICHARD: What is his name?

RATCLIFFE: His name, my lord, is
Tyrrel.

KING RICHARD: I partly know the man: Go call him hither.
(*Exit* RATCLIFFE.)
The deep-revolving witty Buckingham,
Hath he so long held out with me, untir'd,
And stops he now for breath! Well, be it so.
(*Enter* DERBY.)
How now, Lord Stanley? What's the news?

DERBY: Know, my loving lord,
The Marquess Dorset, as I hear, is fled
To Richmond.
(DERBY *stands aside*.)

KING RICHARD: Come hither, Catesby. Rumour it abroad
That Anne my wife is very grievous sick;
I will take order for her keeping close.
Inquire me out some mean poor gentleman,
Whom I will marry straight to Clarence' daughter –

The boy is foolish, and I fear not him.
Look how thou dream'st! I say again, give out
That Anne, my Queen, is sick and like to die.
(*Exit* CATESBY.)
I must be married to Edward's daughter, Elizabeth,
Or else my kingdom stands on brittle glass.
Murder her brothers, and then marry her –
Uncertain way of gain! But I am in
So far in blood that sin will pluck on sin;
Tear-falling pity dwells not in this eye.
(*Enter* RATCLIFFE *with* TYRREL.)
Is thy name Tyrrel?

TYRREL: James Tyrrel, and your most obedient subject.

KING RICHARD: Art thou indeed?

TYRREL: Prove me, my gracious lord.

KING RICHARD: Dar'st thou resolve to kill a friend of mine?

TYRREL: Please you; but I had rather kill two enemies.

KING RICHARD: Why, then thou hast it, two deep enemies.
     Foes to my rest, and my sweet sleep's disturbers.
     Tyrrel, I mean those bastards in the Tower.

TYRREL: Let me have open means to come to them,
     And soon I'll rid you from the fear of them.

KING RICHARD: Thou sing'st sweet music. Tyrrel, say it is
                                                  done,
     And I will love thee, and prefer thee for it.

TYRREL: I will dispatch it straight.
     (*Exit* TYRREL. *Enter* BUCKINGHAM.)

BUCKINGHAM: My lord, I have consider'd in my mind
     The late request that you did sound me in.

KING RICHARD: Well, let that rest. Dorset is fled to Richmond.

BUCKINGHAM: I hear the news, my lord.

KING RICHARD: Stanley, he is your wife's son. Well, look unto
     it.

BUCKINGHAM: My lord, I claim the gift, my due by promise,
     For which your honour and your faith is pawn'd:
     Th'earldom of Hereford and the moveables
     Which you have promised I shall possess.

KING RICHARD: Stanley, look to your wife; if she convey
     Letters to Richmond, you shall answer it.

BUCKINGHAM: What says your Highness to my just demand?
KING RICHARD: I do remember me, Henry the Sixth
    Did prophesy that Richmond should be King,
    When Richmond was a little peevish boy.
    A king . . . perhaps . . . perhaps –
BUCKINGHAM: My lord!
KING RICHARD: How chance the prophet could not, at that
                                    time,
    Have told me – I being by – that I should kill him?
BUCKINGHAM: My lord, your promise for the earldom –
KING RICHARD: Richmond!
BUCKINGHAM: My lord –
KING RICHARD: Ay – what's o'clock?
BUCKINGHAM: I am thus bold to put your Grace in mind
    Of what you promis'd me.
KING RICHARD: Well, but what's o'clock?
BUCKINGHAM: Upon the stroke of ten.
KING RICHARD: Well, let it strike.
BUCKINGHAM: Why let it strike?
KING RICHARD: Because that like a jack thou keep'st the stroke
    Betwixt thy begging and my meditation.
    I am not in the giving vein today.
BUCKINGHAM: May it please you to resolve me in my suit?
KING RICHARD: Thou troublest me; I am not in the vein.
    (*Exeunt all but* BUCKINGHAM.)
BUCKINGHAM: And is it thus? Repays he my deep service
    With such contempt? Made I him King for this?
    O let me think on Hastings, and be gone
    To Brecknock while my fearful head is on.
    (*Exit.*)

SCENE 3

Enter TYRREL.

TYRREL: The tyrannous and bloody act is done;
    The most arch deed of piteous massacre
    That ever yet this land was guilty of.
    Dighton and Forrest, whom I did suborn

To do this piece of ruthless butchery –
Albeit they were flesh'd villains, bloody dogs –
Wept like two children, in their deaths' sad story.
'O, thus', quoth Dighton, 'lay the gentle babes';
'Thus, thus,' quoth Forrest, 'girdling one another
Within their alabaster innocent arms;
Their lips were four red roses on a stalk,
Which in their summer beauty kiss'd each other.
A book of prayers on their pillow lay,
Which once', quoth Forrest, 'almost chang'd, my mind.
But O, the devil' – there the villain stopp'd,
When Dighton thus told on: 'We smothered
The most replenished sweet work of Nature,
That from the prime creation e'er she framed.'
Hence both are gone with conscience and remorse.
They could not speak, and so I left them both
To bear this tidings to the bloody King.
(*Enter* KING RICHARD.)

KING RICHARD: Kind Tyrrel, am I happy in thy news?

TYRREL: If to have done the thing you gave in charge
Beget your happiness, be happy then,
For it is done.

KING RICHARD: But didst thou see them dead?

TYRREL: I did, my lord.
The chaplain of the Tower hath buried them.

KING RICHARD: Come to me, Tyrrel, soon at after-supper,
When thou shalt tell the process of their death.
Farewell till then.

TYRREL: I humbly take my leave.
(*Exit.*)

KING RICHARD: The sons of Edward sleep in Abraham's
                                    bosom,
And Anne my wife hath bid this world good night.
Now, for I know the Breton Richmond aims
At young Elizabeth, my brother's daughter,
And by that knot looks proudly on the crown –
To her go I, a jolly thriving wooer.
(*Enter* RATCLIFFE.)

RATCLIFFE: My lord!

KING RICHARD: Good or bad news, that thou com'st in so
    bluntly?
RATCLIFFE: Bad news, my lord. Ely is fled to Richmond,
    And Buckingham, backed with the hardy Welshmen,
    Is in the field, and still his power increaseth.
KING RICHARD: Ely with Richmond troubles me more near
    Than Buckingham and his rash-levied strength.
    Go muster men. My counsel is my shield.
    We must be brief, when traitors brave the field.
    (*Exeunt.*)

SCENE 4

Enter old QUEEN MARGARET.

QUEEN MARGARET: So now prosperity begins to mellow,
    And drop into the rotten mouth of death.
    A dire induction am I witness to,
    And will to France, hoping the consequence
    Will prove as bitter, black, and tragical.
    (QUEEN MARGARET *retires. Enter* DUCHESS OF YORK *and*
    QUEEN ELIZABETH.)
QUEEN ELIZABETH: Ah, my poor Princes! Ah, my tender
                         babes,
    My unblow'd flowers, new-appearing sweets!
    If yet your gentle souls fly in the air,
    Hover about me with your airy wings,
    And hear your mother's lamentation.
QUEEN MARGARET: (*Aside*) Hover about her; say that right for
                         right
    Hath dimm'd your infant morn to aged night.
DUCHESS OF YORK: So many miseries have craz'd my voice
    That my woe-wearied tongue is still and mute.
    Edward Plantagenet, why art thou dead?
QUEEN MARGARET: (*Aside*) Plantagenet doth quit Plantagenet;
    Edward, for Edward, pays a dying debt.
QUEEN ELIZABETH: Wilt Thou, O God, fly from such gentle
                        lambs,
    And throw them in the entrails of the wolf?

When didst Thou sleep when such a deed was done?
QUEEN MARGARET: (*Aside*) When holy Harry died, and my
    sweet son.
DUCHESS OF YORK: Rest thy unrest on England's lawful earth,
    Unlawfully made drunk with innocent blood.
QUEEN ELIZABETH: Ah, who hath any cause to mourn but we?
    (*She sits down by her.* QUEEN MARGARET *comes forward.*)
QUEEN MARGARET: If sorrow can admit society,
    (*She sits down with them.*)
    Tell o'er your woes again by viewing mine.
    I had an Edward, till a Richard kill'd him;
    I had a Harry, till a Richard kill'd him:
    Thou hadst an Edward, till a Richard kill'd him;
    Thou hadst a Richard, till a Richard kill'd him.
DUCHESS OF YORK: I had a Richard too, and thou didst kill
                                        him;
    I had a Rutland too, thou holp'st to kill him.
QUEEN MARGARET: Thou hadst a Clarence too, and Richard
                                    kill'd him.
    From forth the kennel of thy womb hath crept
    A hell-hound that doth hunt us all to death:
    O upright, just, and true-disposing God!
    How do I thank Thee, that this carnal cur
    Preys on the issue of his mother's body,
    And makes her pew-fellow with others' moan!
DUCHESS OF YORK: O, Harry's wife, triumph not in my woes.
    God witness with me, I have wept for thine.
QUEEN MARGARET: Bear with me: I am hungry for revenge,
    And now I cloy me with beholding it.
    Thy Edward he is dead, that kill'd my Edward;
    Thy other Edward dead, to quit my Edward;
    Thy Clarence he is dead, that stabb'd my Edward;
    And the beholders of this frantic play,
    Th'adulterate Hastings, Rivers, Vaughan, Grey,
    Untimely smother'd in their dusky graves.
    Richard yet lives, hell's black intelligencer;
    That sent them thither. But at hand, at hand
    Ensues his piteous and unpitied end.
    Earth gapes, hell burns, fiends roar, saints pray,

237

To have him suddenly convey'd from hence.
Cancel his bond of life, dear God, I pray,
That I may live and say, 'The dog is dead.'
QUEEN ELIZABETH: O, thou didst prophesy the time would
come
That I should wish for thee to help me curse
That bottled spider, that foul bunch-back'd toad!
QUEEN MARGARET: I call'd thee then vain flourish of my
fortune;
I call'd thee, then, poor shadow, painted Queen,
A dream of what thou wast; a breath, a bubble,
A queen in jest, only to fill the scene.
Where is thy husband now? Where be thy brothers?
Where are thy two sons? Wherein dost thou joy?
Who sues and kneels, and says, 'God save the Queen'?
Where be the bending peers that flatter'd thee?
Where be the thronging troops that follow'd thee
Decline all this, and see what now, thou art:
Thus hath the course of justice whirl'd about
And left thee but a very prey to time.
Thou didst usurp my place, and dost thou not
Usurp the just proportion of my sorrow?
Farewell, York's wife, and Queen of sad mischance;
These English woes shall make me smile in France.
QUEEN ELIZABETH: O thou, well skill'd in curses, stay a while
And teach me how to curse mine enemies.
QUEEN MARGARET: Forbear to sleep the nights, and fast the
days;
Compare dead happiness with living woe;
Think that thy babes were sweeter than they were,
And he that slew them fouler than he is:
Bettering thy loss makes the bad-causer worse.
Revolving this will teach thee how to curse.
QUEEN ELIZABETH: My words are dull: O quicken them with
thine.
QUEEN MARGARET: Thy woes will make them sharp and
pierce like mine.
(*Exit* QUEEN MARGARET.)
DUCHESS OF YORK: Why should calamity be full of words?

QUEEN ELIZABETH: Let them have scope, though what they
will impart
Help nothing else, yet do they ease the heart.
DUCHESS OF YORK: Then in the breath of bitter words let's
smother
My damned son, that thy two sweet sons smother'd.
The trumpet sounds; be copious in exclaims.
(*Enter* KING RICHARD *and his train, marching, with drums
and trumpets.*)
KING RICHARD: Who intercepts me in my expedition?
DUCHESS OF YORK: O, she that might have intercepted thee –
By strangling thee in her accursed womb –
From all the slaughters, wretch, that thou hast done.
QUEEN ELIZABETH: Tell me, thou villain-slave, where are my
children?
DUCHESS OF YORK: Thou toad, thou toad, where is thy
brother Clarence?
KING RICHARD: A flourish, trumpets! Strike alarum, drums!
Let not the heavens hear these tell-tale women
Rail on the Lord's anointed. Strike, I say!
(*Flourish. Alarums.*)
DUCHESS OF YORK: Art thou my son?
KING RICHARD: Ay, I thank God, my father, and yourself.
DUCHESS OF YORK: Then patiently hear my impatience.
KING RICHARD: Madam, I have a touch of your condition,
That cannot brook the accent of reproof.
DUCHESS OF YORK: I will be mild and gentle in my words.
KING RICHARD: And brief, good mother, for I am in haste.
DUCHESS OF YORK: Art thou so hasty? I have stay'd for thee,
God knows, in torment and in agony.
KING RICHARD: And came I not at last to comfort you?
DUCHESS OF YORK: Thou cam'st on earth to make the earth
my hell.
A grievous burden was thy birth to me;
Tetchy and wayward was thy infancy;
Thy age confirm'd, proud, subtle, sly, and bloody.
What comfortable hour canst thou name
That ever grac'd me with thy company?
KING RICHARD: If I be so disgracious in your eye,

Let me march on and not offend you, madam.
Strike up the drum!
DUCHESS OF YORK: I prithee hear one word.
For I shall never speak to thee again.
KING RICHARD: So!
DUCHESS OF YORK: Either thou wilt die by God's just
                                                    ordinance
Ere from this war thou turn a conqueror,
Or I with grief and extreme age shall perish
And nevermore behold thy face again.
Therefore, take with thee my most grievous curse,
Which in the day of battle tire thee more
Than all the complete armour that thou wear'st!
Bloody thou art; bloody will be thy end.
Shame serves thy life and doth thy death attend.
(*Exit.*)
QUEEN ELIZABETH: Though far more cause, yet much less
                                                    spirit to curse
Abides in me, I say Amen to her.
KING RICHARD: Stay, madam: I must talk a word with you.
QUEEN ELIZABETH: I have no more sons of the royal blood
For thee to slaughter.
KING RICHARD: You have a daughter call'd Elizabeth,
Virtuous and fair, royal and gracious.
QUEEN ELIZABETH: And must she die for this? O let her live.
KING RICHARD: I love thy daughter,
And do intend to make her Queen of England.
QUEEN ELIZABETH: Well then, who dost thou mean shall be
her King?
KING RICHARD: Even he that makes her Queen. Who else
should be?
QUEEN ELIZABETH: What, thou?
KING RICHARD: Even so. How think you of it?
QUEEN ELIZABETH: How canst thou woo her?
KING RICHARD: That would I
learn of you.
QUEEN ELIZABETH: And wilt thou learn of me?
KING RICHARD: Madam, with
all my heart.

QUEEN ELIZABETH: Send to her by the man that slew her
$\qquad$ brothers,
 A pair of bleeding hearts; thereon engrave
 'Edward' and 'York'. Then haply will she weep.
 Send her a letter of thy noble deeds:
 Tell her thou mad'st away her uncle Clarence,
 Her uncle Rivers – ay, and for her sake
 Mad'st quick conveyance with her good aunt Anne.
KING RICHARD: You mock me, madam; this is not the way
 To win your daughter!
QUEEN ELIZABETH: There is no other way.
KING RICHARD: Say that I did all this for love of her?
QUEEN ELIZABETH: Nay, then indeed she cannot choose but
$\qquad$ hate thee,
 Having bought love with such a bloody spoil.
KING RICHARD: Look what is done cannot be now amended:
 Men shall deal unadvisedly sometimes,
 Which after-hours gives leisure to repent.
 If I have kill'd the issue of your womb,
 To quicken your increase, I will beget
 Mine issue of your blood upon your daughter.
 I cannot make you what amends I would:
 Therefore accept such kindness as I can.
 What! We have many goodly days to see.
 Go then, my mother; to thy daughter go:
 Put in her tender heart th'aspiring flame
 Of golden sovereignty; acquaint the Princess
 With the sweet, silent hours of marriage joys,
 And when this arm of mine hath chastised
 The petty rebel, dull-brain'd Buckingham,
 Bound with triumphant garlands will I come
 And lead thy daughter to a conqueror's bed.
QUEEN ELIZABETH: What were I best to say? Her father's
$\qquad$ brother
 Would be her lord? Or shall I say her uncle?
 Or he that slew her brothers and her uncles?
KING RICHARD: Infer fair England's peace by this alliance.
QUEEN ELIZABETH: Which she shall purchase with still-lasting
 war.

KING RICHARD: Say I will love her everlastingly.

QUEEN ELIZABETH: But how long shall that title 'ever' last?

KING RICHARD: Sweetly in force, until her fair life's end.

QUEEN ELIZABETH: But how long fairly shall her sweet life last?

KING RICHARD: As long as heaven and nature lengthens it.

QUEEN ELIZABETH: As long as hell and Richard likes of it.

KING RICHARD: Now, by the world –

QUEEN ELIZABETH: 'Tis full of thy foul wrongs.

KING RICHARD: My father's death –

QUEEN ELIZABETH: Thy life hath it dishonour'd.

KING RICHARD: Then by myself –

QUEEN ELIZABETH: Thyself is self-misus'd.

KING RICHARD: Why then, by God –

QUEEN ELIZABETH: God's wrong is most of all:
If thou hadst feared to break an oath by Him,
Th'imperial metal circling now thy head

QUEEN ELIZABETH: Had grac'd the tender temples of my child,
And both the Princes had been breathing here,
Which now – two tender bedfellows for dust –
Thy broken faith hath made the prey for worms.
What canst thou swear by now?

KING RICHARD: The time to come.

QUEEN ELIZABETH: That thou hast wronged in the time o'er-
                                         past:
The children live whose fathers thou has slaughter'd:
Ungovern'd youth, to wail it in their age;
The parents live whose children thou hast butcher'd:
Old barren plants, to wail it with their age.
Swear not by time to come, for that thou hast
Misus'd ere us'd, by times ill-us'd o'er past.

KING RICHARD: As I intend to prosper and repent,
Be opposite, all planets of good luck,
To my proceeding if, with dear heart's love,
Immaculate devotion, holy thoughts,
I tender not thy beauteous, princely daughter.
In her consists my happiness and thine;
Without her follows to myself and thee,
Herself, the land, and many a Christian soul,

Death, desolation, ruin, and decay.
It cannot be avoided but by this;
It will not be avoided but by this.

QUEEN ELIZABETH: Shall I be tempted of the devil thus?

KING RICHARD: Ay, if the devil tempt you to do good.

QUEEN ELIZABETH: Shall I forget myself to be myself.

KING RICHARD: Ay, if your self's remembrance wrong yourself.

QUEEN ELIZABETH: Yet thou didst kill my children.

KING RICHARD: But in your daughter's womb I bury them,
Where, in that nest of spicery, they shall breed
Selves of themselves, to your recomforture.

QUEEN ELIZABETH: Shall I go win my daughter to thy will?

KING RICHARD: And be a happy mother by the deed.

QUEEN ELIZABETH: I go. Write to me very shortly,
And you shall understand from me her mind.

KING RICHARD: Bear her my true love's kiss; and so farewell.
(*Exit* QUEEN ELIZABETH.)
Relenting fool, and shallow, changing woman!
(*Enter* RATCLIFFE, CATESBY *following*.)

KING RICHARD: How now? What news?

RATCLIFFE: Most mighty sovereign, on the western coast
Rideth a puissant navy; to our shores
Throng many doubtful, hollow-hearted friends,
Unarm'd, and unresolv'd to beat them back.
'Tis thought that Richmond is their admiral;
And there they hull, expecting but the aid
Of Buckingham to welcome them ashore.

KING RICHARD: Some light-foot friend post to the Duke of
Norfolk.
Ratcliffe, thyself – or Catesby – where is he?

CATESBY: Here, my good lord.

KING RICHARD: Catesby, fly to the Duke.
Ratcliffe, post to Salisbury.
When thou com'st thither – (*To* CATESBY) Dull
unmindful villain!
Why stay'st thou here and go'st not to the Duke?

CATESBY: First, mighty liege, tell me your Highness' pleasure,
What from your grace I shall deliver to him.

KING RICHARD: O, true, good Catesby! Bid him levy straight

The greatest strength and power that he can make,
And meet me suddenly at Salisbury.

CATESBY: I go.

(*Exit.*)

RATCLIFFE: What shall I do at Salisbury?

KING RICHARD: Why, what wouldst thou do there before I go?

RATCLIFFE: Your Highness told me I should post before.

KING RICHARD: My mind is changed.

(*Enter* DERBY.)

                        Stanley, what news with you?

DERBY: None good, my liege, to please you with the hearing;
Nor none so bad but well may be reported.

KING RICHARD: Hoyday, a riddle! Neither good nor bad –
Once more, what news?

DERBY: Richmond is on the seas.

KING RICHARD: There let him sink, and be the seas on him –
White-livered runagate! What doth he there?

DERBY: I know not, mighty sovereign, but by guess.

KING RICHARD: Well, as you guess?

DERBY: Stirr'd up by Dorset, Buckingham, and Ely,
He makes for England, here to claim the crown.

KING RICHARD: Is the chair empty? Is the sword unsway'd?
Is the King dead? The empire unpossess'd?
Then tell me, what makes he upon the seas!

DERBY: Unless for that, my liege, I cannot guess.

KING RICHARD: Unless for that he comes to be your liege.
Thou wilt revolt and fly to him, I fear.

DERBY: No, my good lord; therefore mistrust me not.
I'll muster up my friends and meet your Grace
Where and what time your Majesty shall please.

KING RICHARD: Ay, thou wouldst be gone, to join with
                         Richmond;
But I'll not trust thee.

DERBY: Most mighty sovereign,
You have no cause to hold my friendship doubtful.
I never was nor never will be false.

KING RICHARD: Go then, and muster men – but leave behind
Your son, George Stanley. Look your heart be firm,
Or else his head's assurance is but frail.

DERBY: So deal with him as I prove true to you.
(*Exit. Enter a* MESSENGER.)
FIRST MESSENGER: My gracious sovereign, now in Devonshire –
As I by friends am well advertised –
Sir Edward Courtney and the haughty prelate,
Bishop of Exeter, his elder brother,
With many more confederates, are in arms.
(*Enter another* MESSENGER.)
SECOND MESSENGER: In Kent, my liege, the Guilfords are in
arms,
And every hour more competitors
Flock to the rebels, and their power grows strong.
(*Enter third* MESSENGER.)
THIRD MESSENGER: My lord, the army of great Buckingham –
KING RICHARD: Out on you, owls! Nothing but songs of
death?
(*He strikes him.*)
There, take thou that, till thou bring better news.
THIRD MESSENGER: The news is that by sudden flood and fall
of waters,
Buckingham's army is dispers'd and scatter'd,
And he himself wander'd away alone,
No man knows wither.
KING RICHARD: I cry you mercy,
I did mistake, Ratcliffe,
Reward him for the blow I gave him.
Hath any well-advised friend proclaim'd
Reward to him that brings the traitor in?
THIRD MESSENGER: Such proclamation hath been made, my
lord.
(*Enter* CATESBY.)
CATESBY: My liege, the Duke of Buckingham is taken:
That is the best news. That the Earl of Richmond
Is with a mighty power landed at Milford
Is colder tidings, yet they must be told
KING RICHARD: Someone take order Buckingham be brought
To Salisbury; the rest march on with me.
(*Flourish. Exeunt all but* DERBY.)
DERBY: Within the sty of the most deadly boar

My son George Stanley is frank'd up in hold;
If I revolt, off goes young George's head;
The fear of that holds off my aid to Richmond.
Towards Leicester does he bend his power;
This letter will resolve him of my mind
And inform him that the Queen hath consented
He should espouse Elizabeth her daughter.
God and good angels fight on Richmond's side
And Richard fall in height of all his pride.

SCENE 5

Enter BUCKINGHAM *with* RATCLIFFE, *to execution.*

BUCKINGHAM: Will not King Richard let me speak with him?
RATCLIFFE: No, my good lord; therefore be patient.
BUCKINGHAM: Holy King Henry, Hastings, Edward's
children,
Rivers, and all that have miscarried
Now for revenge mock my destruction.
This is All Souls' Day, fellow, is it not?
RATCLIFFE: It is.
BUCKINGHAM: Why, then All Souls' Day is my body's
doomsday.
This is the day which, in King Edward's time,
I wished might fall on me when I was found
False to his children and his wife's allies.
This is the day wherein I wish'd to fall
By the false faith of him whom most I trusted.
This, this All Souls' Day to my fearful soul
Is the determin'd respite of my wrongs:
That high All-seer which I dallied with
Hath turn'd my feigned prayer on my head,
And given in earnest what I begg'd in jest.
Thus doth He force the swords of wicked men
To turn their own points in their masters' bosoms.
Thus Margaret's curse falls heavy on my neck:
'When he', quoth she, 'shall split thy heart with sorrow,
Remember Margaret was a prophetess.'

Come, sirs convey me to the block of shame;
Wrong hath but wrong, and blame the due of blame.
(*Exeunt* BUCKINGHAM *with officers.*)

SCENE 6

Enter RICHMOND, BLUNT, ELY *and others, with drum and colours.*

RICHMOND: Fellows in arms, and my most loving friends,
    Bruis'd underneath the yoke of tyranny;
    Thus far into the bowels of the land
    Have we march'd on without impediment;
    And here receive we from our father Stanley
    Lines of fair comfort and encouragement.
    The wretched, bloody, and usurping boar,
    That spoil'd your summer fields and fruitful vines,
    Swills your warm blood like wash, and makes his trough
    In your embowell'd bosoms – this foul swine
    Is now even in the centre of this isle,
    Near to the town of Leicester, as we learn.
    From Tamworth thither is but one day's march:
    In God's name, cheerly on, courageous friends,
    To reap the harvest of perpetual peace
    By this one bloody trial of sharp war.
BLUNT: Every man's conscience is a thousand men,
    To fight against this guilty homicide.
RICHMOND: I doubt not but his friends will turn to us.
ELY: He hath no friends but what are friends for fear,
    Which in his dearest need will fly from him.
RICHMOND: All for our vantage; then in God's name march.
    True hope is swift, and flies with swallow's wings;
    Kings it makes gods, and meaner creatures kings.
    (*Exeunt omnes.*)

SCENE 7

Enter KING RICHARD *in arms, with* NORFOLK, RATCLIFFE, CATESBY *and soldiers.*

KING RICHARD: Here pitch our tent, even here in Bosworth
                                                    field.
   Why how now, Catesby, why look you so sad?
CATESBY: My heart is ten times lighter than my looks.
KING RICHARD: My Lord of Norfolk.
NORFOLK: Here, most gracious
   liege.
KING RICHARD: Norfolk, we must have knocks – Ha, must we
   not?
NORFOLK: We must both give and take, my loving lord.
KING RICHARD: Up with my tent! Here will I lie tonight.
   (*Soldiers begin to set up the King's tent.*)
   But where tomorrow? Well, all's one for that.
   Who hath descried the number of the traitors?
RATCLIFFE: Six or seven thousand is their utmost power.
KING RICHARD: Why, our battalia trebles that account!
   Besides, the King's name is a tower of strength
   Which they upon the adverse faction want.
   Up with the tent! Come, noble gentlemen,
   Let us survey the vantage of the ground.
   Let's lack no discipline, make no delay:
   For, lords, tomorrow is a busy day!
   (*Exeunt omnes. Enter* RICHMOND, BLUNT, ELY *and*
   DORSET. *Some of the soldiers pitch Richmond's tent.*)
RICHMOND: The weary sun hath made a golden set,
   And by the bright tract of his fiery car
   Gives token of a goodly day tomorrow.
   Where is Lord Stanley quarter'd, do you know?
BLUNT: His regiment lies half a mile at least
   South from the mighty power of the King.
RICHMOND: If without peril it be possible,
   Give him from me this most needful note.
BLUNT: Upon my life, my lord, I'll undertake it.
RICHMOND: Good night, good captain.
   (*Exit* BLUNT.)
   Come, gentlemen:
   Let us consult upon tomorrow's business;
   Into my tent; the dew is raw and cold.

(*They withdraw into the tent. Enter, to his tent,* KING
RICHARD, RATCLIFFE, NORFOLK *and* CATESBY.)

KING RICHARD: What is't o'clock?

CATESBY: It's supper time, my lord; it's nine o'clock.

KING RICHARD: I will not sup tonight. Give me some ink and
paper.

What, is my beaver easier than it was,
And all my armour laid into my tent?

CATESBY: It is, my liege, and all things are in readiness.

KING RICHARD: Good Norfolk, hie thee to thy charge;
Use careful watch; choose trusty sentinels.

NORFOLK: I go, my lord.

KING RICHARD: Stir with the lark tomorrow, gentle Norfolk.

NORFOLK: I warrant you, my lord.

(*Exit.*)

KING RICHARD: Catesby!

CATESBY: My lord?

KING RICHARD: Send out a pursuivant-at-arms
To Stanley's regiment: bid him bring his power
Before sun-rising, lest his son George fall
Into the blind cave of eternal night.

(*Exit* CATESBY.)

Fill me a bowl of wine. Give me a watch.
Saddle white Surrey for the field tomorrow;
Look that my staves be sound and not too heavy.
Give me a bowl of wine.
I have not that alacrity of spirit
Nor cheer of mind that I was wont to have.

(*A bowl of wine is brought.*)

Set it down. Is ink and paper ready?

RATCLIFFE: It is, my lord.

KING RICHARD: Bid my guard watch; leave me.
Ratcliffe, about the mid of night come to my tent
And help to arm me. Leave me, I say.

(*Exit* RATCLIFFE *with others.* KING RICHARD *withdraws
into his tent, and sleeps. Enter* DERBY *to* RICHMOND *in his
tent, lords and others attending.*)

DERBY: Fortune and Victory sit on thy helm!

RICHMOND: All comfort that the dark night can afford

Be to thy person, noble Stanley.
Tell me, how fares our loving mother?
DERBY: I, by attorney, bless thee from thy mother,
Who prays continually for Richmond's good.
So much for that. The silent hours steal on:
In brief, for so the season bids us be,
Prepare thy battle early in the morning.
I, as I may – that which I would, I cannot –
With best advantage will deceive the time,
And aid thee in this doubtful shock of arms.
But on thy side I may not be too forward,
Lest, being seen, my son, thy brother, George,
Be executed in his father's sight.
Farewell; the leisure and the fearful time
Cuts off the ceremonious vows of love.
Be valiant, and speed well.
RICHMOND: Good lords, conduct him to his regiment.
I'll strive, with troubled thoughts, to take a nap
Lest leaden slumber peise me down tomorrow
When I should mount with wings of victory.
Once more, good night, kind lords and gentlemen.
(*Exeunt.* RICHMOND *remains.*)
O Thou, whose captain I account myself,
Look on my forces with a gracious eye;
Put in their hands Thy bruising irons of wrath,
Make us Thy ministers of chastisement,
That we may praise Thee in the victory.
To Thee I do commend my watchful soul:
Sleeping and waking, O defend me still!
(*He sleeps. Enter the* GHOST OF PRINCE EDWARD, *son to
Henry VI.*)
GHOST OF PRINCE EDWARD: (*To* KING RICHARD) Let me sit
                                    heavy on thy soul tomorrow.
Think how thou stab'st me in my prime of youth
At Tewkesbury; despair therefore, and die.
(*To* RICHMOND) Be cheerful, Richmond, for the wronged
                                                        soul
Of butcher'd Edward fights in thy behalf;
King Henry's issue, Richmond, comforts thee.

(*Exit. Enter the* GHOST OF HENRY VI.)

GHOST OF HENRY VI: (*To* RICHARD) When I was mortal, my
anointed body
By thee was punched full of deadly holes.
Think on the Tower and me; despair, and die;
Harry the Sixth bids thee despair and die!
(*To* RICHMOND) Virtuous and holy, be thou conqueror:
Harry, that prophesied thou shouldst be King,
Doth comfort thee in thy sleep: live, and flourish!
(*Exit. Enter the* GHOST OF CLARENCE.)

GHOST OF CLARENCE: (*To* RICHARD) Let me sit heavy in thy
soul tomorrow —
I, that was wash'd to death with fulsome wine,
Poor Clarence, by thy guile betray'd to death —
Tomorrow in the battle think on me,
And fall thy edgeless sword; despair and die.
(*To* RICHMOND) Thou offspring of the house of Lancaster,
The wronged heirs of York do pray for thee.
Good angels guard thy battle; live, and flourish!
(*Exit. Enter the* GHOSTS OF RIVERS, *and* GREY.)

GHOST OF RIVERS: (*To* RICHARD) Let me sit heavy in thy soul
tomorrow,
Rivers that died at Pomfret; despair and die.

GHOST OF GREY: Think upon Grey, and let thy soul despair.

BOTH: (*To* RICHMOND) Awake, and think our wrongs in
Richard's bosom
Will conquer him: awake, and win the day.
(*Exeunt* GHOSTS. *Enter the* GHOST OF HASTINGS.)

GHOST OF HASTINGS: (*To* RICHARD) Bloody and guilty,
guiltily awake,
And in a bloody battle end thy days.
Think on Lord Hastings; despair, and die.
(*To* RICHMOND) Quiet, untroubled soul, awake, awake:
Arm, fight, and conquer for fair England's sake.
(*Exit. Enter the* GHOSTS *of the two young* PRINCES.)

GHOSTS OF THE PRINCES: (*To* RICHARD) Dream on thy
cousins, smother'd in the Tower:
Thy nephews' souls bid thee despair and die.

(*To* RICHMOND) Sleep, Richmond, sleep in peace, and
wake in joy;

Live, and beget a happy race of kings.

(*Exeunt. Enter the* GHOST OF ANNE, *his wife.*)

GHOST OF ANNE: (*To* RICHARD) Richard, thy wife, that
wretched Anne, thy wife,

That never slept a quiet hour with thee,

Now fills thy sleep with perturbations.

Tomorrow in the battle think on me,

And fall thy edgeless sword; despair and die.

(*To* RICHMOND) Thou quiet soul, sleep thou a quiet sleep;

Dream of success and happy victory.

Thy adversary's wife doth pray for thee.

(*Exit. Enter the* GHOST OF BUCKINGHAM.)

GHOST OF BUCKINGHAM: (To RICHARD) The first was I that
help'd thee to the crown;

The last was I that felt thy tyranny.

O, in the battle think on Buckingham,

And die in terror of thy guiltiness.

Dream on, dream on, of bloody deeds and death;

Fainting, despair; despairing, yield thy breath.

(*To* RICHMOND) I died for hope ere I could lend thee aid,

But cheer thy heart and be thou not dismayed.

(*Exit.* KING RICHARD *starts out of his dream.*)

KING RICHARD: Give me another horse! Bind up my wounds!

Have mercy, Jesu! – Soft, I did but dream.

O coward conscience, how dost thou afflict me!

The lights burn blue; it is now dead midnight.

Cold fearful drops stand on my trembling flesh.

What do I fear? Myself? There's none else by;

Richard loves Richard, that is, I and I.

Is there a murderer here? No. Yes, I am!

I am a villain – Yet I lie, I am not!

Fool, of thyself speak well! Fool, do not flatter.

My conscience hath a thousand several tongues,

And every tongue brings in a several tale,

And every tale condemns me for a villain:

Perjury, perjury, in the highest degree;

Murder, stern murder, in the direst degree;

All several sins, all us'd in each degree,
Throng to the bar, crying all, 'Guilty! guilty!'
I shall despair. There is no creature loves me,
And if I die, no soul will pity me –
And wherefore should they, since that I myself
Find in myself no pity to myself?
(*Enter* RATCLIFFE.)

RATCLIFFE: My lord!

KING RICHARD: Zounds! Who is there?

RATCLIFFE: Ratcliffe, my lord, 'tis I. The early village cock
Hath twice done salutation to the morn;
Your friends are up and buckle on their armour.

KING RICHARD: O Ratcliffe, I have dream'd a fearful dream!
What thinkest thou – Will our friends prove all true?

RATCLIFFE: No doubt, my lord.

KING RICHARD: O Ratcliffe, I fear, I fear!

RATCLIFFE: Nay, good my lord, be not afraid of shadows.

KING RICHARD: By the Apostle Paul, shadows tonight
Have struck more terror to the soul of Richard
Than can the substance of ten thousand soldiers
Armed in proof, and led by shallow Richmond.
'Tis not yet near day; come, go with me;
Under our tents I'll play the eavesdropper,
To see if any means to shrink from me.
(*Exeunt* RICHARD *and* RATCLIFFE. *Enter the lords to*
RICHMOND *sitting in his tent.*)

LORDS: Good morrow, Richmond.

RICHMOND: Cry mercy, lords and watchful gentlemen,
That you have ta'en a tardy sluggard here.

LORDS: How have you slept, my lord?

RICHMOND: The sweetest sleep, and fairest-boding dreams
That ever enter'd in a drowsy head
Have I, since your departure, had, my lords.
Methought their souls whose bodies Richard murder'd
Came to my tent and cried on victory.
I promise you my heart is very jocund
In the remembrance of so fair a dream.
How far into the morning is it, lords?

LORDS: Upon the stroke of four.

RICHMOND: Why then 'tis time to arm and give direction.
   (*His oration to his soldiers:*)
   More than I have said, loving countrymen,
   The leisure and enforcement of the time
   Forbids to dwell upon. Yet remember this:
   God, and our good cause, fight upon our side.
   Richard except, those whom we fight against
   Had rather have us win than him they follow.
   For what is he they follow? Truly, gentlemen,
   A bloody tyrant and a homicide;
   One rais'd in blood, and one in blood establish'd;
   One that made means to come by what he hath,
   And slaughter'd those that were the means to help him;
   A base foul stone, made precious by the foil
   Of England's chair, where he is falsely set;
   One that hath ever been God's enemy.
   Then, if you fight against God's enemy,
   God will, in justice, ward you as his soldiers;
   If you do sweat to put a tyrant down,
   You sleep in peace, the tyrant being slain;
   If you do free your children from the sword,
   Your children's children quit it in your age.
   Then, in the name of God and all these rights,
   Advance your standards, draw your willing swords!
   Sound, drums, and trumpets, boldly and cheerfully!
   God, and Saint George! Richmond and victory!
   (*Exeunt omnes. Enter* KING RICHARD, RATCLIFFE *and
   soldiers.*)
KING RICHARD: Who saw the sun today?
RATCLIFFE: Not I, my lord.
KING RICHARD: Then he disdains to shine, for by the book
   He should have brav'd the east an hour ago.
   A black day will it be to somebody.
   Ratcliffe!
RATCLIFFE: My lord?
KING RICHARD: The sun will not be seen today!
   The sky doth frown and lour upon our army:
   I would these dewy tears were from the ground.
   Not shine today? Why, what is that to me

More than to Richmond? For the selfsame heaven
That frowns on me looks sadly upon him.
(*Enter* NORFOLK.)
NORFOLK: Arm, arm, my lord: the foe vaunts in the field!
KING RICHARD: Come, bustle, bustle! Caparison my horse.
Call up Lord Stanley; bid him bring his power.
I will lead forth my soldiers to the plain,
Our archers shall be placed in the midst.
Norfolk, shall have the leading of the horse.
They thus directed, we will follow
In the main battle, who puissance on either side
Shall be well winged with our chiefest horse.
This, and Saint George to boot! What think'st thou,
Norfolk?
NORFOLK: A good direction, warlike sovereign.
This found I on my tent this morning.
(*He shows him the paper.*)
KING RICHARD: (*Reads:*) 'Jockey of Norfolk, be not so bold;
For Dickon thy master is bought and sold.'
A thing devised by the enemy.
Go, gentlemen; every man unto his charge!
Let not our babbling dreams affright our souls;
Conscience is but a word that cowards use,
Devis'd at first to keep the strong in awe.
Our strong arms be our conscience, swords our law.
(*His oration to his army:*)
What shall I say, more than I have inferr'd?
Remember whom you are to cope withal:
A sort of vagabonds, rascals, and runaways;
A scum of Bretons and base lackey peasants,
Whom their o'ercloyed country vomits forth
To desperate adventures and assur'd destruction.
And who doth lead them but a paltry fellow,
A milksop! One that never in his life
Felt so much cold as over-shoes in snow.
Let's whip these stragglers o'er the seas again,
Lash hence these overweening rags of France,
Fight, gentlemen of England! Fight, bold yeomen!
Draw, archers, draw your arrows to the head!

Spur your proud horses hard, and ride in blood!
Amaze the welkin with your broken staves!
(*Enter* LOVELL.)
What says Lord Stanley? Will he bring his power?
LOVELL: My lord doth deny to come.
KING RICHARD: Off with his son George's head!
NORFOLK: My lord, the enemy is past the marsh!
After the battle let George Stanley die.
KING RICHARD: A thousand hearts are great within my bosom.
Advance our standards! Set upon our foes!
Our ancient word of courage, fair Saint George,
Inspire us with the spleen of fiery dragons!
Upon them! Victory sits on our helms.
(*Exeunt omnes.*)

SCENE 8

Alarum; excursions. Enter CATESBY.

CATESBY: Rescue, my Lord of Norfolk, rescue, rescue!
The King enacts more wonders than a man.
His horse is slain, and all on foot he fights,
Seeking for Richmond in the throat of death.
Rescue, fair lord, or else the day is lost!
(*Alarums. Enter* KING RICHARD.)
KING RICHARD: A horse! A horse! My kingdom for a horse!
CATESBY: Withdraw, my lord; I'll help you to a horse.
KING RICHARD: Slave! I have set my life upon a cast,
And I will stand the hazard of the die.
I think there be six Richmonds in the field;
Five have I slain today instead of him.
A horse! A horse! My kingdom for a horse!
(*Exit.*)

SCENE 9

Alarum. Enter KING RICHARD *and* RICHMOND; *they fight;*
RICHARD *is slain. Retreat and flourish. Enter* RICHMOND,
DERBY *bearing the crown, with divers other lords.*

RICHMOND: God, and your arms, be prais'd, victorious
friends:
The day is ours; the bloody dog is dead.
DERBY: Courageous Richmond, well hast thou acquit thee!
Lo, here this long usurped royalty;
Wear it, enjoy it, and make much of it.
RICHMOND: Great God of heaven, say Amen to all!
But tell me, is young George Stanley living?
DERBY: He is, my lord.
RICHMOND: Proclaim a pardon to the soldiers fled
That in submission will return to us;
And then, as we have ta'en the sacrament,
We will unite the white rose and the red.
Smile, heaven, upon this fair conjunction.
England hath long been mad, and scarr'd herself;
The brother blindly shed the brother's blood;
The father rashly slaughter'd his own son;
The son, compell'd, been butcher to the sire.
All this divided York and Lancaster –
O! now let Richmond and Elizabeth,
The true succeeders of each royal house,
By God's fair ordinance conjoin together,
And let their heirs, God, if Thy will be so,
Enrich the time to come with smooth-fac'd peace,
With smiling plenty, and fair prosperous days.
Now civil wounds are stopp'd; peace lives again.
That she may long live here, God say Amen!
(*Exeunt omnes.*)

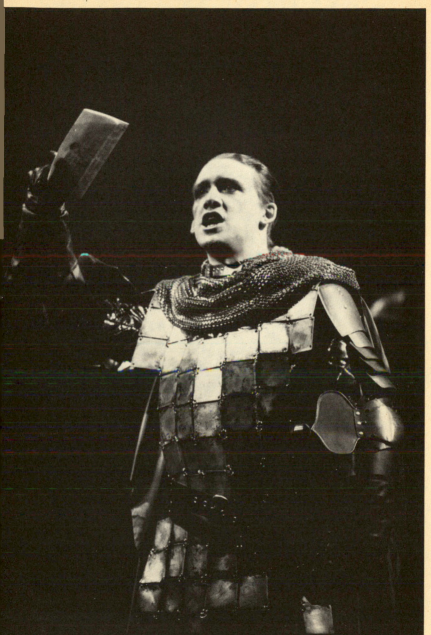